THE GHOST
AND THE BABY

The Ghost of Marlow House

The Ghost Who Loved Diamonds

The Ghost Who Wasn't

The Ghost Who Wanted Revenge

The Ghost of Halloween Past

The Ghost Who Came for Christmas

The Ghost of Valentine Past

The Ghost from the Sea

The Ghost and the Mystery Writer

The Ghost and the Muse

The Ghost Who Stayed Home

The Ghost and the Leprechaun

The Ghost Who Lied

The Ghost and the Bride

The Ghost and Little Marie

The Ghost and the Doppelganger

The Ghost of Second Chances

The Ghost Who Dream Hopped

The Ghost of Christmas Secrets

The Ghost Who Was Say I Do

The Ghost and the Baby

The Ghost and the Halloween Haunt

HAUNTING DANIELLE - BOOK 21

USA TODAY BESTSELLING AUTHOR
BOBBI HOLMES

The Ghost and the Baby
(Haunting Danielle, Book 21)
A Novel
By Bobbi Holmes
Cover Design: Elizabeth Mackey

Robeth Publishing, LLC

robeth.net

ISBN: 978-1-949977-41-7

Dedicated expressly to my readers who have shared with me their thoughts on my books through emails, blog comments, and social media. You are the energy that fuels my muse. Thank you.

ONE

Daisy Faye Morton stood in her bedroom on the second floor, looking down at the street from the corner windows. To her right was Marlow House, vacant since she was three years old. She had no memory of anyone ever living there, yet she had met its owner two years earlier when Brianna O'Malley had come to inspect the property. O'Malley had been practically a girl at the time —the same age as Daisy was now.

Turning her attention to the street, she spied the postman walking toward her house. Her father had made a point of telling her not to leave the house today until the mail arrived. If there had been somewhere she wanted to go, she would have made up some excuse for her father about why she hadn't waited. Yet she had nowhere to go this morning; plus he had piqued her curiosity, especially after that unfortunate incident when he had walked in on her and her gentleman friend borrowing his office. It was his own fault, she thought. After all, her father was supposed to be in Portland that day.

Between the shouts, Daisy had reminded her father that she was no longer a girl. But it wasn't just the compromising position that had infuriated him, it was the other man's age—*old enough to be your father*—Elmer Morton had roared. Daisy found that quite hypocritical, considering what the age difference had been between her own parents.

As for the fact the man was much older than her, that was hardly her fault; after all, most of the eligible men were off at war. There was of course her sister's beau, Kenneth Bakken, who had just been released from the army, returning home with a missing leg. There was also Daisy's old beau, Lewis Samson, who was 4-F and was unable to serve his country.

Just as the postman started up her walkway, Daisy darted from the room and headed downstairs to answer the door. She was alone in the house. Her only sibling, Maisy Faye, was at some boring Red Cross meeting, and her father was at work. When she threw open the front door a few minutes later, the postman had just stepped up on the porch and was about to ring the bell.

"Good morning," he greeted her. "Is it Daisy or Maisy?"

"I'm Daisy," she said brightly, playfully snatching the mail from his hands and sending her blond curls bobbing. "Remember, I'm the pretty one!"

He laughed at her comment—not because she wasn't pretty, but because she and her sister Maisy were identical twins.

Several minutes later, Daisy was alone again in the entry hall, sorting through the mail, wondering what her father thought so important about today's delivery. In the stack of mail there was only one envelope addressed to her, and curiously, the return address was her father's attorney.

Staring at the unopened letter, Daisy frowned. "Why is he sending me something?"

After tossing the rest of the mail on the entry table, Daisy hastily opened the envelope addressed to her and pulled out the letter. She began to read.

"No!" she shouted a moment later. "He can't do this!"

Angrily clutching the letter in her right hand, she looked frantically around the entry hall, trying to figure out how to get to the funeral home, cursing her sister for taking the car today. She needed to straighten this out with her father—*now*—and it was not something she could do on the phone. Nor could she wait for him to come home tonight.

Daisy briefly considered calling Lewis and asking him to drive her to the funeral home, but then she would have to tell him why, and knowing Lewis, he wouldn't stop until he got the truth. One thing she hated about Lewis, he could always see through her lies. Of course, that never stopped him from pursuing her. She couldn't tell him what was in the letter—she needed to fix this before anyone found out.

The only option, she would have to walk to the funeral home. Hastily she slipped on her jacket and hat, grabbed her handbag, and shoved the attorney's letter into her jacket pocket. Leaving her house a few minutes later, she angrily made her way down the street, replaying in her mind the contents of the letter. If she had a gun, she would be sorely tempted to shoot her father. Yet the only problem, she realized it was too late for that. On the bright side, if she managed to fix this, she could always shoot him later—a thought she found somewhat comforting.

MORTON FUNERAL HOME was located on the south side of Frederickport in a large two-story Victorian. Elmer Morton had lived in the house with his first wife, and after she had died and he met his second wife, he moved into the house next door to Marlow House, where he had raised his two daughters, Daisy and Maisy.

Slightly out of breath from the brisk walk, Daisy stood outside the funeral home and looked up to the second floor and the window of her father's office. She knew he was alone, considering his newly hired assistant was off sick, and the woman who helped in the office didn't work on Wednesdays, and there were no strange cars parked out front. Digging one hand in her coat pocket, she took hold of the crumpled letter and then made her way up the walk.

The front door was not locked. It never was during business hours. As soon as she opened the door, bells jingled, heralding her arrival. The moment she stepped inside, the scent of lilies overwhelmed her, and she cringed. Since she was a small child, she loathed the smell of lilies. Although she had to admit it smelled better than the embalming room. Shivering at the thought, she closed the door behind her, sending the bells on another jingle.

Daisy was about to call out for her father when he came walking into the entry from a nearby room. He halted abruptly when he saw her.

"What are you doing here?" he asked.

Elmer Morton looked more like her grandfather than father, with his white hair and deeply creased face and slight hunched build. Wearing a dark suit befitting a mortician and solemn expression, he looked unkindly at his daughter.

Pulling the letter from her pocket, she waved it at him and said, "What do you think?"

"I assume that is the letter from my attorney?" he asked calmly.

Crumpling the letter into a ball, she threw it at him. It landed at his feet. "How could you?"

He looked down at the ball of paper, making no attempt to pick it up. He looked back to Daisy and asked, "Shouldn't you be at home packing?"

"And just where am I supposed to go?"

He shrugged. "It's not really my problem, is it? As you told me, you are an independent woman. Now you can prove it."

"Of course, your favorite, Maisy, doesn't have to move out?" she hissed.

"Maisy has always behaved like a lady. I am tired, Daisy. Tired of your endless antics and vulgar behavior. It's over. You have what you've always wanted, your independence."

"And just like that, you've written me out of your will?" she fumed. "How could you?"

"I wouldn't get too excited about it. I don't plan to go anywhere right away, and the doctor tells me I'm in relatively good health. So perhaps, if you can learn to restrain yourself and prove to me you are capable of acting not just as an independent woman, but a responsible one with some semblance of morals, then maybe you will one day be written back in. But that day is not now."

Red-faced, she glared at her father and immediately recognized his resolve. After a moment of silence, she said, "Fine. Write me out of the will until I prove I can be—respectable enough for you. But why do I need to move out of our house?"

"It's my house, Daisy, not yours. And I don't want you there anymore. As the letter stated, you have one week to move out."

"Move out where? And how am I supposed to pay for a place to live?"

"I would assume an independent woman would get a job. That's normally how it's done. Or perhaps you could just marry your current beau. Oh…that's right, he doesn't have a job, does he?" Elmer turned from Daisy and started down the hallway toward the staircase.

"Where are you going?" she demanded.

"I have work to do. Go home and pack your things," he told her without looking back.

Stunned, she watched her father walk away. Just as he started up the stairs, she ran after him.

"Wait, Father, please, can we discuss this!" she begged.

"I'm done arguing with you," he said wearily, continuing up the staircase, his back to her.

"You can't just throw me out like this! I'm your daughter!"

"Go home, and start looking for a job," he told her, still walking up the stairs. "You'll need one if you're going to find a place to move into before I have you evicted. I'd hate for you to have to live on the streets."

"You can't be serious!" She rushed up the stairs after him. Just as he was about to step onto the second-floor landing, she grabbed the back of his jacket, wanting him to stop and look at her.

Unprepared for the physical contact, Elmer stumbled and lost his balance. Just as he started to fall, Daisy reached out to catch him, but his shoe slipped on the edge of the stairs, accelerating the momentum of the fall. Had Daisy not grabbed hold of the handrail, she too would be toppling down the stairs with her father. His arms flailed in all directions as he tried to grab hold of something, anything to break the fall. Daisy watched in morbid fascination as her father plummeted downward until his head hit the first-floor landing. She could hear his skull crack just before blood began spilling onto the carpet.

Dazed, Daisy walked slowly down the stairs, her eyes riveted to her father's seemingly lifeless body. She couldn't believe what she was seeing. Once she reached the first-floor landing, she knelt by his side and took hold of one wrist, feeling for a pulse. Nothing. Panicked, she rolled him over onto his back and looked down at his lifeless face. He was dead.

She just stared at him a moment. Instead of tears, anger welled up inside her.

"You stupid old man!" she hissed. "How could you do this? I don't want you dead! What am I going to do now? I didn't think it was possible to hate you as much as I do, but at this moment, I've never hated you more! You stupid, stupid clumsy old man!"

Daisy rolled him back over, placing him in the same position he had been in after he had fallen down the stairs. She then ran down the hall and picked up the letter she had thrown at her father.

Shoving it in her pocket, she turned one final time to look at his dead body.

After hurling a final curse in his direction, she slipped out of the funeral home and started back to Beach Drive, doing what she could not to be seen. The last thing she needed right now was for anyone to know she had been with her father when he had fallen down the stairs. Considering what his attorney had sent her today, someone might believe she had pushed her father down the stairs in a fit of anger. But that was not what had happened, she told herself. He had fallen down the stairs on his own. She only wished it had happened a week earlier.

TWO

Pearl Huckabee stood in her bedroom on the second floor, looking down at the street from the corner windows. To her right was Marlow House, vacant when she had been a child. It was vacant now, at least it had been for the last two weeks. From what Pearl understood, Walt and Danielle Marlow were in Hawaii on their honeymoon and would be returning any day now. She smiled in satisfaction, knowing they were in for a surprise when they returned home. It had taken dogged persistence, but Pearl had managed to find a way to end the influx of strangers coming and going next door. If the Marlows had any reservations, they would be forced to cancel them when they returned home. Marlow House Bed and Breakfast was out of business—Walt and Danielle just didn't know it yet.

Motion from her yard caught her attention. Pearl looked down and spied the black cat from next door sitting in the middle of her flower bed, looking up at her. As his gaze met hers, he quietly did his business and then covered it with soil before sauntering off to his own yard. If she didn't know better, Pearl would swear the demon cat had just defiantly used her garden as a litter box while daring her to do something about it.

"You little monster!" Pearl hissed. She turned from the window and headed downstairs.

It hadn't been the first time she had caught the Marlows' cat using her yard in such a disgusting manner. She didn't know who they had left in charge of the animal, but whoever it was, they certainly weren't monitoring its whereabouts. After talking to Danielle about her pet, Pearl had stopped seeing it in her yard. But just days after they left for their honeymoon, the pest showed up in her garden again. Yet it was always when she was upstairs. It was almost as if the cat knew she would be unable to do anything when on the second floor.

After several days of watching the cat use her yard from her bedroom window, she'd decided to outsmart the animal. Pearl had set up a cage-like trap in her yard, baited with tuna, sure to attract the annoying feline. Once in the cage, she planned to haul it down to a shelter—in another town. If she took him to the shelter in Frederickport, Danielle would be sure to get the little monster back.

Yet each morning, when she went to check the cage, the tuna was gone—and so was the cat. It was as if someone was releasing the animal from the cage before she could get to it. As Pearl stormed downstairs, she decided to take care of the menacing feline once and for all. After all, she took care of the bed and breakfast, didn't she? Pearl figured if she didn't act now, then once Walt and Danielle returned, it would be too late to do anything.

Before going outside, she grabbed a pillowcase from the laundry room. She figured she could shove the little beast in the pillowcase, and it shouldn't be too hard to carry it back to her house, shove him —and the pillowcase—into the cage, and then get rid of him once and for all.

Going outside, she grabbed hold of the cage trap and began dragging it toward the wrought-iron fencing separating her yard from Marlow House. There was a loose section she could squeeze through. Leaving the cage on her side of the property line, she slipped through the opening, pillowcase in hand.

THERE WAS no shortage of friends willing to feed Max while Walt and Danielle were on their honeymoon. Lily and Ian were just across the street, Heather was one door over, and Chris lived down the road. Any of them would have been likely candidates. Even Joanne had offered to stop by. Yet it was Marie who had been given the task. She enjoyed feeling needed and it gave her the opportunity to practice her newly acquired levitating skills. As it turned out, Marie was a good choice because she had become something of a night owl in her death, which allowed her to keep a closer eye on Max's antics.

Marie had also offered to bring in the mail, but it was decided envelopes floating up from the mailbox to the front door might shake up some of the neighbors. Therefore, Lily and Ian assumed that chore.

Wearing a new sundress—something she had seen in one of the local dress shop windows and had manage to duplicate—Marie sat at the kitchen table and watched as Max entered through the pet door. The moment he spied her sitting there, he stopped in his tracks and sat down, the metal pet door swinging close behind him.

Arching her brows, she said, "I saw what you did over there."

Max let out a meow and then stood up and sauntered over to the food bowl Marie had just filled.

"Maybe you won't listen to me, but when Walt and Danielle get home, I'm going to tell them what shenanigans you have been up to."

Max, who had just started to eat, paused a moment and looked back at Marie.

"Don't look at me like that," she scolded. "If it weren't for me, you would still be in that cage, and who knows where she would have taken you!"

Max stared at Marie for a moment longer and then resumed eating.

Marie rolled her eyes. "I suppose I should be flattered that you had faith in me. But, Max, I might not be around the next time you find yourself trapped in a cage. And if I counted correctly, she had you trapped seven—no, eight—times."

Max looked back to Marie and meowed again.

Marie shook her head. "Oh pshaw, it wasn't the challenge you liked; it was the tuna!"

The next moment the pet door flew open and a head popped in the kitchen. It was Pearl Huckabee from next door.

"Oh, there you are, you little monster," Pearl said in a soft singsong voice. "Come here, kitty, kitty!"

"What is she doing here?" Marie gasped. Of course, Pearl couldn't see Marie. Unlike many of the neighbors on Beach Drive, she couldn't see ghosts.

Max stopped eating and turned to face the door. He looked from Marie to the gray-haired head sticking in the kitchen through the pet door.

"You stay right there!" Marie warned Max. He started to take a step toward Pearl when Marie snapped, "You heard me, Max! Unless you want to be levitated to the ceiling!" Max froze. He hated to be levitated.

Marie narrowed her eyes and looked back to Pearl, who continued her attempt to coax the cat to her.

"I should have brought some tuna," Pearl grumbled under her breath as Max stared at her, refusing to budge.

"You're trying to catnap Max!" Marie blurted. She then paused and considered what she had just said. "Kidnap—catnap—no, that doesn't work," she mumbled and then rephrased, "You're trying to steal Max!"

Focusing on the swinging pet door resting on the top of Pearl's head, Marie willed it to open wider. It slowly moved up until it lay flat against the door, unnoticed by the intruding neighbor. The next moment it slammed down atop Pearl's head.

"Ouch!" Pearl yelped, inadvertently slamming her head back against the pet door's wooden frame. The metal flapping door slapped against the top of her head again—and again. Now in a panic, Pearl managed to wiggle her head from the opening. Once her entire body and self were back outside, Pearl turned from Marlow House and ran as fast as she could to the section of fence she had crawled through. In her hasty departure she dropped the pillowcase on the back porch, leaving it there.

Sticking her head outside—literally through the door—Marie watched Pearl run back into her yard after squeezing through the loose section of fence. Looking down at the abandoned pillowcase, Marie willed it up off the ground and into the house, through the pet door.

Once the pillowcase was in the house, Marie picked it up and said, "Walt and Danielle need to see this." She looked back at Max, who had returned to his food. "And you need to stay in the house until they get home." She glanced at the kitchen wall clock. "They should be home in a couple of hours."

DANIELLE LEANED back in the passenger seat and watched as Walt steered her Ford Flex down the highway, heading back to Frederickport from the Portland Airport. He wore a white linen shirt and tan slacks, his complexion darker than she had ever seen it—the Hawaiian suntan an alluring contrast to his vivid blue eyes. He looked relaxed, content and happy, which was how she felt. It had been a magical two weeks, and there had been moments during the honeymoon—many of them, actually—when she had managed to forget their strange history, and she and Walt were no different than any other newlyweds in love. Of course, they were no more newlyweds than a normal couple, she reminded herself.

"I have to say you've become an excellent driver," Danielle said, her eyes on Walt.

Hands on the steering wheel, he glanced over to her and flashed a smile and then looked back down the road. "I suppose I could remind you that I started driving over a hundred years ago, but the truth is, driving is definitely different now."

"The traffic?" Danielle asked.

"That and the paved roads. To be honest, I'm a little surprised you don't have a problem with me driving your car."

"We are married," Danielle reminded him. "It's technically our car."

"Does that make the Packard yours?" he asked in a faux pout.

Danielle laughed and then said, "Truth is, it's kind of nice not to have to drive."

"I thought all modern women like to drive their own cars?" he asked.

Danielle shrugged. "Maybe I'm getting lazy." *Or perhaps I rather like the idea of a handsome—incredibly sexy chauffeur driving me around,* she thought, suppressing a giggle.

Walt reached over and gave Danielle's hand a pat. "It's that island lifestyle. Hawaii in person was even better than a dream hop."

"I had such a good time," Danielle said with a sigh. "But I have to admit I'm really looking forward to getting home."

"Me too. I hope Max stayed out of trouble."

"Yeah, I was a little worried about him, but Marie promised to keep an eye on him."

"I think she's rather fond of that cat," Walt said.

"Which is interesting, because if I recall, Marie wasn't especially crazy about cats when she was alive."

"Back then she'd never had a real conversation with one," Walt reminded her.

Thirty minutes later Walt pulled the car into the garage at Marlow House. He was tempted to levitate the luggage from the garage to the house, but Danielle reminded him the new neighbor had prying eyes, so they hauled the luggage inside the old-fashioned way.

Entering through the back door into the kitchen, they were greeted by Marie and Max. Danielle gave Marie a quick summary of their time in Hawaii, and in turn, Marie updated them on Max and their new neighbor.

"She tried to trap him?" Danielle asked after Marie finished her telling.

"Max thought it was a great game. He especially loved the tuna."

"Walt, you need to explain to Max that the next time the tuna could be poisoned!" Danielle told him.

Walt picked up the pillowcase and looked at it. "And you think she intended to put Max in this?"

Marie shrugged. "That's my guess. But I chased her off."

Walt looked down at Max. "You and I have to have a talk."

Staring up at Walt, the cat blinked his golden eyes and then jumped into Danielle's arms and began to purr.

Marie shook her head and mumbled, "He is a spoiled brat."

Holding Max in her arms, Danielle kissed his head. "Yes, I suppose he is."

"I promised Eva I would meet her at the theater after you returned home. You'll find your mail piled on the desk in the parlor." A moment later Marie vanished.

With Max in her arms, Danielle followed Walt to the parlor. Once there, she tossed the cat on the sofa and then took a seat at the desk and began sorting through the mail.

"Anything interesting?" Walt asked.

"Mostly bills, but there are a couple of cards from some of my friends from California. I imagine they're wedding congratulations." Danielle stacked the letters and cards in one pile, and what looked like bills in another. She then paused and looked at one from the city.

"I wonder what this is," Danielle muttered as she tore open the envelope.

Walt glanced up from where he sat on the sofa with Max and noticed Danielle's peculiar expression as she read the letter.

"What is it?" Walt asked.

"It's from the city. Our business license has been revoked."

THREE

"Revoked?" Walt asked.

Danielle nodded and stood up from the desk, her attention still on the letter in her hands. "That's what it says." She walked to the sofa where Walt sat. "Something about a discrepancy with the initial paperwork, and we're to cease and desist until when—or if—we can get the license reinstated."

Walt scooted over on the sofa, pushing Max to one end to make room for Danielle. She sat down next to him and handed him the letter.

"Maybe I should call the chief, see if he knows anything," Danielle suggested. "I really don't want to spend my first day home down at the city office."

"You think he'll know anything?" Walt asked. "It's not really his area."

Danielle stood back up. "He usually keeps informed of this sort of thing. After all, he needs to know if someone is operating an illegal bed and breakfast," she grumbled. After walking to the desk, she picked up the handset to the landline and placed the call.

"Hi, Chief. Yes, we're back," Danielle said a moment later. She glanced over to Walt, who silently listened to her side of the conversation. "Yeah, we had a great time. But the reason I'm calling, we just started going through our mail, and we got something from the city…What, you knew?…Why?…Renton?…She what? Oh, brother…I can't believe this. No, I take that back. Yes, I can. You know that woman was trying to capture Max while we were gone… I don't know…but she even tried to coax him out of our house… Marie told me…So is this thing hopeless?…Okay…What is her problem?…Doesn't like change?…Yeah…No, I understand… Okay…Yeah…I'll tell Walt, and we'll figure out what we want to do…Okay…Yeah…Talk to you later. Thanks." Danielle hung up the phone and returned to the sofa with Walt.

"Well?" he asked.

She sat down next to him. "Apparently, when you start a business in a residential area of Frederickport, you have to send a notice to all your neighbors within a specific proximity to the property and notify them of your intentions and then hold a hearing. If any of the neighbors object at the public hearing, then the license can be denied. There was no hearing for Marlow House."

Walt frowned. "I don't understand. How did you get the license in the first place, and didn't you know about this before you opened?"

Danielle let out a sigh and slumped back on the sofa. "Renton handled everything before we arrived."

"Renton? You mean the man who murdered Cheryl? The one I hit over the head?"

Danielle nodded. "Yes. But back then I knew him as my aunt's trusty attorney. What a joke."

"If Renton didn't arrange for a public hearing, how did he get you a license?"

"I guess he took a shortcut and paid someone in the city to sign off on it—I'm sure with my money, not his. At least, that's what they suspect. But the employee who handled our business license is no longer with the city; he was fired last year. And there is no record of any public hearing."

"I don't understand. Why did all this come up now?"

"Why do you think?" Danielle gave a nod to the south-facing wall. "She didn't just have an issue with Max."

"The new neighbor?" Walt asked.

"Yep. According to the chief, she has been down at city hall asking all sorts of questions about the legalities of running a bed and breakfast—although she kept referring to it as a motel—in a residential neighborhood. I guess someone down there was tired of her badgering them, so they decided to show her the process and in doing so discovered a vital step had been skipped when our license was issued.

"The chief doesn't think the city would have revoked our license over this if our lovely neighbor wasn't making such a big deal out of it. But there was no way for them to sweep this under the carpet. And considering Renton's history, the city understands I probably wasn't aware of his shortcut. But still, I can't operate the B and B without a business license."

Walt tossed the letter on the coffee table and wrapped one arm around Danielle's shoulders, pulling her closer. "Ironic we were just discussing closing the B and B on our flight home."

She leaned against him and let out a sigh. "I know, but to be forced to close, that makes me want to keep it open!"

Walt gave her a little squeeze and then dropped a quick kiss on her head before saying, "But just think, you'll get the last laugh. I don't imagine you'll need a business license for what we were talking about."

Danielle chuckled. "Yeah, you're probably right. So maybe this is a sign?"

"Sign?" he asked.

"That we go ahead with what we talked about on the way home."

"Unless we hold a hearing with the neighbors and hope Pearl doesn't manage to get the license denied, it looks like your bed and breakfast is closed. So we either do nothing or what we discussed," Walt said.

"As much as I hate giving up without a fight, I think with everything that has happened—with what we want for our future—then in some ways Pearl Huckabee has made it all easier for me."

"Gave you the shove you needed to make up your mind once and for all?" Walt asked.

"Yeah. Maybe I should go thank her?" Danielle chuckled.

"I'm sure she would appreciate it," Walt teased.

Kicking off her shoes and propping her stockinged feet on the coffee table, Danielle said, "I wonder why she is such an unpleasant woman. According to the chief, that house has been in her family for years, and she bought it from some cousins."

"I wonder if she's related to Elmer Morton. That might explain her disposition."

Danielle looked to Walt. "Elmer Morton? Who's that?"

"That's who was living next door—in Pearl Huckabee's house—when I died," Walt explained.

"Her maiden name might have been Morton. From what I understand, she's a widow and Huckabee was her husband's name," Danielle said. "So why did you say it might explain her disposition?"

"Morton and I never got along. He was about my grandfather's age. Pious old coot, an avid supporter of prohibition. And I'm pretty sure he was a member of the local Klan."

"Seems like such an oxymoron."

Walt frowned. "In what way?"

"How can you be pious and belong to an organization like the KKK?" Danielle asked.

Walt shrugged. "Sadly, it wasn't uncommon."

"You've never mentioned him before."

"Not much to tell. Morton and I tended to avoid each other. Although, I imagine he got the last laugh when I died and became a customer."

Danielle frowned. "Last laugh?"

"He owned the local mortuary, Morton Funeral Home."

"Morton Funeral Home? It's still here," Danielle said. "The chief mentioned he heard one of Pearl's relatives still lives in Frederickport and was one of the owners who sold the property to her. But he didn't know who it was. I wonder if it's whoever owns the funeral home now."

"It's possible."

"I'm assuming Morton had children, if Pearl is one of his descendants," Danielle said. "What were they like? Did you know them?"

"He had twin daughters. They were babies when I died."

"Babies?" Danielle frowned.

"Yes. Old Man Morton's first wife died in childbirth, giving birth to stillborn twins."

"How sad," Danielle murmured. "But you said he had twin daughters?"

"His second wife was much younger. Much. At the time he was courting her, he lived at the funeral home, but from what I heard, she refused to live there."

"Well, I can't say I blame her."

"Why? You're always hanging out with dead people. Seems like the perfect place for you," he teased.

Danielle playfully elbowed Walt. "Oh hush. Go on with your story."

Max, who had been napping at the end of the sofa, opened his eyes and then jumped down to the floor and sauntered out of the parlor.

"Was it something I said?" Danielle asked as she watched the cat leave the room.

"I think we were making too much noise for him," Walt said.

Danielle rolled her eyes and then turned to Walt. "Go on with your story."

"Morton bought the house next door. The couple who had lived there had passed away, and it had been vacant for a few years. Not long after that he moved in with his new bride. She was pregnant right away, and like his first wife, with twins. Sadly, she also died in childbirth, but this time, the babies lived."

"Oh my gosh, that's heartbreaking. I hate those kinds of stories, especially with Lily being pregnant."

"Lily will be fine," Walt promised, giving Danielle's knee a pat.

"I'd like to think childbirth is safe for women these days, but there are still complications."

"I don't imagine Lily is going to give birth at home with a midwife, as did both of Morton's wives," Walt said.

"And he raised the twins by himself?" Danielle asked.

"He hired a full-time nanny who moved into the house. Initially I assumed he would move back to the funeral home with the babies; it would have been more convenient for him. But Katherine O'Malley knew the nanny, and she told me the wife had made her husband promise on her deathbed not to raise her daughters in a funeral home. I guess she was superstitious, and he honored her wishes, at least while I was alive."

"Considering the age of Pearl Huckabee, one of the twins could be her grandmother or mother," Danielle speculated. "I wonder what happened to them."

"I imagine Marie knew them," Walt suggested. "They would have been a couple of years older than Marie, but they would have gone to school together."

"Funny, when I discussed Pearl with Marie, she didn't seem to know anything about Pearl's family or background."

Walt shrugged. "Maybe she just didn't make the connection. After all, it has been a long time."

"True." Danielle leaned back against the sofa and quietly considered all that Walt had told her.

After a few minutes of silence, Walt asked, "What are you thinking about?"

"There are no kids on Beach Drive. It's funny to think that back when you lived here—in your first life—there was a baby across the street and two little ones next door. And in a few months, there will be a baby across the street again."

"And maybe in the not so distant future, a baby on this side of the street." Walt pulled her onto his lap.

Wrapping her arms around her husband, Danielle dropped a quick kiss on his lips and whispered, "Remember, I said I wanted to be married for at least a year before we start planning babies. And we just came back from our honeymoon."

Walt pulled her closer and returned her kiss—yet not a quick one, as hers had been. His was slower and more deliberate, which she fully appreciated. When the kiss ended, he whispered, "Our one-year anniversary is less than three months away."

Danielle gave him an exuberant hug while whispering in his ear, "So it is."

FOUR

Lily Bartley sat alone at her desk in her classroom at the elementary school, correcting spelling papers. The bell had rung five minutes earlier, and her students had all left. She didn't have a lot of papers to correct today, and she didn't want to take them home with her. Glancing at the wall clock, she wondered if Walt and Danielle were back in Frederickport yet. Danielle had sent her a text message when they had landed earlier that day at the Portland Airport.

Just as Lily turned her attention back to the papers before her, she heard a voice call out, "Mrs. Bartley? Can I come in?"

Lily looked up to the now open door. It was Evan MacDonald. She couldn't believe how much he had grown since she had first met him several years earlier. Tall and lanky—taller than any of the other third graders in his class—he had large brown eyes and eyelashes women spent a fortune to have, yet they never looked quite as good as Evan's. He had been one of her students the previous school year. But he had been a friend first, student second. He was also the youngest son of Police Chief MacDonald. And like her dear friend Dani—and Walt and Chris and Heather—he could see ghosts.

"Come on in, Evan. And it's after hours, so you can call me Lily."

Evan grinned broadly and walked into the class carrying his backpack.

"I was wondering if you knew if Walt and Danielle were back yet," he asked as he approached her desk.

"Dani sent me a text message about three hours ago, telling me they had just landed at the airport. So they might be back home by now."

Standing by Lily's desk, Evan dropped the backpack on the floor and stared at Lily a moment, saying nothing.

Lily looked at him curiously. "Is there something else you wanted to ask me?"

Evan chewed his lower lip and then looked down to the floor. "Umm…never mind. I…I just wondered if Danielle and Walt were back yet."

A smile tugged at the corners of Lily's mouth as she studied Evan a moment before saying, "Come on, out with it. I can tell there's something you're dying to ask me. You look like you're about to explode."

He looked up shyly. "Umm…I overheard my dad talking. I wasn't supposed to hear."

"And?"

"Is it true you aren't going to be a teacher anymore?"

"Ohhh…what else did you hear?" she asked mischievously.

"Are you having a baby?" Evan asked in a whisper.

Lily smiled and reached over and grabbed a nearby chair. She dragged it closer and then motioned for Evan to sit down. He sat down.

"Yes. It is true. But I would appreciate it if you would keep the secret for now. I haven't told my class yet. As for being a teacher, I might be a teacher again—later. I don't know. But for now, I want to be home with the baby."

Evan looked up to Lily, his eyes wide. "Are you going to have a boy or girl?"

Lily shrugged. "I don't know yet. It'll be a couple of months before I find out."

"I hope you have a boy," Evan said.

Lily chuckled. "You wouldn't want me to have a pretty little girl?"

"I guess a girl would be okay. When are you going to be leaving?"

"I plan to finish out this term." She glanced around the room. "Which means I need to pack up my classroom when school gets out this summer. It won't be my room next year."

"If you want any help, I can help you," he offered.

Lily smiled at Evan, noting his sincerity. "Thanks. I appreciate the offer." She glanced around the room again. All of her personal school supplies—the books, games, bulletin board art, reading rug, aquarium, posters—were all relatively new. The school supplies she had accumulated since first becoming a teacher almost a decade earlier had all been given away by her parents when they had thought she was dead. After accepting a class at the Frederickport Elementary School, she had purchased new items to replace what her parents had given away.

Glancing around the room, she was torn as to what to do. Perhaps she should donate them to a new teacher—one who could not afford to purchase supplies for his or her room. Teachers didn't make a lot of money, but Lily was more fortunate than most. Not only had she married a wealthy man, but the settlement she had been awarded after her kidnapping had set her up for life—providing she didn't spend her money foolishly.

"Do you think the baby will be able to see ghosts?" Evan asked, disrupting Lily's train of thought.

"What?"

"Your baby. Marie told me when she was a baby, she could see Eva," Evan told her.

"Ahh…that's right. I remember hearing that. You know, I've even seen a ghost."

"You mean when Walt used to take you on a dream hop?" Evan asked.

Lily grinned. "I wasn't talking about seeing one in a dream. I was talking about seeing a ghost when I was wide awake. Over on Pilgrim's Point there was a ghost, Darlene Gusarov; I saw her."

"I know about her. Eva said she's gone now. That she moved on."

"You sure know a lot about ghosts."

Evan nodded again. "And Walt's wife—the one who tried to kill him—she was at the cemetery, but Eva said she moved on too."

"I guess ghosts aren't meant to stick around indefinitely. Of course, there are always exceptions. Eva has been hanging around for quite a while."

"I wish my mom would have stuck around," Evan said glumly.

Lily reached out and patted Evan's hand. "But you know why she didn't, don't you?"

"Yeah. I was pretty little back then, and Walt said it would have confused me. People would have thought I was crazy."

Lily nodded. "Yep. Pretty much. I imagine it was difficult for your mother to make that choice. But moms try to do what's best for their children."

"That's why you're staying home and not going back to school?" Evan asked.

"A lot of moms decide to keep working after they have babies. It doesn't make them bad moms. We just have to do what works for us. For me, it's staying home. And I'm luckier than most; I can afford to do it."

"I'm glad I got to have you as a teacher. You are my favorite teacher," Evan told her.

"Thanks." Lily thought Evan was being sweet, but told herself not to let it go to her head. After all, he was only in third grade, and he hadn't had that many teachers in his young life.

AFTER LEAVING the school a short time later, Lily went home, parked her car in the garage, and then walked across the street to Marlow House. Ian had gone to Portland and had taken Sadie with him, and Lily didn't expect him to return until the dinner hour.

Thirty minutes later Lily sat with Walt and Danielle in the living room of Marlow House.

"You really aren't going to try to get your business license reinstated?" Lily asked Danielle after hearing what had happened.

"If I still wanted to operate the B and B, I suppose I would. But Walt and I have other ideas for the place, and in some ways, this makes it easier for me. Kind of forces my hand. I told Walt I should probably thank Pearl."

"Yeah, right," Lily scoffed. "The woman is horrid. And I thought you loved running the B and B."

Walt stood up. "I'm going to let you two catch up while I go find Max. I need to have that talk with him."

"Talk with him?" Lily asked after Walt left the room.

"Max is having too much fun tormenting Pearl. He needs to realize she's dangerous," Danielle said.

"True. But I can't say I blame him. Now, back to the B and B. I thought you loved it?"

"I did. We met some great people. But we also had our share of problems."

"Yeah, well…maybe a murder or two." Lily shrugged.

"And I hate to admit it, in some ways, Joe was right."

"Oh no, please. Don't say that," Lily groaned.

Danielle chuckled. "I don't mean right in how he thinks I need a keeper. Although, maybe I do." She chuckled again and then grew serious. "No. Think about it. When I first decided to open the B and B, it was after I had inherited my aunt's estate, and I was trying to start a new life after what had happened to Lucas, and after selling our business. At the time, I had no idea my aunt's estate was worth far more than Renton had let on…"

"Or that you would be inheriting your cousin's estate, or finding the Missing Thorndike or the gold coins," Lily added.

"Exactly. Initially, it was a way to generate income from this property. It sounded fun and would allow me to try something new. Use skills I hadn't really used before while still utilizing some of my marketing skills. But the main thing, I needed the business back then. I couldn't afford—or at least I didn't think I could—afford to just move in here without doing something to make a living."

"But now you don't need to work?"

"I kept telling myself how much I love baking and being a hostess—and I do—and how fun it was to meet new friends—like Will Wayne and Patricia and her brother. But then people from Clint's life showed up, and Walt and I found ourselves making breakfast for guests we didn't even like—guests who were trying to blackmail us! That's just nuts."

"Not to mention Chris's uncles," Lily reminded her.

Danielle nodded. "Exactly. While we were in Hawaii, Walt and I started talking about it. And I realized I had been trying to convince myself I wanted to keep the B and B open—trying to justify it all. But really, it's kinda silly."

"I'm not sure it's silly, exactly," Lily argued.

"Yeah. It is. I'm no longer in a place where I need to run a business to survive. And while a B and B was a fun business—well, at least it was as long as someone wasn't trying to kill us—things are different now. Much more different than when I first decided to open."

"I suppose they are. So what will you do? I can't see you just sitting around the house while Walt writes."

"I want to take a page from Chris."

"Chris?"

"Pay it forward," Danielle explained.

"You've already donated a ton of money to Chris's foundation. Surely you aren't going to just give it all away like he is, are you?"

"Chris isn't actually just giving all his money away," Danielle corrected. "He's using it to generate more money so he can keep helping worthwhile causes."

"Is that what you plan to do?" Lily asked.

"I did love running the B and B. It was fun. And I still want to do it."

Lily frowned. "Okay, you are confusing me."

"In some ways, Walt and I will still be running Marlow House as a B and B. Well, maybe not a B and B exactly. More like an inn, I suppose."

"You really are confusing me now. I thought you just told me you no longer have a business license."

"We aren't going to need a business license for what we intend to do," Danielle explained. "And while I don't like to be perverse, it will be amusing when Pearl Huckabee realizes her plan backfired on her."

FIVE

"Do you need me to pick anything up when I go out?" Danielle asked Walt as she washed the breakfast dishes as he dried.

"No. It looks like Joanne did a good job restocking the pantry and refrigerator." Walt set the plate he had just dried on the stack of clean dishes in the overhead cabinet. They had returned from their honeymoon just the day before and were settling back into their day-to-day life. Yet their new life would no longer include operating a bed and breakfast.

"Which is one reason I'm glad you agree with me about keeping Joanne. I think I got spoiled." Danielle dried her hands on a piece of paper towel and turned to face Walt.

"Not sure about spoiled, but I have to give you credit for good instincts." Walt hung the damp dish towel on its hook.

"Instincts?" Danielle frowned.

"You were the one who decided not to start taking any reservations until after we came back from our honeymoon. It makes this all easier. I imagine we would be on the phone right now, trying to find other accommodations for the guests."

Danielle groaned. "I don't even want to consider that." She walked to the table and picked up her purse and then the pillowcase Marie had showed them.

"What are you going to do with that?" Walt nodded at the pillowcase.

"Return it to our neighbor before I run my errands, of course."

DANIELLE STOOD on Pearl Huckabee's front porch and rang the doorbell. As she waited, she looked out to the street and noticed a pickup truck pull up to the house. It was Craig Simmons, Joe Morelli's brother-in-law. Simmons was also the local landscaper who had done a lot of work for Danielle. She watched as he sat in his truck. It looked as if he were sitting there reading something on his clipboard.

"You?" Pearl said a moment later. She stood behind the front door, peeking outside at Danielle, making no attempt to open the door wider.

"Hello, Mrs. Huckabee," Danielle said cheerfully. She glanced quickly toward the street—Craig was still sitting in his truck, looking at his clipboard—and she then looked back to her neighbor.

"If this is about your bed and breakfast, that's between you and the city," Pearl snapped.

Danielle arched her brows. "My bed and breakfast?" she asked innocently, pretending she had no idea what Pearl was talking about.

"Isn't that why you're here?" Pearl asked, still clutching the edge of her front door, standing inside the house while peering outside.

"I'm here to bring you this." Danielle raised her right hand quickly, dangling the pillowcase in front of her neighbor. Until that moment, Pearl hadn't noticed what Danielle had been holding.

"What's that?" Pearl asked nervously.

"It's your pillowcase. You left it in our yard yesterday." She handed it to Pearl.

"It's not mine," she said quickly, handing it back. "I don't know why you think it's mine."

"Oh yes, it is." Danielle's syrupy voice could have sweetened an entire stack of flapjacks.

"No, it's not. Why would my pillowcase be in your yard?"

"That's kind of what I wondered too." Danielle's tone lost its sweetness.

"Hey, Danielle," came a man's voice.

Danielle glanced behind her. Craig Simmons was coming up the walkway.

"Hey, Craig. Are you doing some work for my neighbor?" Danielle asked.

"That's what I'm here to find out," he said cheerfully.

Pearl, who had been quietly watching, was startled when Danielle turned abruptly back to her and shoved the pillowcase in her hands.

"I don't think you should be crawling through my pet door again," Danielle whispered just loud enough for Pearl to hear. She then turned away from the door and flashed a smile at the landscaper.

"It was great seeing you, Craig," Danielle said cheerfully as she started down the walkway.

ADAM NICHOLS SAT at his desk, sorting through a stack of receipts, when he heard someone say, "Aloha!" He looked up and found Danielle walking into his office from the hall.

Shoving the receipts aside, he smiled up at her. "Welcome home. When did you get back?"

Carrying a candy box in one hand, she walked to his desk. "Yesterday." She handed him the box.

Looking at the offering, he asked, "What's this?" Which was actually a redundant question considering the packaging clearly revealed its contents.

"Chocolate-covered macadamia nuts," she explained, sitting down on a chair facing the desk and dropping her purse to the floor.

"Wow, thanks. Did you have fun? You look great. Tan." He set the box of candy on his desk.

"We had a great time. But it's good to be home."

Leaning back in his desk chair, he said, "Yeah, it's always good to get home. Where's Walt?"

"He had some work to do at the house, so I thought I'd get out, see a few friends, deliver some candy." She flashed him a grin.

"I don't want to be a downer on your first day back from your honeymoon, but I heard something strange about the bed and breakfast."

"You mean that my business license was revoked?" Danielle asked.

"So it's true?"

"Yes, it is." Danielle then went on to tell him all that she knew.

"I feel a little guilty," Adam said after Danielle finished updating him on the situation.

Danielle frowned. "Guilty why?"

"I knew about the hearing requirement. I should have mentioned it to you so you could have looked into it, so it wouldn't come back to bite you, like it has. But I just didn't think it was a big deal. At the time, the only one on Beach Drive who had an issue with the bed and breakfast was Pete Rogers."

"And he wasn't going to force the issue," Danielle said.

"At the time, I didn't know why. But considering what Renton's firm had on Rogers, he knew there wasn't going to be a problem there. And my grandmother, Renton knew she wouldn't have an issue with it; after all, her house was a rental, as were most of the other houses on the street. I'm sorry, Danielle. If you'd had that hearing before your new neighbor moved in, I don't think you would have had a problem getting a license."

"That's okay, Adam. It all worked out." Danielle then went on to tell him what she and Walt wanted to do with the property.

When Danielle was finished, Adam said, "The way the codes are in this town, you're not going to need a business license for what you want to do. Especially if you aren't taking any money."

"That's what we figured."

"I don't imagine your neighbor will be thrilled, but I don't see how she can do anything," Adam said.

"I don't know what her problem is. She's a nasty woman. According to the chief, that house has been in her family for years."

"I know, I was surprised when I heard it sold. Never went on the market. Then I found out she bought it from some cousins."

"Do you know who they are?" Danielle asked. "The chief said one of her relatives still lives in Frederickport, but he didn't know who it is."

"No, sorry. Why?"

"Just curious. But I think it might be the owners of Morton Funeral Home."

"Now that you mention it, I do remember Grandma saying that house was once owned by the Morton family. Didn't know it was still in the family, but it's entirely possible. Look at my grandmother. She hadn't lived in the Beach Drive house since she was a baby, but she owned that house most of her life."

"What do you know about the Mortons?" Danielle asked. "I thought if I knew more about them, I might be able to understand why Pearl Huckabee is such a bitter old woman."

"It's too bad Grandma isn't here anymore. She could have told you a lot. I remember her mentioning the family a few times. There was a bit of a scandal."

"Scandal?" Danielle asked.

"Yeah. There were two sisters—twins. Grandma went to school with them. They were a couple of years older than her. I guess one of the sisters ran off with her twin's fiancé."

"That's rude."

Adam chuckled. "It was. Grandma thought it was done for spite. The one who ran off with her sister's boyfriend had been disinherited by their father. And since she couldn't get any of the family money, she helped herself to her sister's boyfriend. At least, that's how Grandma told the story."

"I wonder if they ever made up?" Danielle asked.

"Not sure. From how Grandma told it, the jilted sister stayed in Frederickport and ran the funeral home. She ended up married to one of her employees. Grandma said she was pretty bitter over what her sister had done; it changed her."

"What happened to the sister who ran off with the fiancé?"

"They seemed to have a more exciting life. It didn't look like the lack of inheritance bothered her much. She traveled all over the world. The sister of one of my grandmother's friends had been a close friend of the twin who ran away, and she'd get letters periodically from her—from Paris, Greece, Italy. I don't think she ever returned to Frederickport."

"If Pearl is related to the Morton family, then it must be through the jilted twin. And if she was that bitter, I suppose it is entirely possible she passed some of that bitterness down to her children or grandchildren."

Adam grinned. "Is bitterness an inheritable trait?"

Danielle shrugged. "Maybe not by DNA, but by how one's raised."

"WAS that Danielle who just drove away?" Melony asked when she walked into Adam's office not long after Danielle left.

Adam, who was still sitting behind his desk, held up the candy Danielle had dropped off. "Yes. And she brought me chocolate macadamia nuts."

"Oh, I love those," Melony said, reaching for the box of chocolates.

Adam snatched them out of her reach. "Mine. You go get your own. In fact, I think she said something about having a box for you too."

"I don't want to wait," Melony said, successfully grabbing the box from Adam's clutch. He frowned but didn't try to take them back.

Melony sat down in a chair, the box in her hand. She looked over at Adam and asked in a less aggressive tone, "Can I?"

Adam rolled his eyes. "Yeah, you can open them."

Melony grinned and started to open the box. "I promise if Danielle gives me some, I will share. Did they have fun in Hawaii?" With the box now open, she stood back up and held it out to Adam. He took a piece. She took one too and sat back down in her chair.

"Sounded like it. She seems in a good place. I think marriage agrees with her."

After taking a nibble of her piece of candy, Melony asked, "So you've come to terms with Walt?"

Adam shrugged. "He's an alright guy. And she definitely seems happy."

"With Lily pregnant, I wonder if Danielle is going to get pregnant soon." Melony popped the rest of the piece of candy in her mouth.

"I don't know why that would matter."

"They are best friends. Sometimes girlfriends like to plan having kids at the same time. Unless I'm the girlfriend." Melony took another piece of candy and then set the box on Adam's desk.

"That's just because you don't want kids," Adam teased.

"True. But neither do you," Melony countered.

"What do you mean you don't want kids?" Marie gasped. She had just popped into the office moments earlier, just in time to hear Melony and Adam announce that neither one of them wanted children.

SIX

After Danielle left Pearl's house that morning, Craig Simmons introduced himself to Danielle's neighbor. Pearl had called him the day before, requesting he come over to give her a bid on some work. She stepped out onto the front porch and began telling him what she needed done in the front yard. He busily jotted down notes on a pad of paper as he listened to her instructions.

"I think that covers everything I want done in the front yard. Now, let me take you to the backyard," Pearl told him.

"What about that tree?" He pointed to a large tree in the front of the property not far from the sidewalk.

"What about it?"

"You should consider having it trimmed. That one branch could come down in a good wind."

"I don't want to deal with the trees yet. I'm sure it will be fine for another year. I need to get the rest of the yard finished first. I'm not made of money. That branch has been there for as long as I can remember; I'm sure it will be fine for a couple more years."

"Okay. But you might want to think about it." He then shook the pen in his hand. "My pen died. Let me grab another one from my truck."

"Fine. I'll meet you around back," she told him.

As Craig went to his truck, Pearl headed for the backyard, walking along the wrought-iron fencing separating her property from Marlow House. Just as she stepped behind some bushes, blocking her view of the street, she spied motion in the tree along the property line. The tree itself was on Marlow property, but one of its branches arched onto her side of the property line, and sitting on the branch looking down at her was the Marlows' black cat.

Pearl glared up at him. "You sneaky little animal." On impulse Pearl leaned down and snatched up a large rock from the ground. She then hurled it at the cat. Pearl had played softball most of her life, quitting about ten years earlier. However, she still had a good arm and was capable of hitting any target if she set her mind to it.

It happened so fast she would later question what she had actually witnessed. Her aim had been perfect. Unless the cat moved at the last second, the rock should have hit square between his eyes, and considering the size of the rock and the velocity, it could have killed him. Yet just before the rock hit its target, it reacted like a boomerang, changing course, heading back in her direction. Frozen from shock, Pearl didn't have time to duck to avoid the incoming missile, but once again it changed course, this time veering off several inches to one side, whizzing by her head, brushing the tip of her ear.

The cat did not budge from his perch and continued to stare down at her. Nearby rustling caught her attention, and her gaze moved from the cat toward the neighbor's yard. She found herself staring into the intense blue eyes of Walt Marlow. He stood several feet from the tree, watching her, his face expressionless. She knew he had seen what she had tried to do. For a fleeting moment she imagined Walt Marlow had somehow caused the rock to change course and almost hit her. That, of course, she told herself, was a ludicrous thought. The only reasonable explanation, the rock must have hit somewhere on the tree and then ricocheted back in her direction.

"Okay, I'm ready, Mrs. Huckabee. What do you need done back here?" Craig said the next moment as he came walking down the side of the yard from the front.

"Umm…come, I'll show you," Pearl said hastily, turning from Walt.

WALT STOOD in the side yard of Marlow House and watched as Pearl led Craig to the back of her property. He shook his head in disgust and then walked to the tree and put out his arms to Max. The cat looked down at him and then leapt into Walt's outstretched arms.

"When are you going to listen to me?" Walt asked as he cradled the cat.

Nuzzling Walt's hand, Max began to purr.

"Stop trying to change the subject," Walt told him.

Max stopped purring. He looked up in Walt's eyes and meowed. Leaning over, Walt set the cat on the lawn and released him. Max looked up to him and blinked.

"Why didn't I hit her with the rock? I'm not going to hit women with rocks."

Max blinked again, his attention fully on Walt, who stood over him.

"Yes, I know she almost hit you. If it hadn't been for me, she would have knocked you out of that tree and over to Marie's side."

Max meowed.

"You need to stop pushing it, Max."

Walt turned from the cat and headed to the back of the property, near the garage.

Max trailed alongside Walt and meowed.

Still walking, Walt glanced down at the cat and silently conveyed, *I think I will do a little eavesdropping. See what our neighbor has planned for her yard.* Lingering by the woodpile at the side of the garage, Walt straightened the firewood while listening to what was being said next door.

PEARL POINTED to an area near the back fence. "I'd like to have the lawn removed. It's scraggly anyway. I would like to have a sitting area put in. Maybe a patio made from pavers. Do you do that sort of thing?"

"Yes, we do."

"And over there..." She pointed to the two rows of rosebushes along the north fence, bordering the Marlow property line. "I don't want you to touch that. None of that area."

"Are you sure? Those bushes look dead. I could take them out for you and plant something else."

"No. Absolutely not. They were my grandmother's prize roses. I'm going to bring them back to life."

Craig frowned at the scraggly rosebushes, woody and dried looking without a single bud. "They're going to need resuscitating," he muttered under his breath.

Walt, who was still standing by the woodpile in his yard, glanced over to his neighbor's yard. He couldn't recall the last time he'd seen flowers on those plants. Shaking his head, he made his way to the front of his property, Max trailing behind him like a dog.

Craig walked over to one of the rosebushes and knelt down. He gently wiggled one of its branches. It snapped off. He looked up at Pearl. "Mrs. Huckabee, I hate to tell you this, but these rosebushes are dead. I could always replace them with new ones if you have your heart set on roses."

She shook her head adamantly. "No. I'm afraid I can't have you do that. They were my grandmother's prize roses. When we were little, she always told us they were never to be removed. She made all us grandchildren promise to never disturb this area of the yard. She was so proud of those roses."

"But they're dead," he reiterated.

"They aren't dead. They're just dormant."

WALT HAD BEEN in the house just a few minutes when the doorbell rang. When he answered the door, it was Bill Jones, handyman and friend of Adam Nichols. Wearing worn denim jeans, a blue work shirt and a black baseball cap, Bill carried a clipboard in his hand.

"Mr. Jones," Walt greeted him, opening the door wider.

"Hi. Danielle called, said she had some fencing she needed repaired," Bill told him.

"Yes, in the side yard. I'll show you."

By the time Walt and Bill got to the side yard, Craig Simmons had just gone into the house next door with Pearl.

Bill nodded toward Pearl's house. "I see you have a new neighbor."

"Yes. Not the most friendly of neighbors."

"I used to do some work for the last owners. Peculiar bunch."

"Really? I didn't know Adam was the manager of that property."

Bill shook his head. "He wasn't. I do side jobs for people who aren't in his rental program—like Marlow House."

Walt nodded. "Of course." Walt glanced over to Pearl's house. "I understand the new owner is related to the previous owner. Why do you say they are a peculiar bunch?"

Bill shrugged. "I know the house was passed down in the family a couple of generations. Last owners were cousins who had inherited the property from their parents. Didn't get along very well. I can only recall a few times they even used the house. But they'd have me maintain the yard. Last time I was over here, there were a bunch of dead rosebushes in the backyard, and I offered to take them out. But they wouldn't let me touch them."

"They're still there," Walt told him.

"Maybe the new owner will take them out," Bill suggested.

"Doesn't sound that way. She seems pretty sentimental about them."

Bill rolled his eyes. "Yeah, the previous owners were too. So, where is that fence you want me to fix?"

Walt took Bill over to the section of the fence where Pearl had climbed through the day before.

"You think you can fix it?" Walt asked after Bill inspected the section.

"Sure. I can do it." Bill glanced down at the damaged piece. "Looks like someone's been going through that opening." He pointed to the ground. "You can see where the broken piece has been dragged, and there's a footprint."

"Which is why we want to have it repaired."

Bill glanced over to Pearl's house. "You think the new neighbor went through there?"

Walt shrugged. "Someone did. What do you think it will cost to repair?"

Bill threw out a price.

"When can you start?" Walt asked.

"I can start now. I need to get some measurements first. But I should be able to get it fixed by tomorrow."

"Wonderful."

"I guess now that you're married to Danielle, you can authorize this?" Bill asked.

Walt flashed Bill a smile. "Yes. But if you would feel better calling Danielle first, you can reach her on her cellphone."

Bill shrugged. "Nah, that's okay. I'll take your word for it. I'll go measure it now."

PEARL WALKED Craig Simmons back outside and said goodbye to him, while he promised to get her an estimate the next day. As he made his way down the walkway to the street, she spied movement by the fencing between her house and Marlow House. Looking that way, she noticed someone crouched by the fence. It looked as if he was peering into her yard. It wasn't Walt Marlow. It was another man wearing a black baseball cap and blue shirt. Reaching her hand in her pocket, she felt for her cellphone.

Glancing toward the street, she saw Craig wasn't to the sidewalk yet. If she had a problem with this man, she was sure she could call for help and Craig could get to her. With narrowed eyes she stomped over to the man crouching by the fence.

"What are you doing there?" she demanded.

He looked up at her. "I'm going to fix this fence after I see what I need. Looks like someone has been crawling through this opening."

"It's probably that menacing cat of theirs! It's always in my yard!"

"I don't think cats wear shoes," Bill said, pointing to the footprint in the dried mud. He then glanced at Pearl's shoes. "Looks like your size."

She scowled at him and then turned abruptly, hurrying back to her house.

SEVEN

The next stop on Danielle's list was the Glandon Foundation Headquarters, to say hello to Chris and Heather and bring them each a box of chocolate-covered macadamia nuts from Hawaii. When she pulled up in front of the building and parked, she noticed several trucks parked out front—one from a local electrician and another from a local contractor. As she got out of her car, she wondered what they were doing here.

Wearing skinny jeans, knee-high boots, a beige knit cowl-neck sweater, its hem falling at her hips, with two boxes of candy under one arm and a purse draped over the opposite shoulder, Danielle opened the front gate and started up the walkway. She was greeted by Chris's pit bull, Hunny, who came darting out from the side of the building, tail wagging, excited to see her.

"Hey, Hunny," Danielle cooed, pausing a moment to say hello. She leaned down to pet the dog and was greeted by sloppy kisses as Hunny jumped up and down.

"She's totally out of control," came a woman's voice from the front porch. Danielle glanced up from the excited dog and spied Heather standing in the now open front doorway.

Heather Donovan lived two doors down from Marlow House, on the other side of Pearl Huckabee. She worked for Chris Glandon, aka Chris Johnson, and like Chris, Danielle and Walt, she could see ghosts. On first impression people often classified Heather as Goth, which Heather thought a ridiculous assumption. Just because she wore her long jet-black hair straight, often pulled into braids or pigtails, with straight-cut bangs falling along her eyebrows, and she preferred black nail polish and lipstick, there was no reason to imagine she liked sleeping in coffins. Heather had no idea if Goths actually slept in coffins, that was just what she imagined. And to her coffins meant dead people, and she saw enough of those without inviting them into her bed.

Today Heather wore thigh-high black high-heeled boots over black yoga pants, with a poncho-like dark blue knit blouse. She had skipped applying any lipstick that morning, but her long fingernails wore black polish. Instead of braids or pigtails, she wore her hair down straight, its length silky and shiny from an early morning shampoo.

"Hey, Heather!" Danielle greeted her, starting on her way again toward the house.

"Welcome home. I saw the lights on at Marlow House last night. I was tempted to come over and say hi, but figured you probably wanted time to settle in."

"You should have." Danielle walked up the front steps and greeted Heather with a quick hug while Hunny pranced around their feet, wanting more attention.

"You stay out here a while," Heather scolded the dog, pushing her back outside when the two women walked into the building. The door closed behind them, leaving Hunny outside.

Danielle handed Heather a box of candy. "For you."

"Awesome! Love these. Thanks. So how was Hawaii?"

"It was wonderful. So relaxing. The weather was great. Walt actually has a suntan!"

"No longer ghostly white?" Heather snickered as she led the way into the waiting area.

"I must say a tan does something for those blue eyes of his," Danielle said with a dreamy sigh.

Heather rolled her eyes. "You sound like a lovesick newlywed."

"I am." Danielle grinned. "But Walt reminded me our real first wedding anniversary is less than three months away."

"You look great. All that sunshine must agree with you," Heather said as she sat down on a chair and started to open the box of candy.

"We had an amazing time. It was weird. It was like we were…

normal for once." Danielle sat in the chair next to Heather.

Heather arched her brow at Danielle as she removed a piece of candy from the box. "Normal? You guys will never be normal. Does this mean you didn't run into any spirits over there?"

"Not that we noticed."

"Really? I always heard the islands had all sorts of spirits." Heather bit off half of the piece of candy and while chewing, mumbled, "This is really fresh."

Danielle set the other box of candy on the side table and glanced to the doorway leading to the hall. "Where is Chris?"

"He's upstairs with the contractors. He should be down in a minute."

"What's he doing with the contractors? Did something break?"

Heather offered a piece of candy to Danielle. After she declined the offer, Heather took a second piece and then put the lid back on the box before setting it on the table. "No, nothing's broken. But Chris has finally decided to do it—he's remodeling the rest of the house, creating office space."

"Really? Do you need more office space?"

"We will if Chris does what he's been thinking about for the last six months. Like you know, only a fraction of what the foundation does is run out of this office. And he still has his family's corporation. He's planning to move everything here, to Frederickport. Centralize in one location. Well, as much as he can."

"Wow. He's come a long way. I remember when I first met him he hadn't set up the foundation yet. Of course, he was still giving away money." Danielle glanced around. "This house is certainly large enough to be turned into office space, but can he legally do that? This is a residential area. I know he was able to get a variance for the office when he bought the place, but that's because no customers or real foot traffic would be coming or going. But if he is going to remodel—and even if clients don't come here, you would still have employees who would be using all those offices he intends to create. Can he legally do that?"

"Apparently he can. I'll let him tell you how he pulled it off. Typical Chris." Heather chuckled.

"The reason I ask, Marlow House Bed and Breakfast lost its business license."

"So it's true?" Heather asked.

"You heard?"

Heather nodded. "Yeah. Adam said something to Chris about it, and Chris was tempted to give you a heads-up, but we talked about it and decided there was no reason to ruin your honeymoon. There was nothing you could do about it from there, and we weren't even sure how true it was."

Voices from the hallway caught their attention. Danielle glanced over to see Chris walking two men out of the building and telling them goodbye. After he closed the front door, he turned toward the doorway leading to Danielle and Heather.

"Welcome home!" Chris greeted her as he walked into the room.

"Aloha," Danielle said as she stood. She picked up the unopened box of candy and handed it to Chris. "I come bearing gifts."

"Oh, sweet!" Chris said, taking the box.

"Yes, they are." Danielle grinned.

Chris gave her a quick hug. Several moments later Danielle sat back down in her chair with Chris sitting across from her and Heather.

"I was just hearing about your plans. I would love to know how you got permission," Danielle said.

Heather looked to Chris. "It's true about Marlow House. Danielle was just telling me about it."

Sitting on the chair with the unopened box of candy on his lap, Chris looked to Danielle and asked, "What happened?"

Danielle went on to tell Chris and Heather about losing the business license and why. When she was finished with her telling, Chris shook his head and let out a low whistle. "That new neighbor of ours is a piece of work."

"She's a witch," Heather said. "I don't even let Bella outside when I'm at home unless I'm outside with her."

"I want to know how did you get your neighbors to agree to what you have planned for this house?" Danielle asked Chris. "I am assuming you went through the process."

"I did." Chris grinned. "First, I promised all the parking would be on my property—not on the street. There is plenty of room for what parking we'll need, and it will all be concealed behind a wall."

"That's it?" Danielle asked.

"It also cost me a fortune to get them to agree," Chris said with a snort.

"Don't tell me you paid off your neighbors?" Danielle asked.

"Yes and no." Chris picked up the box of candy and set it on the coffee table.

"Go ahead, tell her," Heather urged.

"I went to each neighbor," Chris explained, "and offered to make a million-dollar donation to their favorite charity."

"You didn't?" Danielle couldn't help but laugh.

Chris shrugged. "My main business these days is giving away money to worthy causes. This time, I figured I'd use it to get what I wanted. The catch was, it had to be a legitimate nonprofit charity. And the money would only be given if all the neighbors agreed and the city approved my application."

"Wow. Talk about putting on the peer pressure," Danielle said dryly.

"It was kind of interesting to see what causes the different neighbors found important. And they were pretty excited about it," Heather said.

"And you did all this in the last two weeks?" Danielle asked.

"I've been working on it for a while," Chris explained. "I didn't say anything to you before because you had a lot on your plate with the wedding and all."

"You mentioned Pearl might be related to the Morton Funeral Home family?" Heather asked.

"According to Walt, that's who lived in the house when he died. And Pearl claims the house has been in her family for years. So that's what we're wondering. She supposedly has relatives who still live in Frederickport."

"The owners of the Morton Funeral Home are one of the neighbors on this street," Heather told her.

"Really?" Danielle looked from Heather to Chris, back to Heather.

"In fact, we have all the paperwork on the donations back from all the neighbors—except for them," Heather explained.

"What do you know about them?" Danielle asked. "I'd love to figure out why Pearl is such a nasty person."

"You mean Norman Bates and his scary old mother?" Heather began to laugh.

Danielle looked at Heather with a frown. "What?"

Chris rolled his eyes and shook his head at Heather. He looked at Danielle. "His name is Norman Bateman, and he lives with his elderly mother, Faye Bateman, down the street."

"I swear he looks just like Anthony Perkins in *Psycho*," Heather told Danielle. "And he acts just like him!"

"He does not," Chris argued.

"Does too," Heather insisted.

"Do they just own the funeral home, or does he work there?" Danielle asked.

"He's the funeral director," Chris explained. "And he has always been very pleasant to me."

Heather shrugged. "So was Anthony Perkins in the movie—just before he hacked up poor Janet Leigh in the shower."

"He's not married? Does he have any kids? If he's related to Pearl, I wonder how," Danielle asked.

"He's not married now, but he might be a widower or divorced, for all I know," Chris told her. "And considering his age, if he has children, they're probably adults by now. He's never mentioned kids or grandkids before."

"Does he have siblings?" Danielle asked.

"I have absolutely no idea," Chris said. "We aren't that friendly."

"No. You're just giving him a million dollars to give away," Heather said with a snort.

"As long as it's for a good cause, I'm okay with it," Chris said. He then looked at Danielle. "If you're that curious about the Batemans, Heather has to go over to the funeral home tomorrow to pick up his papers on his donation. He promised to have them ready by then. Why don't you go with her?"

"Oh yes," Heather said quickly. "Please do. I really don't want to go to a funeral home alone."

"Don't be silly," Chris scoffed.

"I don't blame her," Danielle told Chris. "I've never been thrilled about going to a cemetery."

"You've been to the local cemetery lots of times," Heather reminded her.

"True. But I really didn't want to go the first time I went. And I wouldn't have been there if Angela's ghost hadn't been playing tricks with my car and phone. But since then, it's not so bad. I have a better sense of what to expect now. Each cemetery is different, with varying degrees of hauntings."

"That's how I feel about going to the funeral home," Heather told her.

"I suppose two of us would be better than one. I'll go with you. I'm curious to find out more about Pearl's family."

EIGHT

"You want Chris to pay off Pearl?" Heather teased. "I'm sure he has another million he's dying to give away."

Danielle chuckled. "No, that's okay. For one thing, I don't imagine Pearl would change her mind, even for her favorite charity."

"I doubt she has a favorite charity," Heather grumbled.

"Are you going to try fighting it?" Chris asked.

Danielle shook her head. "Ironically, when we were in Hawaii, Walt and I discussed closing the B and B."

"I thought you loved it?" Heather asked.

"I did." Danielle went on to repeat all that she had told Lily as to why they had come to that decision.

"I understand," Chris said when she finished her telling. "What do you want to do? You mentioned you and Walt had decided on something else with Marlow House."

"We'd like to use it to help raise money for charities. It could be a place where I can host charity luncheons—dinners—barbecues. Maybe provide free housing for charity benefits—work with you."

Chris grinned. "I love that idea."

"Oh! What about the high school's fundraiser?" Heather said excitedly. "They could sell raffle tickets for spring break!"

"High school fundraiser?" Danielle frowned.

"Do you remember Elizabeth Sparks?" Chris asked.

"Isn't she the art teacher the police department uses sometimes to make police sketches?" Danielle asked.

"Yes. She's trying to raise money for the high school's art department. Funding for the arts has been drastically cut," Chris began. "She remembered the foundation had purchased the portraits and had them on loan at the museum. She wondered if the foundation might consider a donation to the art department."

"Are you donating?" Danielle asked.

"I've come to believe it's best when communities take an active role in fundraising, without one corporation or benefactor always stepping up. So I told her if she put together a fundraiser, I would match whatever they raised. I think it's important to get the students involved. If they want to save their art department, I think they should fight for it," Chris explained.

"They haven't come up with an idea yet," Heather told Danielle. "They want something original. This would be original. The students could sell raffle tickets—and the winners could spend Easter week at Marlow House."

"I like that idea." Danielle smiled. "We have four rooms to offer. People might be more inclined to buy tickets if there was more than one winner."

"That's, of course, if you can do something like that without a business license?" Heather said.

"I think so, since I'm not renting out the rooms. But I'll stop by the city office on my way over to see the chief and find out for sure."

"I HATED SENDING you that notice. I wanted to call you personally, but I heard you were gone on your honeymoon, and I didn't want to call your cellphone and disrupt your holiday," the woman at the city clerk's office explained to Danielle. "But I had to get the notice out immediately."

"That's alright," Danielle assured her. "I understand. The reason I'm here, I was wondering…" Danielle went on to explain what she wanted to do with Marlow House.

"That is so nice of you!" the woman said after Danielle finished explaining.

"Do I need any kind of license?" she asked.

The woman shook her head. "No, you don't."

"Are you sure? I'd hate to get this going and find out I can't do it."

"I'm positive. A few years ago one of our residents, who normally does not rent her house out, had a raffle to raise money for her church. The winner got the beach house for a week that summer. It was perfectly legal. I remember double-checking the codes back then, and nothing has changed."

"Wonderful." Danielle grinned.

"And if the high school takes you up on your offer, make sure you have one of the students stop by here to sell some tickets. I have family coming then, and I would love the chance to put them up at Marlow House. In fact, before I discovered there was a problem with your business license, I intended to see if I could make reservations with you for spring break."

"I hope you understand I had no idea Mr. Renton had taken any shortcuts. He was supposed to handle everything for me before I arrived in town."

"Oh, I do. To be honest, I never cared much for Mr. Renton. But he finally had to deal with karma."

"I suppose it was karma," Danielle agreed.

"Anyway, remember to have the students bring me some tickets if you go through with the fundraiser."

"I'll do that. Thanks for the information." Danielle started to turn away when the woman called her back.

"I noticed you never got around to putting up a sign in front of Marlow House."

"I kept meaning to do it, but something always came up and I got sidetracked."

"Since you'll be working with Elizabeth Sparks, I thought you might ask her about her boyfriend making you a sign."

"Sign?" Danielle frowned.

"Elizabeth's boyfriend makes signs for people all over the country. He does much of it over the internet. Some of them are quite beautiful. I always thought one of his signs in front of Marlow House would be fitting. It could say Marlow House and the year it was established. Of course, if it were still a bed and breakfast, it would say Marlow House Bed and Breakfast, but you couldn't do that now."

"I wouldn't need a permit for a sign like that?"

"No. According to the city ordinance, it would be considered a historical marker, which doesn't require a permit and is encouraged. They do require approval, but I know you wouldn't have a problem getting one of his signs approved. And it would be great publicity for you if you want to continue offering Marlow House for charity functions."

"I think I would like that. Thanks for the suggestion. Do you know what his name is or how I can contact him?"

The woman shook her head. "I'm sorry. I can't recall his name offhand. But if you're going to be talking to Elizabeth anyway, she can give you his name and number."

DANIELLE ENTERED the police department fifteen minutes later carrying a stack of cellophane-sealed boxes of chocolate-covered macadamia nuts. As she walked by the dispatcher, she dropped off a box, said hello, and chatted for a moment before heading for the chief's office.

"Welcome home!" MacDonald greeted her when Danielle walked into the office. He stood up from his desk and looked to the boxes of candy and asked, "Are those all for me?"

"Ha ha," Danielle said with a grin. "Three are. Well, one is for you and the other two are for your boys." She set the candy on the desk. "I have a box for Joe and Kelly, and one for Brian. Are they here?"

"No."

Danielle took a seat in one of the chairs facing the chief. He sat back down behind his desk.

"The boys are going to be thrilled, each getting their own box of candy. I just need to make sure they don't eat it all at once."

Danielle grinned. "The joys of parenthood!"

"Now you're reminding me of his grandparents. Give them a noisy toy that I have to deal with. But in this case, an entire box of chocolate."

Danielle shrugged. "What can I say? I like to stir up things. Would you mind giving Joe and Brian the candy when they get back?"

"Sure. If I don't eat them first." He grinned.

"And here you are acting like it's the boys who would eat all the candy," Danielle snickered.

The chief flashed Danielle a smile. "It was sweet of you to think of us while you were on your honeymoon."

"I'll admit I sort of took the easy gift route. I figured who doesn't love chocolate-covered macadamia nuts?"

"You didn't have to get us anything. But I do appreciate it." He leaned back in his chair. "Where is Walt? Tired of hanging out with each other?"

"I had some errands to run, and he had some work to do at home. Plus, I called Bill to stop by and look at the fence between our house and Pearl's. It needs to be repaired. Walt stayed home so he could talk to him about it."

"How is your new neighbor? What did you decide to do about the B and B?" MacDonald asked.

Danielle spent the next ten minutes updating the chief on all that had happened since she and Walt had arrived back in Frederickport.

"I'm glad it's working out for you. This will make Joe happy." He chuckled.

Danielle shook her head. "He never could understand why I kept it open. Especially after the inheritances."

"I'll admit I did wonder myself when you might start questioning keeping it open—especially now that you and Walt are married and after some of your recent experiences."

"You mean like our guests trying to blackmail us or kill us?"

"Yeah, pretty much." The chief nodded.

Danielle let out a sigh and leaned back in the chair. Her hand absently went up to the locket hanging from the gold chain around her neck, fiddling with it. Until that moment, it had been hidden under the cowl neckline of her sweater.

"You're wearing the locket." The chief beamed. "You do like it."

She glanced down at the locket, rubbing one thumb over it. "I love it. And…well…there is something about the locket you don't know. I didn't have time to tell you when you gave it to me, what with getting married and then leaving on our honeymoon."

"Tell me what?"

Letting go of the golden heart locket, she looked at the chief. "First, I need to ask you something. When you gave it to me, you mentioned you purchased it at an antique shop. How did you happen to be there?"

"Remember when I went to Vancouver with the boys? When Claudia Dane was claiming to be married to Clint."

"Yeah. It was some family gathering, right?"

The chief nodded. "One day we took some of the kids down to get ice cream, and there was an antique shop next door. One of the cousin's wives wanted to look in the shop while the kids picked out their ice cream. At the last minute I decided to go into the shop with her. It was fate, I think. The minute I walked in, I almost felt like something made me look at the jewelry in the glass case. I don't know why. I don't normally check out women's jewelry—I'm not even dating anyone right now." He laughed.

"It was fate, Chief." Danielle smiled softly.

Cocking his head to one side, he studied her curious expression. "So what did you want to tell me about the locket?"

"The night before my wedding I had a dream. My parents were there. Mom was helping me into my wedding dress. My father came into the room and he gave me a present—a gold heart locket. One that looks exactly like this one." She touched the locket again. "It even had an engraved M. Exactly like this one."

The chief stared blankly at Danielle. He blinked his eyes. "Are you saying your father's spirit guided me to buy that locket? That it was his wedding gift to you?"

Danielle nodded. She then grinned and said, "But I don't think Dad's going to pay you back for it."

NINE

It was their third day back home. Danielle had just gotten off the phone with Elizabeth Sparks, who loved the idea of the fundraiser. With Easter about six weeks away, they decided to have the tickets printed immediately. That would give the students three weeks to sell the tickets, announce the winners, and give the winners almost three weeks to make any necessary travel plans. Danielle worried they were cutting it a little short, yet figured whatever they raised would help the art department while kick-starting her and Walt's new plans for Marlow House. She also obtained the contact information for Elizabeth's boyfriend, which she gave to Walt.

"Elizabeth said he might be able to come over today and talk to you about the sign," she told him.

"Don't you want to be here?" Walt asked.

"I think you have a better eye for what kind of sign would look best for Marlow House. Something that fits the era when the house was built."

"Are you insinuating I'm old?" Walt teased.

Danielle grinned at Walt before giving him a quick kiss and slipping on her jacket. "You do have an intimate knowledge of that era."

Walt, who stood facing Danielle, reached out and tenderly buttoned the top of her jacket. She stood patiently, waiting for him to finish.

"You do know I was born almost thirty years after this house was built," he asked.

"I love you, Walt," Danielle said as he finished slipping the last button through its buttonhole.

Walt arched his brows and asked with a smile, "What does that have to do with what we were talking about?"

"Nothing. But I just like saying it."

"SECOND DAY I've seen you without Walt. Is the honeymoon over?" Heather teased as she climbed into Danielle's car fifteen minutes later.

"Actually the honeymoon ended three days ago." Hands on the steering wheel, engine running, Danielle watched as Heather shut the door and fastened her seatbelt.

"So the romance is over?"

"I thought we were talking about honeymoons?" Danielle asked. "The romance is still there. Even for us old married couples. You know our real first anniversary is just around the corner."

"I know. That's what you told me yesterday. So what are you going to do for your first anniversary?" Heather asked as Danielle drove the car out into the street and headed down the road.

"Not a clue. After all, we just got back from our honeymoon."

"Seriously, I did sort of expect Walt to come with us today. You two are always together."

"He had to stay home and take care of some stuff at the house. Bill's fixing our fence."

"Where Pearl came through?" Heather asked.

Danielle nodded. "Yeah."

"Good. I need to check the fence between her house and mine. Her trying to go through your dog door is beyond creepy."

"I wonder if she is related to Norman Bateman," Danielle said.

"Considering her creep factor, she probably is," Heather grumbled. "By the way, thanks again for coming with me today. When Chris told me he needed to pick up the papers at the funeral home, I really didn't want to go alone, but I knew he was meeting with more contractors today. And considering my recent raise, I really need to try to be a better employee. Ugh."

Danielle glanced at Heather and then looked back down the road. "You got a raise?"

"Crazy but true. I really don't know why Chris puts so much trust in me. I'm his assistant, and when the new employees arrive and fill the new offices, according to Chris, I will be…well…their supervisor."

"Really?" Danielle said.

Heather shook her head in disbelief and dropped her head on the headrest as she stared out the front windshield. "I know. What in the world was Chris thinking?"

DANIELLE STEPPED into the front foyer of the Morton Funeral Home with Heather and looked around at the dark paneled walls and vintage decor. From what she understood, the Victorian house had been built about ten years after Marlow House. She wondered if the upholstered furniture—several sofas and chairs in the waiting area—were original pieces, yet obviously reupholstered, considering their pristine condition.

On one wall she spied several portraits. She wandered over to take a closer look when she heard a male voice say, "Ms. Donovan, thank you for picking this up."

Danielle glanced to the man who had just stepped into the foyer from a connecting room. He walked toward Heather, his right hand extended. If Danielle weren't mistaken, it was Norman Bateman. *He does look sort of like Anthony Perkins in* Psycho, she thought, *albeit an older version.*

Heather shook the man's hand and then nodded to Danielle. "I brought my friend along. Mr. Bateman, this is Danielle Boatman…I mean Danielle Marlow."

"Ahh, the infamous Danielle Marlow of Marlow House," Mr. Bateman said as he took Danielle's hand in his for a brief informal handshake.

"Infamous?" Danielle asked with a chuckle.

"A few of my clients have come from Marlow House," Bateman explained. "Often under suspicious circumstances."

"I try to help the local economy."

Bateman laughed. "A woman with a dark sense of humor. I rather like that."

Danielle blushed. "I guess I probably shouldn't have said that—sort of slipped out."

Bateman flashed Danielle a smile. "I promise I won't tell. But it is nice to meet you."

Danielle nodded to the first portrait on the wall—of a man. "Who's this? He looks a little like you."

Standing next to Danielle and Heather, Norman looked up to the portrait. "It's my grandfather, Elmer Morton. He founded Morton Funeral Home."

"Were you close?" Danielle asked. "You obviously followed in his footsteps."

Norman shook his head. "I'm afraid he passed away before I was born. But my father was also in the business. So I suppose I followed in both of their footsteps."

Danielle moved toward the next portrait. It was of two young women—obviously twins—with short blond curls and vivid blue eyes. "Who are they?" She was fairly certain she already knew, but she asked anyway.

"One is my mother and the other is my aunt Daisy. As you can see, twins."

"They were beautiful," Danielle said, staring at the portrait. She glanced briefly at Norman and asked, "I understand your mother is still alive."

"Yes. She just turned ninety-five. Still sharp as a tack," he told her.

"Wow. Good genes." Still studying the portrait, Danielle asked, "And your aunt Daisy? Is she still alive?"

Norman shook his head. "No, I'm afraid not. Aunt Daisy died about ten years ago."

"I understand they used to live in the house next door to Marlow House," Danielle said. "We were neighbors."

"That's true," Norman said with a grin. "In fact, I tried buying the house back a number of times over the years. I heard it has a new owner now."

With a frown Danielle looked to Norman. "Your family didn't own the house anymore?"

"No. My mother sold it after her father died. At the time, she thought it was too big a house to live in alone—and I think it just had too many memories for her. But she later regretted selling it. Over the years she tried buying it back—and made a few offers. In later years, I tried buying it for Mother. I knew how much it meant to her. I think because her family was all gone and she was trying to recapture what she had lost. But the family who owned it didn't want to sell. From what I understand, it has had a number of owners since my mother sold it, but all from the same family."

"That's true. That's why I assumed it was from the Morton family," Danielle said.

Norman shook his head. "No. And as far as Mortons go, I'm the last one in my grandfather's line—aside from Mother."

"Your aunt didn't have any children?" Danielle asked.

"No. She was married, but her husband died fairly young, and they never had children. She never remarried."

"Did they live in Frederickport?" Danielle asked.

"No. In fact, I never met her. She and her husband left Frederickport right after they were married and never returned. But I felt like I knew her through her letters. She traveled all over the world. A fascinating woman."

"It must have been hard for your mother," Heather said. "I understand twins are closer than most siblings. To have her sister so far away."

Danielle remembered what Adam had told her: *One of the sisters ran off with her twin's fiancé.*

"While my aunt never returned to Oregon, she and Mother kept in touch over the years. I think Mother always imagined her sister would eventually return. It was difficult for her when she got the news Aunt Daisy had passed away."

Danielle wondered if the ex-fiancé dying young had made it easier for Norman's mother to make up with her sister—which Danielle assumed must have happened if they had kept in touch all those years, as Norman said. Or perhaps it was falling in love and marrying Norman's father that had helped her put her sister's betrayal behind her. One thing she did learn today—none of those people were related to Pearl Huckabee.

Danielle turned from the portrait to Norman. "I understand that part of the family who owned the house next door to me before the recent sale still lives in Frederickport. Do you happen to know who that might be? I'll admit I am a little curious about the family. Especially since they've owned the house for so long."

"I've never met anyone from the family personally. In fact, the only contact I've ever had with them is through my attorney at the time when I made my offers. He tracked the owners down for me. Although, my mother once knew who they were. If any of them still live in town—and if she knows about it—I don't recall her ever mentioning them."

"Umm...would you mind telling me who your attorney is? I'd love to contact the family."

"I'm afraid it won't help. It was Clarence Renton."

"Ummm...Clarence Renton?" Danielle groaned.

Norman nodded. "And if those newspaper articles I read were accurate, you above anyone else know how Mr. Renton's career ended."

"I DIDN'T SEE A SINGLE GHOST," Heather said with a sigh of relief as she buckled herself into the passenger seat in Danielle's car.

"Me neither. Of course, we didn't accept Mr. Bateman's offer to tour the facility. I wouldn't be surprised if there are a few spirits hanging around that place." Danielle pulled the car into the street and headed toward home.

"That's why I told him we needed to get back for another appointment when he offered to give us the tour. I didn't want to push our luck," Heather said with a shiver.

"At least we know Pearl's bitterness doesn't come from some Morton family scandal."

"So Norman's aunt stole his mother's boyfriend?" Heather asked.

"Fiancé, according to Adam. While they are not related to Pearl, I have to admit I am curious to hear more about their story."

"I'm sure Marie will be able to tell you more," Heather suggested.

"That's what I'm thinking."

"If Norman's attorney had been someone other than Renton, were you seriously going to see if he could put you in contact with the family? I can't even imagine why. What did you want to say to them?" Heather asked.

"I just said that. Sort of popped out," Danielle told her.

"Like it popped out when you said you like to stimulate the economy by killing off your guests?"

"I didn't say it like that!"

"It was implied." Heather shrugged.

"I'm just curious to learn more about Pearl's family—try to figure out why she's the way she is. Figured the attorney might be able to tell me who they are. Not sure what I would do once I found out."

"You could always stop by the prison and see if Renton's ghost is hanging around. See what he knows," Heather teased.

"Funny. By the way, I didn't think Norman was a bit creepy."

"I think he liked you. Just be careful. And when you're taking a shower, keep an eye on the shower curtain," Heather warned.

TEN

When Danielle returned to Marlow House from the funeral home, she found Walt in the library, jotting down ideas on a legal pad for his current book.

"I stopped and picked up some burgers for lunch," Danielle announced when she entered the room, holding up two to-go paper sacks.

Walt looked up from his writing and smiled. "You must have read my mind. I was just about to get up and make myself a sandwich."

Danielle handed Walt one of the paper sacks. "This is better—and easier."

Walt set his notepad and pen on the nearby table and took the paper bag from Danielle.

"Find out anything interesting at the funeral home?" he asked.

"Just that Pearl isn't related to the Mortons," Danielle said as she sat down on the sofa next to Walt. She then went on to tell him what she had learned.

Danielle was just about finished recounting the morning when Marie suddenly appeared in the room.

"Marie!' Danielle said with surprise. "You and Eva must've been having a good time at the theater. We haven't seen you since we first got home."

Marie shook her head in agitation and began to pace before them. "I was only with Eva the evening after you got home. I've spent the last couple of days at the cemetery."

"Cemetery?" Walt frowned. "What were you doing there?"

Marie stopped pacing and faced them. "Trying to make some sense of life."

"In a cemetery?" Danielle asked.

"I heard something that has shaken me up—made me question why—why am I allowed to stay? Why am I able to harness energy while not being confined as Walt was? What is the reason for any of it?"

Walt and Danielle exchanged quick glances and then looked back to Marie. "What happened? Is this about Marlow House closing? If it is, we're okay," Danielle said.

Marie frowned. "What do you mean Marlow House is closing?"

"Umm…our business license was revoked, but—" Danielle began, only to be cut off by Marie.

"No, no." Marie waved her hand dismissively. "This is about Adam."

"Adam?" Danielle asked. "What's wrong with Adam?"

"I stopped over to see him, and Melony was there. Melony does not want children!" Marie cried before flopping down in one of the chairs facing the sofa.

"Oh…" Danielle muttered.

"And do you know what is worse?" Marie asked.

Danielle shook her head. "No. What?"

"Adam doesn't want children either! How can he not want children? What about my great-grandchildren?"

"You do have another grandson," Walt reminded her.

"But he isn't Adam! That's why I stayed, to make sure he would get married, settle down, have babies. And I thought that was going to happen with Melony—that I would be able to see them start their life together."

"Is it Melony or Adam who doesn't want children?" Walt asked.

"It's both of them," Marie grumbled. "If it was just Melony, I would start looking for someone else for Adam. But Adam claims he doesn't want them either. So what would be the point? And I do so like Melony. How can she not want children? Maybe if she wanted them, she could change Adam's mind. If anyone could change

Adam's mind, it would be Melony. But they actually agree on this! What am I to do?"

"I'm just curious why you went to the cemetery," Walt asked.

"To visit my parents. I needed someone to talk to. Of course, I didn't expect to actually see them, they have moved on, but I did come across a couple of lingering spirits. Unfortunately, they were absolutely no help. I didn't even bother discussing this with Eva, she told me once she never wanted children, so how would she understand?"

"Maybe she could help you understand Adam and Melony's point of view?" Danielle suggested.

"I'm not sure how that's going to help," Marie grumbled.

"Marie, I understand your disappointment," Danielle began gently. "But you have to know deep inside that it would be wrong for Adam to have children if it was not something he really wanted. It would be wrong for the children too. Maybe they will change their minds—but maybe they won't."

"Why don't they want children?" Marie asked sadly.

Danielle considered the question a moment. "I can't speak for them. But maybe in Melony's case it has something to do with her own childhood. Same for Adam. Neither one had a great relationship with their parents. Maybe they're afraid. Maybe they don't feel capable of being good parents. Or maybe they just don't want kids. Marie, it is a big responsibility. And if someone doesn't want children, they shouldn't have them."

Marie let out a sigh. "Maybe they'll change their minds."

They sat in silence for a few minutes while Walt and Danielle quietly ate their burgers. Suddenly Marie sat up straight and blurted, "What do you mean your business license was revoked?"

Danielle went on to update Marie on what had happened to her business license and what they planned to do with Marlow House.

"I could have told you Pearl wasn't related to the Morton family," Marie said.

"What happened to Elmer Morton?" Walt asked.

Leaning back in the chair, Marie crossed her ankles. Folding her hands in her lap, she said, "It was probably twenty years after your death; he fell down the stairs at the funeral home. He was alone when it happened, and when he didn't go home that night, Maisy Faye went looking for him. She was the one to find him at the bottom of the stairs. They said he had been dead for a couple of hours."

"Maisy Faye?" Walt muttered. He then smiled and said, "Maisy Faye. I knew a Maisy Faye once. Beautiful young woman, with golden curls. I haven't thought about her in years…"

"It definitely was not the same Maisy Faye. This one was one of the twins, and I think she was about three when you died," Marie told him.

With arched brows Danielle looked to Walt. "Hmmm…do I need to be jealous? The way you say Maisy Faye's name sounds like there was a little something going on," she teased.

Walt's faraway look quickly passed and he flashed Danielle a sheepish smile. "No. There was nothing between us…at least…I don't think so."

"You don't know?" Danielle couldn't help but chuckle.

He shrugged. "Her face came to me immediately when Marie mentioned the name—and I remember her voice. But I can't recall exactly where I knew her. Maybe in college—or she might have been one of Angela's friends."

"Whoever she was, it was a different Maisy Faye," Marie said matter-of-factly.

"From what Norman Bateman told me, the twins were Maisy Faye and Daisy Faye. But his mother, Maisy Faye, goes by Faye now," Danielle explained.

"I don't recall ever knowing the babies' names. Someone might have told me, but if they did, I don't remember. I was never on friendly terms with Elmer," Walt said.

"Adam told me a little about their story. How Daisy ran off with Maisy's fiancé," Danielle said.

"Ahh yes, it was quite the scandal back then," Marie said. "Especially with the disinheritance."

"So what was that all about?" Danielle asked.

"The twins were a few years older than me," Marie began. "Identical twins. One of my friends used to call them pinup girls—because of their extraordinary looks—and figures. Mr. Morton was raising them on his own. Daisy was the trial, always testing the limits, wild as a March hare. Frankly, I expected her and one of her beaus to be walked down the aisle at the end of a shotgun, considering her reputation. But Maisy was such a sweet thing. She took care of the house, looked after their father, never got in trouble, and was engaged to a war hero."

"And then Daisy stole Maisy's boyfriend?" Danielle asked.

"Yes, but before that happened, Mr. Morton went to his attorney and had Daisy written out of the will. He'd had it with her. I'm not sure what happened exactly—what was the final straw—but there were rumors he walked in on Daisy in a compromising position with a man. Some said it was a married man. But you know rumors."

"Did Mr. Morton fall down the stairs after Daisy ran away with Maisy's boyfriend?" Danielle asked.

Marie shook her head. "No. A few days after his attorney wrote up the papers, there was the accident at the funeral home. Daisy was supposed to move out of the house next door—her father had basically evicted her. But after he died, Maisy begged her to stay on. With her father's unexpected death, she didn't want to stay at the house alone. The lawyer said that since the house was Maisy's now, Daisy could stay if her sister wanted."

"Did they ever suspect Daisy might have had something to do with her father's fall?" Walt asked. "After all, he did disinherit her."

Marie shook her head. "No. According to the family attorney, Mr. Morton was willing to put Daisy back in the will if she straightened up. Maisy had more to gain with her father's death, and she would never have hurt him. Plus, Mr. Morton was not a young man, and he had a bad leg, so a fall wasn't especially surprising."

"How long after their father's death did Daisy run away with Maisy's boyfriend?" Danielle asked.

"It was about two months later. The two girls were staying together at the house next door. When her sister was not around, Daisy would shamelessly flirt with Kenneth, her sister's boyfriend. Everyone was talking about it. But poor Maisy seemed utterly clueless. And then one day they were gone. Just like that. They left a note telling Maisy they were sorry but that they had fallen in love."

"She loses her father, then her fiancé and her sister?" Danielle said sadly.

"It changed her. Which I can understand, I suppose. She became bitter, withdrawn. Maisy stopped seeing her friends. She sold the house—although, from what I understand, she had already sold it before her sister ran off. At the time she planned to move into a new house as a new bride—with her new husband. She hadn't expected her beau to run off before the wedding. Maisy did move into the new house, but alone."

"She obviously got married, had a son," Danielle said.

Marie nodded. "Yes. After her father died, she let the man who worked for him run the mortuary, but he was out of his element. It was too much of a job for him. She ended up rehiring someone who had once worked for Mr. Morton. From what I understand, he had left Morton Funeral Home to take a better job in Portland. But Maisy managed to talk him into coming back and taking over the business. About a year after her sister's betrayal, they were engaged. They built a new—larger—more impressive home, where they moved into after their marriage. That's the one she still lives at, with her son, Norman. In fact, it's right down the street from the Glandon Foundation."

"What happened to Norman's father?" Danielle asked.

"He died years ago. He was much older than Maisy."

"Were they happy?" Danielle asked.

"I suppose. Although, we were never friends. We had both grown up in Frederickport, basically knew each other most of our lives. But as to the state of her marriage, I have no idea."

"According to Norman, the sisters stayed in contact until Daisy's death."

Marie nodded. "I had heard that. In some ways it always surprised me because of how Maisy withdrew from all her friends after Kenneth ran off with Daisy. And it wasn't just Maisy who was forever changed by Daisy's actions. Millie Samson's brother-in-law killed himself over it all."

"Why?" Walt asked.

"It was Millie's husband's older brother, Lewis. It was before Millie was married. Lewis and Daisy had dated off and on. He was crazy about her. And when she took off with Kenneth Bakken, he drove his car off Pilgrim's Point. It was heartbreaking for the family, especially for Millie's husband. He worshiped his older brother. But like I said, that was before he and Millie were married."

"According to Norman, Kenneth Bakken died fairly young," Danielle said.

"Yes. It was a couple of years after they ran off. They were in another country—I can't remember where—maybe Greece—but he got sick, died. Family was heartbroken. After he ran away with

Daisy, he never again saw his family or the friends he left behind. And from what I heard, he only sent a few postcards."

"Why?" Danielle asked.

"Kenneth had always been well respected. Frankly, I think he was ashamed. Daisy could be very seductive. I always wondered if he ever came to regret what he had done. Maybe even right before he died. But by then, Maisy had already started a new life; she was married. Although I could be wrong and maybe Kenneth was perfectly happy with his choice. I just always thought it was sad that he didn't reconcile with his family before he passed away."

ELEVEN

It had been over three weeks since Walt and Danielle had returned from their honeymoon, and April was just around the corner. The raffle for the local high school's art department would be ending soon, and Walt and Danielle hoped the new sign would be delivered before spring break.

Walt was on the side patio with Danielle, helping to clean up the outdoor kitchen after a recent rain, while discussing what work needed to be done in the yard and if they should do it themselves or hire Craig Simmons.

"I ran into Craig in the hardware store," Danielle told Walt as she wiped down the covered barbecue. "He's pretty busy right now. I guess he's going to do some work for Pearl, but he can't start until after spring break."

"I was wondering what was happening with that," Walt said as he repositioned the patio chairs. "I saw him over there and heard him say something about getting her a bid on the work. I haven't seen anything going on over there since then, figured Pearl changed her mind."

Danielle paused a moment, a damp rag in one hand, and glanced over to Pearl's house. "No, she didn't change her mind. He just can't do it right away."

"It would be nice if he could talk her into pulling out those dead rosebushes in back," Walt said.

"I don't know why she wants to keep them. But who knows why she does anything she does?"

Hands now on his hips, Walt surveyed the side yard. "You know, I wouldn't be opposed to doing the outside work myself. We don't need to hire Craig."

"Seriously? I thought you said you never worked in the yard before, always hired someone."

Walt shrugged. "I don't know. I think after being stuck inside for almost a hundred years, looking out at all this, it might be rewarding to work in the soil. Trim up the bushes, get the yard in shape for summer."

"I don't mind working outside. And now that we don't have guests every week, I wouldn't be opposed to working in the yard with you," Danielle said.

NEXT DOOR TO MARLOW HOUSE, Pearl stood at the corner windows in her upstairs bedroom and looked down at her neighbors' house. Walt and Danielle were in their side yard cleaning up. Pearl didn't understand why anyone in Oregon would want an outdoor kitchen, considering their annual rainfall. But she didn't really care about the Marlows' outdoor kitchen now that she knew it would no longer be used to entertain bed and breakfast guests. She couldn't imagine how noisy summers might be in the Marlows' side yard if they were still operating a business. When Pearl looked out her bedroom window, she didn't want a bunch of strangers looking up at her. If she had her wish, Marlow House would be vacant, as it had been when she had been a child. Turning from the window, Pearl headed downstairs.

Just as she reached the first-floor landing, the doorbell rang. Picking up her step, she hurried to answer the front door. When Pearl opened it a few moments later, she found two teenage girls standing on her front porch. One was a short brunette; the other a tall willowy redhead. Each wore jeans and a Frederickport High School sweatshirt.

"What do you want?" Pearl asked the teenagers.

"Hello," the brunette chirped. "We're selling raffle tickets to raise money for the high school art department."

"I don't need any raffle tickets," Pearl grumbled as she started to shut her door on the girls.

"But you could win a week at Marlow House Bed and Breakfast!" the other teenage girl said quickly.

Pearl paused a moment and then instead of shutting the door all the way, she opened it again. Frowning at the girls, she said, "Marlow House Bed and Breakfast is no longer open."

"But it is!" the brunette insisted, holding up the raffle tickets. "And we're selling chances for a free week at Marlow House for spring break! I know it's just next door, but if you win, you could give the prize to a friend or family member or stay there yourself and enjoy a gourmet breakfast every morning and dinner every evening."

Pearl snatched one of the tickets out of the girl's hand. "Let me see that." With a frown, she stared at it.

"There will be four winners because they have four rooms. So if you bought more than one ticket, it would be possible to win more than one room!" the brunette told her.

Staring at the ticket, Pearl shook her head. "No, this is not right. Marlow House Bed and Breakfast closed down. They can't be renting rooms." She handed the ticket back to the girl and said, "You can't sell these."

"We've been selling them all month. Raffle ends tomorrow; this is your last chance to buy one," the redhead told her.

Pearl shook her head. "You will obviously have to give the people their money back because this raffle is illegal. And if you don't, I will have to talk to the police chief."

"Police Chief MacDonald?" The redhead frowned. "He bought two tickets."

"Then he doesn't know! I'll just have to go down to the city and talk to Mrs. Keats," Pearl snapped. "She'll take care of this!"

"Mrs. Keats? Umm, that's Cindy's mom. She bought four tickets," the brunette told her.

Pearl slammed the door shut on the girls.

SOMEONE WAS RINGING the doorbell at Marlow House, and it appeared the person's finger was glued to the doorbell, considering it kept ringing over and over again. Walt and Danielle had come in from outside five minutes earlier, and Walt was in the library, and Danielle was in the kitchen. Upon hearing the insistent ringing, they both stepped out into the entry hall at the same time and looked at each other and then glanced toward the door. The doorbell stopped ringing, but now someone was pounding on the front door.

"Who in the world could that be?" Danielle asked as she hurried to answer it, Walt by her side.

"Don't open it until you see who it is," Walt warned.

When they reached the door, Danielle peered out the peephole. There, standing on her front porch, pounding insistently on the door, was Pearl Huckabee.

"It's Pearl," Danielle whispered. She looked around quickly and asked, "Where's Max?"

"He's sleeping in the library."

Danielle nodded and then opened the door to Pearl, who was just preparing to knock again.

"What's with the pounding?" Danielle asked. "Is there a fire or something?"

"If you think I'm going to sit around and watch you flagrantly break the law, you are mistaken!" Pearl shouted at Danielle.

"Mrs. Huckabee, if you have something to say, say it. But if you yell at my wife one more time, I am shutting this door, and if you don't leave our property, I am calling the police," Walt told her sternly.

Pearl glared at Walt. "Oh please, *our property.* You just married her for her money. Everyone knows. Just because your last name is Marlow, it doesn't make this your house. It's your wife's house, you gigolo."

"Like my husband said, if you have something to say, say it. But if you are going to come onto *our* property and treat me or my husband with disrespect, I am going to ask you to leave, and if you don't, we will call the police," Danielle told her.

"Yes, I have something to say!" Pearl hissed. "If you continue to illegally operate Marlow House as a bed and breakfast, I am going to take you to court. And if the city of Frederickport refuses to enforce their laws, then I am going to sue them too!"

"I don't know what you are talking about. Marlow House Bed and Breakfast no longer has a business license. We can't—and we aren't operating a business here anymore. So I really don't know what all this is about," Danielle said sweetly.

"Oh, really? Then can you explain why two teenagers just knocked on my door trying to sell me raffle tickets? And according to them, the prize is a week at Marlow House Bed and Breakfast."

Danielle shrugged. "The girls misspoke. The prize is a week at Marlow House—not Marlow House Bed and Breakfast."

"Are you trying to be funny?" Pearl snapped.

"Funny? No. Marlow House Bed and Breakfast is no longer in business. We can't operate without a business license."

Pearl glared at Danielle. "You're talking double-talk. I don't care what you call it—Marlow House, Marlow House Bed and Breakfast, Marlow House B and B, Marlow House Motel, or Marlow House Flophouse, you can't be operating a house in a residential neighborhood as a motel."

"Mrs. Huckabee, if you were to have houseguests stay with you for a week, would you consider yourself a motel?" Walt asked calmly.

"What a ridiculous question. Of course not. I don't charge my houseguests to stay with me."

"And we are not charging the winners of the raffle to stay here," Danielle said calmly.

"But you're selling raffle tickets!" Pearl argued.

Danielle shook her head. "No. The high school is selling the raffle tickets; we have just donated the prize."

"Double-talk!" Pearl shouted before turning abruptly, her back now to Walt and Danielle, as she hurried down the walkway to the sidewalk.

"I could trip her, but I won't," Walt said as he and Danielle stood in the open door watching Pearl stomp away.

"That's because you are a gentleman," Danielle said primly as she slammed the door shut. She then turned to Walt and said with a grin, "A gigolo, but still a gentleman."

THIRTY MINUTES later Pearl stood at the window of Mrs. Keats at the city office.

"Umm, Mrs. Huckabee, what can I do for you?" Mrs. Keats asked.

"You do remember me?" Pearl asked sharply.

How could I forget? Mrs. Keats thought, but instead smiled weakly and said, "Yes. How can I help you today?"

"I'd like to know how is it that Marlow House continues to operate as a bed and breakfast if it no longer has a business license?"

"Umm, I'm not sure what you're talking about. Are you saying Danielle is taking guests? I find that very hard to believe."

"Do you have a daughter named Cindy?"

Mrs. Keats frowned. "What does Cindy have to do with this?"

"Did you buy raffle tickets for spring break at Marlow House?"

Mrs. Keats let out a sigh and smiled. "Oh, is that what this is about? Danielle is no longer running the B and B. In fact, she told me they had been considering closing for some time. The high school is raising money for their art department by selling raffle tickets, and Danielle has generously donated the rooms in Marlow House for spring break as the prize."

"But people will be staying there. It's no different than operating a bed and breakfast," Pearl insisted.

"Oh, but it is. Danielle—you—in fact, anyone on Beach Drive is welcome to let whoever they want stay in their bedrooms, within reason. Now, if you start charging for that privilege, then we need to talk business license. But there is nothing illegal about the raffle, or with Danielle donating her rooms to the winners…Now…is there anything else?" Mrs. Keats smiled sweetly.

Pearl stared dumbly at the woman. It took a moment for it all to register. Finally, Pearl let out a grunt and said, "If there is nothing I can do about it, I suppose I should be grateful it is just for that one week." She turned abruptly and stomped out of the office.

"Who was that? She seemed upset," one of Mrs. Keats's coworkers asked.

"Remember when Danielle Marlow came in the other day and talked to our supervisor about doing more Marlow House raffles for other charities?" Mrs. Keats asked.

"Yes. I love the idea. Why?"

"The lady who just left, she isn't going to love it."

TWELVE

It was the last Monday in March, and Walt and Danielle were on their way to Adam Nichols's office. Sitting in the passenger seat of the Packard, Danielle leaned back against the car door and watched Walt as he drove the vintage vehicle down the road. She was amazed at how natural and comfortable he appeared—not remotely apprehensive behind the wheel.

Today he wore the denims Lily and Ian had given him for Christmas. But instead of the flannel shirt that had come with the pants, Walt wore a pressed white long-sleeved shirt and leather vest. He reminded her a bit of a cowboy in the clothes. But not one who rode the range—the kind who sat in some Texas boardroom making a fortune off oil rigs or cattle ranches. She had found the vest in a vintage shop. And while it wasn't the type Walt the spirit had worn with his three-piece pin-striped suits, it reminded Danielle of him. Now all he needed was a pair of cowboy boots and hat.

"You're staring at me," Walt said with a chuckle, his eyes darting to Danielle and then back down the road.

"I like looking at you."

"That's supposed to be my line."

"You like looking at yourself?" Danielle teased.

Walt grinned. "You know what I meant."

Danielle let out a satisfied sigh and repositioned herself in the seat, now leaning back and looking out the front windshield. "It is going to be nice having guests again next week. While I've enjoyed having the house to ourselves, I've missed the bed and breakfast."

"I'm surprised to say I have too. Never imagined I would feel that way when you first told me what you planned to do with Marlow House."

"You were dead at the time. What did you know?"

Walt chuckled. "You have a point."

Danielle let out another sigh.

"What's with all the sighs?" Walt asked as he turned down Main Street on the way to Adam's office.

"I keep thinking of Pearl and what makes her tick. I'd hoped Marie knew something about her family." After Marie had told Danielle and Walt about what had happened to the Morton twins, Danielle had hoped she would be able to tell them something about Pearl's family, who had moved into the house after it had been sold. Marie could not recall the family, yet she suggested someone who might know something—Millie Samson.

Walt pulled the Packard up in front of the museum and parked.

"What are we doing here?" Danielle asked.

"Marie told us Millie Samson might know something," Walt reminded her. "While I'm not sure learning about Pearl's family is going to help us deal with our neighbor, I know your curiosity is driving you crazy."

Making no attempt to get out of the car, Danielle glanced over to the museum. "She might not even be here."

"Or she might be," Walt reminded her.

"I don't want her to think I just dropped by the museum to pump her for information on our neighbor."

"I'm sure you can come up with a good story," Walt said as he opened his car door. "You're good at that."

"True," Danielle conceded as she got out of the vehicle.

They started toward the museum. Danielle paused a moment and pointed to a car parked nearby. "Looks like we're in luck. That's Millie's car."

"Hello, Danielle, Walt," Millie greeted them several minutes later when they walked into the museum gift shop. The elderly woman stood behind the counter, affixing price tags on newly arrived inventory.

"Afternoon, Millie. We were on our way to Adam's office, and I remembered those Marlow House Bed and Breakfast brochures the museum handed out for me, and thought I'd pick them up."

"Oh yes, I was going to call you and see what you wanted me to do with them." Millie reached under the counter and retrieved a stack of brochures. "I didn't want to just throw them away. I thought you might get that business license worked out and reopen."

"Not sure about that," Danielle said, taking the stack of brochures from Millie.

"It really is a shame you had to close. I heard your new neighbor is the one who caused such a ruckus."

"She is definitely opposed to a B and B in the neighborhood," Danielle said. "Umm…I can't recall who mentioned it, but someone said you knew Pearl's family."

"Pearl?" Millie frowned.

"Pearl Huckabee, our new neighbor. The one opposed to the B and B," Danielle explained.

Millie shook her head. "I don't think I've ever met her."

"From what I understand, the house has been in her family for years. They bought it from the Mortons—the ones who owned the funeral home."

"Really? Yes, I did know that family. I can't recall their name. But I know it wasn't Huckabee. I was about twelve when they moved into the house. The wife was in Mother's bridge group. She had two daughters about my age. Her husband was a traveling salesman." Millie paused a moment, chuckled and shook her head.

"What's funny?" Danielle asked.

"I didn't really know the girls very well; they went to a private Catholic school. But I remember going to the beach with them once —with our mothers. When I was alone with the girls, they told me their father had died." Millie chuckled again.

Danielle arched her brows. "Umm…and that was funny?"

Millie shook her head quickly. "Oh, no! I guess that did sound strange. No, it was what my mother told me later when I got home that night. She said their father had not died—he had run away with some woman and never came home from one of his business trips. I always thought that so odd the girls would rather say their father had died than their parents had divorced. But they were Catholic; maybe that was why. I am assuming the parents got a divorce. Although, it is entirely possible they stayed married. I know his wife never remarried."

"Did the daughters seriously believe he had died?" Danielle asked.

Millie shook her head. "Not according to my mother. But that's what the family told people. Of course, my mother knew the truth."

"Perhaps that house has some kind of curse," Walt suggested.

"Curse?" Millie frowned.

"From what I understand, the previous owner was jilted by her fiancé when he ran off with her sister. And then the same thing basically happened to the next owner," Walt explained.

"Oh my, I've never thought of that before, but you are right!" Millie said. "And the Morton twins..." Millie shook her head. "You have no idea how all that affected my poor husband."

"Your husband?" Danielle asked. Marie had told her about the connection between Millie and the Mortons, but Danielle couldn't tell Millie that.

"My husband's older brother was in love with the Morton girl who ran away. When she took off with another boy, he was devastated. He killed himself."

"That's tragic," Danielle said.

"Bruce never believed it was suicide. He insisted Lewis would never have killed himself over a girl," Millie told them. "Of course, Bruce was just a young boy at the time, and he idolized his older brother."

"I'm assuming Bruce was your husband?" Walt asked.

Millie nodded. "Yes."

Walt studied Millie a moment before asking, "Did they suspect foul play?"

Millie shook her head. "No. He died after his car went off Pilgrim's Point. The police believed he intentionally drove off the cliff, but my husband never believed it. It drove him crazy for people to think his brother had killed himself. And it was devastating for my in-laws."

"Why did the police believe it was intentional and not an accident?" Walt asked.

"There was a witness who saw the car drive off the cliff. They claimed it hadn't been speeding. And there were no skid marks at the scene, which substantiated the witness's claim."

"Maybe he had been drinking," Danielle suggested.

"No. The coroner report said he hadn't been drinking. Bruce suggested he fell asleep at the wheel, but considering the time of the accident, the police didn't buy that scenario. Plus, he had made quite a scene several days earlier when he found out Daisy—that was the twin he was in love with—had taken off with someone else. He refused to believe it was true. The police felt that when he realized it was true, he snapped and couldn't deal with it and took his life."

"Do you think he committed suicide?" Danielle asked.

Millie smiled sadly. "I feel disloyal to my husband to suggest it was suicide. But I'm afraid there really is no other explanation, especially if you look objectively at all the evidence. And my husband was looking at it all through the eyes of a very young and naive boy who had his older brother on a pedestal and couldn't imagine him ever doing something like that. Bruce used to say, *Lewis would never do that to me. He always promised to be here for me.*"

"So tragic…" Danielle murmured.

"Yes. Yes, it was." Millie took a deep breath and then smiled at Danielle. "Back to your neighbor, you say she might be related to my mother's friend?"

"Pearl claims the house has been in her family for a long time, so I would assume so. I heard she has some relatives who live in town, but they aren't on friendly terms."

"Well, if she is related to my mother's friend—it could be Ruby Crabtree," Millie suggested.

"Ruby Crabtree, the one who owns the Seahorse Motel?" Danielle asked.

"Yes. Ruby and I talked about it once. This was a number of years ago. I don't recall how the conversation came up, but we were talking about Mother's friend whose husband had run off, yet preferred to pretend he was dead, and Ruby told me the woman was her aunt. Ruby's father was the woman's brother, but they had been estranged for years, up until Ruby's father passed away."

"Her aunt?" Danielle frowned. "Considering Ruby's age, I would assume your mother's friend would be more Ruby's grandmother's age."

"Ruby's father was much older than her mother—old enough to be Ruby's grandfather."

"Do you know if Ruby had ownership in the house?" Walt asked.

"The house next door to you?" Millie asked.

"Yes," Danielle answered for Walt. "From what we understand,

Pearl bought the house from some relatives. According to what we've heard, they didn't all get along. I have to wonder if Ruby is one of the cousins who sold the house to Pearl."

Millie shrugged. "I seriously doubt it. Like I said, they had been estranged for years, up until the time Mother's friend passed away. I would assume that when she died, she would leave the house to her two daughters, not to a niece—especially a niece she had nothing to do with. According to Ruby, she really didn't know her aunt. And she certainly didn't mention inheriting any property from her. I would assume your neighbor Pearl is probably a granddaughter of Mother's friend, considering her age."

"If Ruby isn't one of Pearl's Frederickport relatives who owned a share of the property, I wonder who it is?" Danielle said.

"You did say you were on your way to Adam Nichols's office. I'm sure he knows—or can easily find out, considering he is a real estate broker," Millie reminded them.

THIRTEEN

Marie decided to follow Eva's example and conjure up her own imaginary chair when needed. At Marlow House, alone with Walt and Danielle, there was no problem utilizing her energy to pull out a chair for her to use, but in Adam's office, it would be a problem for her grandson if he started seeing chairs moving about. Yet, even when alone at Marlow House with the mediums, Eva did not have the luxury of repositioning a real chair, because her energy was used on glitter and glam, and the Universe had not seen fit to help her move tangible objects. Marie had no idea why she had been given the gift—assuming it was a gift—but she was most appreciative.

One advantage of an imaginary chair, it could float in the air, allowing Marie to look down at the living people while avoiding the annoyance of one walking through her—or sitting on her. She hated when that happened.

Looking down at Adam, she watched as he sat at his computer keyboard. He was alone in the office—or so he thought. His assistant, Leslie, had gone to the post office, leaving Adam to his own devices. Since most of his work was caught up, he had idle time on his hands, and Marie knew what that meant.

Instead of interrupting the power to his computer when he attempted to visit one of *those* websites, Marie had stumbled on a new tactic, using her energy to intercept Adam's search and replace it with her own. Instead of scantily clad women appearing on the computer monitor, images of families with young children, men with babies, and fathers frolicking with their children popped up on the screen. This perplexed Adam even more than the power going out. Marie saw it as her campaign to change Adam's mind about having children.

Adam practically flew out of his desk chair a few minutes later when Walt and Danielle came walking into his office with a cheery *hello*. Both Marie and Adam had been so focused on the computer—Marie manipulating it and Adam trying to figure out what was going on—that neither was prepared for the visitors.

Both Danielle and Walt stopped in their tracks at the doorway when they spied Marie sitting in an invisible chair floating over Adam's desk. It was a peculiar sight and took great strength on Danielle's part not to comment on the spectacle.

"Oh…you surprised me." Adam sounded flustered as he turned off his computer.

"Umm, whatcha doing?" Danielle asked as she entered the room. The question was more for Marie than Adam, yet Adam didn't know that.

He shrugged. "Nothing. But it was acting weird again."

"Still losing power?" Danielle glanced up to Marie, who looked as if she had just been caught pilfering quarters from the collection plate at church.

"Craziest thing, when I do a search, pictures keep popping up that don't match the search—babies and toddlers and families and more babies."

With an arched brow, Danielle glanced up to Marie, who only returned a sheepish shrug.

"What were you searching for?" Walt asked.

Adam sat up abruptly in his chair. "Nothing in particular. Which reminds me, how is Lily doing? I haven't seen her for a while."

"She hasn't had morning sickness for weeks, and she claims she's starting to show. But frankly I don't see it. According to Ian, she's always tired and hungry."

"Great combination," Adam said with a chuckle and then asked, "Now, what can I do for you?"

"I guess I'll go now," Marie said abruptly just before vanishing.

"I brought you that list of potential customers who had inquired about rooms," Danielle explained as she and Walt took a seat facing

Adam's desk. "I thought you might be able to help them." She leaned forward, handing him the paper.

"I still can't believe you're closing the B and B for good," Adam said as he accepted Danielle's offering.

"Not really closing it. More like reinventing ourselves." Danielle smiled and settled back in the chair.

"Chris told me about how you plan to expand the room raffles for charity," Adam said as he glanced over the paper Danielle had just handed him. He then tossed it on his desk.

"Yes. After we see how the spring break fundraiser goes, we'll move ahead on the project," Danielle told him.

"By the way, have you talked to Chris this morning?" Adam asked.

"I did early this morning," Walt told him. "But he had an incoming call, and I told him we were leaving anyway and would talk to him later."

Adam glanced from Walt to Danielle. "So you don't know? His uncle Loyd passed away last night."

Danielle arched her brow. "Really? I know his cancer had advanced fairly quickly."

"Couldn't have happened to a nicer man," Walt grumbled.

Adam looked at Walt, unable to stifle a chuckle.

"Walt," Danielle scolded, "a man is dead."

"So? He tried to kill you," Walt said angrily.

Adam chuckled again. "I can't say I disagree with Walt. Loyd did try to kill you and Chris. Those uncles are pure evil. I can't believe Simon actually expected Chris to intervene and have Loyd moved somewhere more comfortable."

"I suspect he would have," Danielle said. "Knowing Chris. But fortunately for him, the prison had already made plans to move him, considering his condition. I think Chris was conflicted by Simon's request."

"I just hope Chris cuts off all communications with Simon," Walt said. "He doesn't need that in his life."

Adam studied Walt for a moment and smiled. When he had first met Walt—or Clint as he then wanted to be called—Adam thought he was a major jerk. But he had to admit, the man had changed since his accident, and Adam did not doubt Walt's feelings toward Danielle. Even Walt's obvious protective attitude toward Chris,

Adam found an interesting change. Perhaps Melony was right —*again*.

They chatted a few more minutes about Chris's uncles; then Danielle changed the conversation.

"When I first asked you about the previous owners of Pearl's house, you weren't sure if she was related to the Morton family," Danielle began.

"She's not. Since we talked about it, I looked into it a little," Adam explained.

"Yeah. I know she's not. I met Norman Bateman, the son of one of the Morton twins. He told me the house was sold before he was born, and not to a relative."

Adam nodded. "Yeah. That's what I found out too. I looked into the property records. The owners after the Mortons were a Mr. and Mrs. Darin Burnette. A couple of years before Mrs. Burnette's death, the husband's name was taken off the deed. When she died, the house went equally to their two daughters. One of the daughters sold out her share to her sister. The house was then in the name of that sister and her husband. When they died, the house went to their three children, who apparently have also passed away. Their children then inherited the property. Seven different people were on the deed, and I am assuming they are the great-grandchildren of the Burnettes—from the daughter who bought out her sister."

"Do you know if any of them live in Frederickport?" Danielle asked.

"Yes. One of them had a local address. The name wasn't familiar, and I don't remember it. But if you want me to look it up again, I will," Adam offered.

"Sure. I doubt I will do anything with it, but if you can get it," Danielle said.

Adam turned his computer back on and began a search. "Nice to see no baby pictures are popping up," he muttered as he continued looking for the property record. Danielle and Walt quietly exchanged glances.

"Here it is," Adam said at last. "One of the owners who sold out to your neighbor is an Andy Delarosa."

Danielle shrugged. "Never heard of him."

"He lives on your side of town." Adam looked at the computer monitor again and then frowned. "By his address, I'm pretty sure he lives next door to Presley House."

"Or what was Presley House. Last time I went by there, it was still a vacant lot," Danielle said.

Adam looked up from the computer. "Is there some reason you're thinking of talking to him?"

Danielle shrugged. "Probably not. I was curious about my neighbor Pearl, and why she's so cantankerous. I had this crazy idea I might learn more about her from her relatives who sold her the property, but what do I do? Walk up to this Andy guy, knock on the door, and ask, why is your cousin Pearl such a shrew?"

"So how is this Pearl related to him?" Adam asked Danielle.

"Any chance one of the names on that deed was Pearl Huckabee?" Walt asked.

"Pearl Huckabee, that's who's on the deed now," Adam said.

Danielle turned to Walt. "Why would her name have been on the deed before?"

Walt shrugged. "We didn't consider that maybe she owned a share of the house with her cousins and she just bought them out."

Adam shook his head. "No. Her name wasn't on the deed before."

"Then my assumption, if she really is related to the previous owners, and the house has been in her family for years, as she claims—she's the child of the Burnette daughter who sold her share to her sister," Walt explained.

HAND IN HAND, Walt and Danielle walked to the Packard after leaving Adam's office. Just as they reached the vehicle, a short woman with curly red hair stepped out from one of the shops, blocking their path. Danielle and Walt stopped abruptly. Danielle immediately recognized the woman. She always thought she looked like an angry Strawberry Shortcake doll. It was Ruby Crabtree.

"Ruby?" Danielle said in surprise.

Standing before the couple, Ruby eyed them up and down curiously. "Is it true? Is the bed and breakfast staying closed for good?"

"We plan to use it for some charity events, but it no longer has a business license to operate as a bed and breakfast," Danielle explained.

"Interesting," Ruby mused.

"Funny we should run into you like this. We were just talking about you today," Danielle told her.

Ruby arched a red brow. "You were?"

"I understand you might be related to our new neighbor—the one who is opposed to having a B and B in the neighborhood."

"Ahh, you mean Pearl Huckabee. I just want you to know, I think it's a shame she got you closed down. This town needs places like yours. Never thought it hurt my business. Some people like staying in motels; others like places like your B and B."

"So you are related?" Danielle asked.

"Suppose we are. I don't know her. Never met her. But it doesn't really surprise me she got your place shut down."

"Why is that?" Walt asked.

"Contrary bunch, if you ask me. Her grandmother was my father's sister. Dad used to say he couldn't blame his brother-in-law for running off on his sister. He was surprised he stuck around as long as he did," Ruby said with a snort.

"Is Pearl your cousin?" Danielle asked.

"Her mother was. But I never knew them, even though we lived in the same town. You see, my aunt converted to Catholicism, and my father was a good Protestant. He never forgave his sister for joining the Pope's church. I remember when I was in grade school, going by the house and seeing a bunch of kids playing in the yard. They would have been cousins. But I never went up and introduced myself. After she died, the house went to my cousins. One of the girls bought out her sister. Her kids eventually inherited the property, and when they passed away, it went to their children. Sickly branch of the family. My cousin's kids all died fairly young. From what I hear, their children who inherited the property never got along and rarely used the house. I know this because one of them lives in Frederickport, Andy Delarosa. I suppose he is my second cousin." Ruby shrugged. "Or maybe third?"

"You know Andy Delarosa?" Danielle asked.

"Yes. Do you?" Ruby asked.

"No. I just heard he was related to Pearl," Danielle explained.

"He stopped by the motel and introduced himself after he inherited a share of the property. About five years ago, I think. He's a young fellow. To be honest, he's a bit of an airhead. He was curious about the family, not so much that he cared a hoot about genealogy, but what he could use to his advantage. Not sure what he thought that was exactly. According to him, that side of the family never got along much. Of course, I couldn't give him any information. He told me about his mother's cousin who wanted to buy the house. That was Pearl. I guess she's wanted to buy that house for years."

FOURTEEN

After talking to Ruby, Danielle decided to put her neighbor out of her mind and move forward. With the bed and breakfast officially closed and Walt keeping Max in check, Danielle didn't imagine there was any reason for Pearl to confront her again—at least not until the new sign was installed or the raffle winners arrived for their week at Marlow House. The next two weeks went by quickly, and during all that time, Danielle hadn't had a single confrontation with Pearl. Easter was less than a week away, and in five days the raffle winners would be arriving to collect their prize.

It was late afternoon on the last Monday of March, and down the road from Marlow House, on the other side of the street, Andy Delarosa sat in a parked truck, watching Pearl's house. Andy had borrowed a friend's truck. He didn't want to risk Pearl recognizing his car, and a truck was better suited for what he needed to do. Slumped down in the driver's seat, he peered over the steering wheel and watched. He had run into Pearl at the community center last week, when she had been signing up for a quilting class. According to the information on one of the flyers he had picked up, the first class was to start this afternoon. He had been wondering how he was going to get Pearl out of her house so he could do what he needed to do—before it was too late. Running into her at the community center had been providence—providing she went to the class today.

Andy had been sitting there for about fifteen minutes when he spied Pearl's car backing out of the driveway. He smiled and turned the key in the ignition. With the truck's engine now running, he slumped down further in the seat and watched as Pearl drove by, heading to town. Glancing in his rearview mirror, Andy sat up a little straighter and steered the truck out from the side of the road and headed down the street, in the opposite direction Pearl had gone.

Instead of entering Pearl's driveway, Andy continued up the street, made a right turn, and then another right and drove down the alleyway, heading back toward the rear entrance of Pearl's property. As he drove by Marlow House, he took note of the new garage. As a child he had crawled through loose posts in the wrought-iron fencing separating the two properties to make a fort behind Marlow House—where the garage now stood. Back in those days the yard had been a virtual jungle with its overgrown bushes and foliage, a tangle of brush and vines. He had kept his annoying cousins out of his fort by convincing them Marlow House was haunted.

Andy parked the truck behind Pearl's house. He was thankful she hadn't done any real yard work yet. The overgrown trees along the back of the property line would conceal the truck from view so he could do what needed to be done.

LILY BARTLEY PASSED her neighbor Pearl Huckabee on her way home from school Monday afternoon. She gave Pearl a friendly wave. Their eyes met briefly, and Pearl failed to acknowledge the gesture—not with a smile or return wave. It didn't surprise Lily, but she felt better about herself, knowing she was at least trying to get along with the grouchy neighbor.

When she pulled her car into her driveway a few minutes later, she already knew Ian was not home. Nor was Sadie. So instead of going into her house, Lily got out of her car and headed across the street to Marlow House to see Walt and Danielle. The moment she walked up on the porch, the front door opened before she even had a chance to ring the bell.

"Hello, Lily," Danielle cheerfully greeted her, opening the door wider for her friend to enter.

"Wow, that is service," Lily said with a laugh as she walked into the house.

"I was looking out the parlor window and saw you coming up," Danielle explained as she shut the door behind Lily. "Walt's in the parlor. Come on in. We're waiting for the sign people; that's why I was looking out the window."

Lily followed Danielle into the parlor. "You're getting the sign today?" She then looked at Walt, who was just standing up from the sofa as she entered the room. "Hey, Walt."

"Yes, they're supposed to be here any minute," Danielle told her.

"Hi, Lily. You want to sit on the sofa?" Walt asked, still standing.

"Nah, go ahead and sit down, Walt. I kinda prefer the chairs."

Lily took a seat across from the sofa as Walt sat back down, and Danielle sat next to him.

"You are looking radiant, Lily," Walt told her.

"You mean fat?" she grumbled.

Danielle laughed. "Hardly, Lily. You aren't even showing yet."

"Well, tell that to my jeans that wouldn't zip up this morning," Lily said.

"I think you look beautiful," Walt told her.

Lily flashed Walt a grin. "You're sweet. And I suppose it is silly to complain about not being able to zip my pants. That's sort of what happens when you get pregnant."

"You ready for your trip?" Danielle asked. Lily and Ian were planning to spend spring break in California with Lily's parents.

Lily shrugged. "Not really. I haven't started packing yet—but I have started my packing list."

"What's a packing list?" Walt asked.

"My mother always starts packing for a trip a month in advance. Well, maybe not a month, but at least two weeks," Lily explained. "Used to drive me nuts. I prefer to pack the night before we leave. But I don't want to be stressed that I might forget something. So I start a list—writing down everything I want to take. So when I pack, I just go down the list, and that way I don't forget anything even if I pack at the last minute."

"Unless you forget to put something on the list," Walt reminded her.

Lily shrugged. "Yeah, well, that can happen." Lily turned to Danielle and asked, "So you get your sign today?"

Danielle glanced to the parlor window. "They called about ten minutes ago, said they're on their way over."

"Good news, I passed our lovely neighbor Pearl on the way home. Looks like she was headed to town. Or, if we are really lucky, an extended trip out of town." Lily grinned.

Danielle let out a sigh. "Good. I was rather dreading her seeing them put the sign up. I can just see her coming over here and giving the installers a hard time. Seems like she has an opinion on everything we do, and it is usually a negative one. I would rather the sign be installed before she sees it."

JUST AS PEARL parked in front of the community center, she heard her cellphone make a sound, signifying an incoming text message. She turned off the car's ignition and then fished the cellphone from her purse. Looking at the message, she let out a curse. The quilting class had been cancelled.

"Now they tell us?" Pearl grumbled as she shoved her phone back in her purse. Turning her ignition back on, she decided to stop at the Burger Shack before heading home. She didn't feel like cooking dinner tonight, but she had skipped lunch. An early dinner of a take-out burger sounded like a good idea.

Just as Pearl was about to pull into her driveway thirty minutes later, she noticed a large truck parked in front of Marlow House and some activity in the front of the property. Curious, she drove past her house, slowing down as she started to pass by Marlow House. Her eyes widened in surprise as she spied several men preparing to install a large sign by the front gate.

"This is a residential neighborhood," Pearl grumbled as she quickly parked her vehicle in front of the truck. Hastily getting out of her car, she hurried toward the house. Waving her hands wildly, she shouted, "Unless that is a for sale sign, you need to take it down right now!"

Confused, the men installing the sign paused a moment and looked Pearl's way as she hurried to them. Pearl failed to notice Walt, Danielle, and Lily, who stood on the sidelines watching—first the men putting up the sign and then Pearl.

"Keep doing what you are doing; ignore her," Danielle told the men as she made her way to the gate.

Pearl, who stood just outside the gate leading up the walkway to Marlow House, attempted to push her way in, but the gate stubbornly refused to budge. In her failed attempt to enter, she didn't notice Walt silently watching her—and in his own way stopping her from coming closer.

"They can't do that!" Pearl shouted as the men continued with their installation.

"You seriously need to stop coming over here and yelling at people," Danielle told Pearl. She stood just a few feet from the angry neighbor, the closed gate separating them.

"And this is a residential neighborhood. You can't put that sign up!" Pearl declared.

With a weary sigh, Danielle pulled a folded piece of paper from her jacket pocket. One of the men had given it to her when he had first arrived. She handed it to Pearl.

"What's this?" Pearl frowned, taking the paper and unfolding it.

"The city of Frederickport requires approval of any signs—in residential and commercial areas. As you can see, they have approved this sign for Marlow House."

Now reading the document, Pearl began to shake her head. "No." She looked back up at the sign. The men were almost finished with the installation. "That is going to draw undue attention to Beach Drive. This is a residential area, and we have a right to our privacy. How can we get that with tourists driving up and down our street, blocking traffic? No. You need to take that down!" She shoved the paper back to Danielle.

"You seriously need to mind your own business, Pearl," Danielle told her as she took back the paper and returned it to her pocket.

"It's Mrs. Huckabee to you!" Pearl snapped.

"Fine. You seriously need to mind your own business, Mrs. Huckabee. And if you come over here yelling at me again, I am going to the police station and taking out a restraining order on you," Danielle threatened.

"You can't do that! I have my First Amendment right to speak my mind!" Pearl argued.

"And I have the right to install a historical marker on my property. Now please leave."

PEARL WAS STILL FUMING when she parked her car in her driveway a few minutes later. *Is it really so much to ask for it to go back to how it used to be on Beach Drive?* she asked herself. Why couldn't Marlow House be vacant like it had been when she was a child. She climbed out of her car and started for her front door; then she heard what sounded like someone attempting to start their vehicle. Pausing a moment, she listened. The sound of gears grinding made her cringe as whoever it was made another unsuccessful attempt to start their vehicle.

Instead of going into her front door, she made a detour and headed to the back of her property. It almost sounded as if whoever was making that horrible sound was parked in her backyard—or the alleyway behind it. When she reached the back of her property, she froze—not because she saw a vehicle, but because of what someone had done to her grandmother's rosebushes. Branches had been cut from some of the bushes, and in the center of the rose garden, one bush had been removed completely, leaving a gaping hole in the ground.

Then she heard it again—someone attempting to start an engine. But this time it started. Pearl ran to the back fence. Just as she reached it, she spied the back of a black pickup truck speeding away down the alley before disappearing.

FIFTEEN

Brian Henderson stood with hands on hips, looking down at the gaping hole where the rosebush had been. He looked to his right and then his left. Two rows of rosebushes had been planted along the wrought-iron fence separating Pearl's property from Marlow House. Brian assumed they had seen better days. The missing one had been plucked from the center of the row farthest from the fence. Before digging it up, the thief had apparently cut off a branch from various rosebushes. Or at least, that was what Brian concluded given the fact freshly cut branches littered the ground.

Kneeling by one rosebush, he picked up the closest branch on the ground, careful not to get pricked by a thorn. Examining the rosebush, he found where it looked as if the branch might have been cut. Holding the branch to that spot, he shook his head. "Not sure what we have here. Some vigilante gardener?" Brian asked before dropping the branch back on the ground and standing up to face Pearl.

"He was obviously looking for the healthiest rosebush," Pearl told him.

Brian glanced down at the bush he had just inspected. "I hate to tell you this, but it looks to me like they're dead. Maybe you should have just let the guy take them all out."

The moment Brian made the comment, he realized it was a mistake by Pearl's glare.

"This is not funny, Officer Henderson! Someone has vandalized my property, and you seem to think they did me some sort of favor, and I should be grateful!"

"No, of course not. I'm just trying to understand why anyone would want to steal a dead rosebush."

"Because they didn't take a dead rosebush!" Pearl marched over to where the missing rosebush had been and picked up the branch that apparently had been cut from that plant. She shoved it at Brian.

"What am I looking at?" Brian asked, hesitant to take the branch from her, considering the thorns and the way she was waving it about.

"It's green. See." She held up the cut end for Brian to examine.

He arched his brows. "So it is."

"I want you to find the person who did this!"

"You said you saw a black truck. Did you get a license number?"

She shook her head. "No. They drove away too fast. But the more I think about it, I know who it has to be."

"And who is that?"

"Andy Delarosa. It has to be him. He's the only one who lives in town. Of course, it might be another one of them. I suppose it could be any of them."

"Andy Delarosa? Who is he? And when you say them, who do you mean?" Brian asked.

"The previous owners of this property. They're cousins of mine—second cousins. Their parents were my first cousins."

"Why would they tear up your rosebush?"

"These are my grandmother's prizewinning roses."

Brian glanced over the plants and arched his brows. They looked like dead bushes to him, but he said nothing. Instead, he looked back to Pearl and asked, "Why would your cousin steal one now? If he wanted it, why not take it before selling you the property?"

Pearl looked at Brian as if he were daft. "They never got along. Couldn't agree on anything. That's why they sold me the house. They obviously couldn't decide what to do with Grandma's roses, so one of them came over here and helped himself." Pearl paused a moment and glanced over her backyard. "If they hadn't done it before the house closed, I suppose I should be prepared for others showing up and trying to steal more of them."

"I'll go talk to this Andy Delarosa and see what I can find out. Do you have his contact information?" he asked.

"I don't have his phone number or address. I know he lives on this side of town. Someone mentioned it once."

"I'm sure I can find him," Brian said, writing down the name in his notepad.

"Oh, I do remember something one of the cousins said about where Andy lived. They said his house was like Grandma's, next door to a haunted house."

"Haunted house?" Brian frowned.

Pearl pointed next door. "Marlow House. When we were kids, we used to say it was haunted."

"Ahh, and your house used to belong to your grandmother?"

Pearl nodded. "They said the house next door to Andy's was haunted, just like the one next door to this one. But that supposed haunted house burned down a couple of Halloweens ago."

"You mean Presley House?" Brian asked.

Pearl considered the question a moment and then said, "Yes. I believe that's what they called it. Andy lives next door to Presley House—or where it once stood."

"Okay, I'll go have a talk with him. See if I can find out what happened here."

"One more thing, Officer Henderson."

"Yes?"

"It's about Marlow House. Did you see they put up a sign in the front of the property?"

"Yes. I noticed it when I drove up."

"And that is legal?" she asked.

Brian shrugged. "It's a historical marker. The city encourages those in Frederickport, and frankly, I expected Danielle to put one up after she moved here."

"Well, I don't like it!" Pearl snapped.

ACROSS TOWN, Faye Bateman sat in her parlor gazing out the large picture window, watching as the sun set over the ocean. She sipped a cup of tea. This house had been her home since she had married, and now that she was a widow, she shared it with her son. Norman was rarely home, spending hours at work, and Faye was often alone, save for the domestic who came for six hours each day.

The woman spoke no English, so she was hardly a companion for Faye. However, she was an excellent cook, kept the house spotless, the laundry clean, and before she left each day, she would bring Faye a cup of herb tea. It was her way of letting Faye know she was going home, and that dinner was in the oven. Faye typically waited until her son got home from work before eating the dinner that had been prepared for them.

At first glance Faye looked more like an aging movie star than the elderly mother of the local funeral home director. Instead of gray hair, hers was white blond, falling several inches above her shoulders and worn in soft waves, reminiscent of something Doris Day or Marilyn Monroe might have worn in one of their movies. Faye's weekly trip to the beauty shop kept the style and look consistent. She had worn it that way for over fifty years.

Even when confined in her house—which she found more the norm these days—Faye got dressed each morning and applied her makeup. She had not been raised to lounge around in the house in a robe and uncombed hair.

Her once vivid blue eyes had since faded to gray. Yet even if they had maintained their youthful look, the endless creases lining her once smooth complexion would have been a distraction, making the eyes appear much smaller than they had once been.

In her youth she had stood five feet seven, but the last time she had been measured, her height had come in under five feet four. Part of the deficit was from the curvature of her spine, making it impossible for her to stand at her full height.

Age is not kind, Faye had told her son on more than one occasion. She recognized the unkindness of it all more astutely than others her age, because while her body continued to deteriorate, her mind remained sharp.

Faye had just finished her tea when Norman unexpectedly walked in the room.

"You're home early," Faye said as she set the now empty cup on the side table.

Holding an envelope with his right hand, he sat down in a chair next to his mother. "I was able to leave a little early today and thought I would figure out what I should do with this." He tossed the envelope on the table between them.

She eyed the envelope but didn't bother picking it up. "What's that?"

"Remember those raffle tickets Heather Donovan was selling? The ones for a room at Marlow House over spring break?" he asked.

"You mean the ones you felt obligated to buy since her employer donated so much to your favorite charity?"

"The same. I certainly didn't need a week at Marlow House, and I didn't expect to win. But I did." He laughed.

Faye arched her brow and reached for the envelope. "And you just found out about it now?"

"They announced the winners a week or two ago. That's why I was surprised when someone from the art department contacted me. I guess there was a mix-up with the person who was supposed to call me. It's a good thing this didn't happen to one of the winners from out of town. It might be too late for them to make travel arrangements."

"And what are you going to do with it?" Faye asked.

"If spring break wasn't starting this Saturday, I'd tell them to draw someone else's name."

"No," Faye said, shaking her head as she removed the prize certificate from the envelope and unfolded it. "I have another idea."

"What is that?"

"You could give it to your mother," Faye said, now reading the certificate.

"You want to use it?"

Holding the document with both hands, the envelope resting on her lap, she looked up at Norman. "Yes. I would love to use it. Do you know I grew up next door to Marlow House, and I've never been inside? I've always wanted to see what it looked like inside."

"I know you wanted to go to their open house," he said.

"Yes, and something always seems to come up when they have one. I was sick once, and then I was out of town another time." She refolded the paper and slipped it back in the envelope.

"Then it's yours, Mother. According to the information, they're providing breakfast and supper—no lunch."

"Two meals a day is perfect," she said.

"And you'll be right next door to your old house," he told her.

"I suppose that new woman moved in already."

"She did some time ago," Norman told her.

"I don't understand how she managed to buy that house. We've been trying to pick it up for years."

"It just wasn't meant to be, Mother. From what I understand, they didn't even put it on the market. They sold it to one of their relatives."

"Why didn't they give us the chance to make an offer? It's not like we haven't inquired enough times over the years."

"I don't even know why you want the house now," Norman said. "I can't imagine you would want to move into it. You love this house. You don't want to move."

"Perhaps, but someday if you finally stop being so picky and find a woman to marry and settle down with, I don't think your new wife would want your old mother to be hanging around, getting in the way. This house would be perfect for you to start a family—you know, a man at your age can still have children. Look at my father. And I would have been very comfortable back at the house on Beach Drive. I would be going home."

Norman stared at his mother a moment and thought, *I can't believe you seriously think there's still a chance I'll settle down with any woman.*

SIXTEEN

It was early Saturday morning, and Walt and Danielle stood across the street in the Bartley driveway, chatting with Lily while Ian loaded suitcases in the trunk of his car. Sadie stood nearby, tail wagging, watching Ian's every move.

"I really appreciate you keeping Sadie this week, especially since you'll be having guests," Lily told them.

"Don't be silly. Sadie is always welcome, with or without guests in the house," Danielle said.

"If we were driving we would take her." Lily glanced over to the golden retriever, who hadn't taken her eyes off Ian. "She knows something is up."

"I already discussed it with her," Walt told Lily.

Looking back to Walt, Lily smiled. "And what did you tell her?"

"That you and Ian are visiting your family in California, and it was a long drive, so you decided to fly. I explained it really wasn't safe for dogs to fly on airplanes. I told her she was staying with us."

"So she's okay with that? The way she keeps looking at Ian…"

With a cringe he said, "I probably should have left out the part about it not being safe for dogs to fly, and just said that they aren't allowed on planes."

"Why is that?" Lily asked.

"Because she started worrying about you and Ian. If it's not safe for her to fly, why is it safe for you? I finally convinced her it is safer for you to fly because you don't have to travel in the luggage compartment. It took her a while to understand."

Lily glanced back to Sadie and said, "Considering how she's staring at Ian, not sure you convinced her."

"Just don't let anything happen to you two while you're gone, or she will never trust me again," Walt said.

"Well, that's about it," Ian called out as he slammed the trunk closed. He walked to the three, Sadie trailing next to him.

"Did I tell you my sister is having a surprise baby shower for me while I'm there?" Lily asked Danielle when Ian reached her side.

"It can't be a surprise if you know," Danielle said.

Ian draped an arm around Lily's shoulder. "You know my mother-in-law can't keep a secret."

"It's only because Mom wanted to make sure I brought something to wear—and she told me I need to have my hair fixed before the shower." Lily shook her head at the idea.

"Fixed? Is it broken?" Danielle teased.

"Cute." Lily rolled her eyes. "Mom wants me to have it done at a beauty shop the day before the shower. I guess she expects me to show up at the surprise shower with my hair perfectly done, wearing a new outfit and my makeup on, and act all surprised."

"But that's how you always look." Ian gave Lily's cheek a quick kiss.

"Yeah, right." Lily laughed.

Ian glanced at his watch. "We'd better get going."

"You guys have a great time," Danielle told them.

"I hope so," Lily said. "I would sort of like to stay home, but come summer, I'll be home all the time."

Ian removed his arm from Lily and then turned to Sadie. He knelt down in front of the dog, looking into her face. "You be a good girl for Walt and Danielle."

Sitting before Ian, Sadie looked in his eyes and let out a pitiful whimper.

"Oh, girl, you like staying with Walt and Danielle," Ian told her as he stroked the dog's neck.

"It's my fault," Walt said with a sigh. He stepped closer to the pair and looked down at Sadie. "I promise, Sadie, they won't make Lily and Ian sit in the luggage compartment."

Ian frowned up at Walt. "What?"

With a chuckle, Lily grabbed hold of Ian's right hand and gave it a tug. "I'll explain in the car. We need to go."

Walt's words must have soothed Sadie's concerns, for in the next moment the dog let out a bark and began wagging her tail.

ON FRIDAY JOANNE had changed all the bed linens at Marlow House and had put out fresh towels. In spite of the fact the bed and breakfast had closed, she still came over several times each week, so minimal cleaning was required before the guests started arriving. She planned to come over on Saturday afternoon to help with dinner and prep the food they planned to serve on Easter Sunday.

It was Saturday afternoon, but Joanne had not yet arrived, nor had any of the guests. Walt and Danielle sat in the living room. Sadie napped on the floor by Walt's feet while Max found a quiet corner behind the curtains to snooze.

"Did I miss saying goodbye to Ian and Lily?" Marie asked as she popped into the living room. Sadie lifted her head sleepily and gave Marie a brief *woof* before resuming her nap.

Danielle wasn't sure how Marie had intended to tell them goodbye, since neither Ian nor Lily could see or hear her. But she reserved comment and instead said, "They left early this morning."

"Have any of your guests arrived?" Marie asked.

"Not yet." Danielle glanced at her watch.

"So how did the raffle do? Did they sell a lot of tickets?" Marie asked.

"It did extremely well," Danielle told her. "Especially considering it was all pretty rushed. I was afraid it would be difficult to sell tickets because once they announced the winners, they didn't have a lot of time to make travel plans—or even get the time off from work. But they made more than ten thousand dollars. Actually twice that, since the Glandon Foundation matched whatever they raised."

"That much?" Marie asked.

"Yep. Just in ticket sales it was double what I would have made on those rooms if I had simply rented them out."

"How much did they sell the tickets for?" Marie asked.

"Twenty bucks each," Danielle told her.

Marie arched her brows. "People were willing to pay that much for a chance to stay here?"

"While it would be flattering to imagine Marlow House was such a coveted prize, I suspect most people who bought a ticket were thinking more about supporting the high school art department," Walt interjected.

"Chris told me he talked a Portland radio station into buying a hundred tickets, which they gave out as prizes on their radio show. In fact, one of the winners came from those tickets. A couple from Portland."

"Excellent!" Marie smiled.

"Oh, and you'll never guess who one of the winners was," Danielle said.

"Who?"

"Faye Bateman…or as she was known when she lived next door, Maisy Faye Morton," Danielle told her.

"Faye Bateman bought a raffle ticket?" Marie asked in surprised.

"Her son did. Apparently he bought several from Heather. Heather said he only bought them to be nice and never expected to win. But when he did, he gave it to his mother. She's never been in Marlow House and has always wanted to see it."

"That's not true. She was here once," Walt interjected.

Danielle looked to Walt. "When?"

"Not long after the twins were born. Her father hired a nanny, and the woman had some problem and stopped by here asking for help. She had the babies with her. I remember she had them in the same carriage. They were such little things. I don't think it was long after they were born."

"I seriously doubt she remembers that time," Danielle said with a chuckle.

"I imagine you're right." Walt grinned.

The doorbell rang and the next moment Sadie jumped up, prepared to bark. Walt quickly put a stop to that, and Sadie reluctantly lay back down on the floor, letting out a little grunt as she did.

Several minutes later Danielle opened the front door to her first raffle guest, Faye Bateman. The elderly woman wore a long velvet jacket over a floor-length dress. The formal attire reminded Danielle of what might have once been considered standard apparel for any properly brought up woman from local society's upper station. She wore an emerald green velvet pillbox hat atop her platinum blond hair, and by her side was her son, Norman, a suitcase in his hand.

"Welcome," Danielle greeted them, opening the door wider. She glanced over their shoulders and noticed the dark clouds rolling in.

"Danielle, I would like you to meet my mother, Faye Bateman. Mother, this is Danielle Marlow, your hostess for the week."

"I am so happy to meet you," Danielle told Faye as the elderly woman stepped into the entry.

"I imagine you think I'm a silly old woman to be staying here when I have a house on the other side of town."

"Certainly not," Danielle insisted.

Faye looked around the enormous dark-paneled entry, taking in the sight. "But I have always wanted to see inside Marlow House."

"I'm very glad you came. I'm putting you in the downstairs bedroom. I hope you don't mind. But then you don't have to worry about the stairs—and it does have its own private bathroom, unlike the rooms upstairs."

"That's fine. I just hope you'll take me on a tour of the house—I want to see everything. Even upstairs."

Fifteen minutes later Faye's suitcase was deposited in her room, her son had said his goodbyes, and she was in the living room being introduced to Walt.

"You are the author?" Faye asked, taking Walt's hand in hers and giving it a pat.

"Oh my, she looks so old," Marie muttered from the sidelines.

Danielle flashed Marie a harsh look.

"Well, she does," Marie said unapologetically.

"You've heard of me?" Walt asked.

"I've not just heard of you, I read your book. And loved it."

"That's not all she loves," Marie grumbled. "I don't think she's going to give Walt his hand back."

"I'm glad you enjoyed it," Walt told her.

"And you do look like him. I heard you did," Faye told him.

"I assume you're talking of the original Walt Marlow? My distant cousin?" Walt asked, leading her to a chair so she could sit down.

"I saw the portraits at the museum. Of course, over the years I saw photographs of him, but the portrait is quite magnificent," Faye said.

"I'll go get us some tea," Danielle announced.

Walt flashed her a smile, but Faye's eyes never left Walt.

"I do believe Maisy Faye is smitten with our Walt," Marie told Danielle.

Danielle resisted the urge to chuckle at Marie's words and left the room to get the tea. With a shrug, Marie followed Danielle to the kitchen.

"Did you know I used to live next door?" Faye told Walt. "I was just a baby when your cousin died. And growing up, this house was always closed up." She glanced around the room. "But it always fascinated me. Had I been a little braver, I might have broken in to have a look. But I must admit, back then I thought the house was haunted."

"We only have friendly ghosts, Mrs. Bateman," Walt assured her.

Faye laughed. "That is good to know. But please, call me Faye."

"I will." Walt flashed her a smile.

"I saw you on an interview. Do you still have amnesia?" she asked.

"Yes. But it's only what happened before the accident that I don't remember. I'm making new memories, and I'm quite happy with my life now."

Faye reached over and gave his hand a pat. "Trust me, when you get to be my age, you realize there are some things that happen in your life that are best forgotten. Sometimes a fresh start is a blessing."

"I couldn't agree more," he said softly.

"I remember you mentioning in the interview you used to go by your middle name, but after the accident you started using your first name again," she noted.

Walt nodded. "Yes. When I woke up from my coma, my first name seemed more natural."

"I guess we have that in common—I mean going by our middle names. Faye is actually my middle name. But I don't ever see me using my first name again."

"Why is that?" Walt asked.

Faye shrugged. "It's very old-fashioned. I just never really liked it."

"Can I ask what it is?" Walt already knew, but she didn't know that.

She looked at him a moment and finally said, "Maisy. Maisy Faye."

"I knew a Maisy Faye once."

"Did you? I can't say I've ever met another Maisy, much less Maisy Faye. Who was she?"

"Someone I knew a long time ago. I can't remember much about her, aside from her name. That and how she looked. She was quite beautiful. Big blue eyes and blond curls. And sweet. I remember she was sweet."

"I suppose you can't remember who she was because of your amnesia?" Faye asked.

"Umm…yes. That's correct."

SEVENTEEN

"Should I be worried about this other Maisy Faye?" Danielle teased Walt after Faye went to her room to freshen up. She had walked into the living room with the tea earlier, just in time to hear Walt's comment.

"Maybe, if I could actually place her," Walt countered with a grin.

"Come on, you remember she was sweet—her big blue eyes—and you say you can't place her?" Danielle taunted.

"No, I can't. And I find it quite annoying." His smile turned to a frown, as if he was trying to recall his memories about the other Maisy Faye. "Sometimes it feels as if I really do have amnesia."

Danielle reached over and patted Walt's knee. He sat next to her on the sofa. "It'll come back to you. You have over a century of memories to recall; it's not surprising you've misplaced a few."

Walt's smile returned. He grabbed hold of Danielle's hand and gave it a gentle squeeze. "Where did Marie go?"

"Not really sure. She said she would stop by later and check out the rest of our guests. From what I understand, she hadn't seen Faye for years and was quite shocked at how she looks."

"The woman is ninety-five," Walt reminded her.

Danielle shrugged. "I guess the wrinkles surprised her. To me Faye looks like someone who has smoked all her life."

"And managed to live to ninety-five?" Walt asked. "And here I gave up my cigars."

Danielle arched her brow at Walt. "There is always the exception, the smoker who beats the odds. And it's possible she was never a smoker, and she just has wrinkles. Like you said, she is ninety-five. And if she did once smoke, I don't think she does now. I can always smell that on someone."

The doorbell rang. Again Sadie lifted her head from where she had been sleeping by their feet, and again Walt told her to stay. As Danielle stood up from the sofa, she glanced to the living room window. The blind was open, but little light came through the glass pane.

"Looks like it is getting pretty dark out there," Danielle noted.

"The weather report did say it was going to be a big storm."

"Wonderful," Danielle grumbled. "I was hoping for a week with lots of sunshine."

When Danielle went to answer the front door a minute later, she found two young women—teenagers—standing on the porch, each holding a suitcase. Danielle knew immediately who they were. Both were students from the local high school, sisters. The eldest sister, a senior, had recently turned eighteen and was one of the raffle winners. The girls, a pair of slender brunettes—more cute than beautiful—looked like twins. If Danielle had to guess which was the oldest, she would have a fifty-fifty chance of guessing correctly.

"Hello. I assume you're Brenda and Tammy Owen?" Danielle asked as she opened the door wider.

"Yes. I'm Brenda and this is my younger sister, Tammy. Are you Danielle Marlow?"

"I am. Please come in. Welcome to Marlow House."

By the time Danielle got the sisters situated in the bedroom upstairs with the twin beds, the doorbell rang again. This time Walt answered it.

"Welcome to Marlow House," Walt greeted after opening the front door. Standing on the porch was a thirty-something couple. They introduced themselves as Jose and Juanita Alvarez from Portland. A few minutes later Walt took them up the stairs, where they met Danielle midway. She took over for Walt, taking the Alvarezes to their room while Walt went to answer the door again.

When Walt opened the door this time, rain was falling and a crack of lightning lit up the afternoon sky. Shivering on the porch was a lone fifty-something man, suitcase in hand. Walt hurried him into the house and took his wet overcoat, hanging it on the nearby coat rack to dry. He was just introducing himself to Walt when Joanne arrived to help prepare the evening dinner.

IT HAD BEEN over two months since Marlow House had operated as a bed and breakfast. And while they were no longer open for business, they had a full house. In the kitchen Joanne prepared that night's dinner. In the past bed and breakfast customers typically received just breakfast, yet the raffle winners would receive breakfast and dinner during their stay. Tonight it was fried chicken, mashed potatoes, gravy, homemade biscuits, green beans, asparagus, and apple pie and ice cream for dessert.

Because of the storm—growing in intensity—Danielle insisted Joanne go home before serving dinner, not wanting her driving in the dark while the roads were so slippery and wet. Rain was not unusual for Frederickport, but it was coming down uncommonly hard, and the weather report warned of flash flooding.

By the time Danielle set the table, Joanne had already left for home. Danielle and Walt welcomed their guests. Eight of them sat around the large dining room table, with Walt seated at the head of the table and Danielle at the end. At one time Danielle had taken her place at the head of the table, but since her marriage to Walt, she insisted he take the place of honor. In Danielle's heart, the house—and table—had belonged to Walt long before it had ever been hers.

Danielle handed the man to her right the platter of fried chicken and asked, "I understand you are a teacher at the high school, Mr. McGhie?"

"Yes, I'm an English teacher. But please call me Jonah, and this looks delicious, by the way." He helped himself to some chicken and then held the platter for Faye so she could select a piece.

"I was in Mr. McGhie's class last year." Brenda spoke up. "I had no idea one of our teachers would be here!"

"I promise there will be no pop quizzes this week," he teased.

Brenda giggled and then took the platter from him, passing it in front of Faye.

"Is your wife coming later?" Tammy asked. She sat across the table from her sister, waiting for the chicken to come her way while she helped herself to some biscuits and passed them on.

"No. It's just going to be me this week," he said happily. "And I imagine you will only see me during the meals."

"You aren't staying?" Tammy frowned.

"I'll be in my room. You see, I'm working on my book."

"You're an author too?" Faye asked as she added green beans to her plate. "Walt here is a very successful author."

"Oh, yes, I know." Jonah blushed.

"Not sure how successful. Let's just say my first book was well received," Walt said as he passed a platter of food on.

"You came here to write?" Danielle asked.

"I've been working on my book a couple of years. But it's always difficult to find someplace quiet to work. My wife's a teacher too, and her mother lives with us. She suggested I rent a motel for Easter week, lock myself in and write with no distractions. It sounded like a wonderful idea, but frankly, a little extravagant. But then she bought a ticket for the raffle, and to our surprise, she won. I told her we both should come, but she insisted I use this week to write, and it's always difficult to leave her mother alone for so long."

"Or you could have sent your mother-in-law here and had a romantic week at home with your wife," Faye interjected with a laugh. "That's what my son did. Although the truth is, I practically snatched the prize certificate out of his hand. I've been wanting to see inside Marlow House, and so far, it has not disappointed!"

"I'm glad you decided to come," Danielle told her with a smile.

Jonah looked across the table and asked Jose, "You mentioned you're from Portland. How did you happen to buy a ticket?"

"They were giving away raffle tickets on a radio station I listen to. You have to call in and answer a question. I knew the answer, managed to get through, and here we are." Jose grinned and then stabbed his pile of mashed potatoes with a fork.

"I'm just so happy he won," Juanita said. "It was a little tricky getting the time off work, but we did it."

Thunder shook the house. Everyone stopped eating and talking a moment and looked up to the ceiling.

"That storm does not sound good," Faye said with a shiver.

"I'm glad we got here before the rain started," Jose said.

"I was planning a big Easter dinner for tomorrow and really

hoped we could eat outside, but I don't think that is going to happen," Danielle said as she resumed eating.

"I like the thunder and lightning. Makes this feel like a real haunted house," Brenda said.

"Brenda!" Tammy scolded.

"Oh, come on, you know they all say Marlow House is haunted," Brenda returned. "Not that I really believe in ghosts, but it does make it more fun staying here."

The adults laughed and Walt asked, "So tell me, were you young ladies involved in the raffle sales?"

"Not really," Brenda said. "But I had friends who were selling tickets. According to the rules, you had to be eighteen to be eligible to win, so they weren't really selling to other students. I thought it would be neat to win. I knew it was a long shot, but what the heck? And look, I won!"

"And she asked me to come with her," Tammy said with a grin.

"You know, when I was a young girl and lived next door, we thought the house was haunted too," Faye said.

"You lived next door?" Jonah asked.

"I THINK it's a pretty nice group," Walt said as he sat on the edge of the mattress in the attic bedroom, removing his shoes.

Danielle stood at the window looking out at the lightning streaking across the night's sky. "I agree. A very eclectic group, but they all seemed to get along. I really enjoyed this evening."

"It's too bad Faye isn't our neighbor instead of Pearl. She told me this afternoon she had been trying to buy back the house next door for years, but they would never sell."

"Why did she want to buy it back?" Danielle turned from the window and faced Walt.

"Faye told me she had second thoughts on selling the property and tried to cancel the sale, but Pearl's grandmother refused. She wanted the house. And over the years, after the woman died, Faye approached the family and tried to buy it back."

"I wonder why she sold it in the first place."

"I imagine she put the house up for sale because she was planning to start a new life with her fiancé. They probably wanted to move into their own house, not her childhood home. But then he ran off with her sister, and Faye had already sold her house," Walt suggested.

"You're probably right. With him gone, what was the point of moving? And it would be pretty painful to move into a house they had picked out together."

Walt pushed his shoes under the bed. "It really is a shame those cousins of Pearl's didn't give Faye a chance to bid on the house. I have a feeling Faye Bateman has far more money than Pearl Huckabee and could have easily given top dollar for it. So not only would we have a better neighbor, they would have made more money."

"Wouldn't that have been nice?"

"Plus, Faye doesn't seem to have a problem with Sadie or Max," Walt added.

Sadie, who was sitting in the corner of the room when Walt said her name, looked up in his direction. The next minute thunder shook the house. The golden retriever catapulted from the corner, landing in the center of the bed, her body shaking.

Walt looked down at the frightened dog. "I have a feeling Sadie is sleeping with us tonight."

The next moment Max appeared from where he had been hiding under the bed. He jumped up on the mattress, curling up next to Sadie.

"Where are we supposed to sleep?" Danielle asked.

EIGHTEEN

Pearl opened her eyes and looked up at the ceiling. All was quiet. It had finally stopped raining. The morning sun streamed through the bedroom windows. Rolling out of bed, Pearl grabbed her robe off the rocker and slipped it on. She tied the robe's belt around her waist as she stumbled to the window and looked outside. The sky was clear blue with no sign of rain clouds. But when her gaze dropped downward to the ground, her heart sank. A river of mud flowed through her side yard, and fallen tree branches littered the area.

She groaned and looked over to the Marlows' side yard. It looked no different than it had before the storm. She didn't see any downed limbs or mud on their side of the fence. Pearl started to put her slippers on but changed her mind. She wanted to assess the damage to her property, and she didn't think walking around in her slippers outside after a major storm was a terrific idea. Instead, she quickly dressed for the day and put on her gardening shoes.

Pearl was happy to find the front yard had suffered little damage from the storm. But in the side yard a river of mud flowed around the gardening shed. She headed to the backyard to see where the mud had originated. A few minutes later she found the problem and groaned again. Water poured from a broken pipe, telling her the rain was not the primary source of the mud river. A fallen limb from one of her dead trees in the backyard had caused the break.

The gaping hole left behind from the stolen rosebush was now filled with water, and the soil in her backyard had shifted significantly, completely changing its appearance. Her first thought was the landscaper she had hired. He was supposed to start work in a few weeks, but now, would she need to get a new bid for the work?

Glancing around the yard, she immediately knew this was going to cost her considerably more money than the bid Craig Simmons had originally given her. Limbs and branches littered the backyard, taken down by last night's fierce storm. Craig had warned her several of her trees needed branches removed, but she had refused to believe him—just like with the rosebushes. Craig had his work cut out for him.

Somewhat dazed and overwhelmed at the carnage, she glanced back over to the broken pipe and realized it was still pouring more water into her yard. Jolted into action, she rushed to the outside valves and turned off the water to her irrigation system. A few minutes later, only a trickle spilled out from the broken pipe before it stopped altogether.

Taking one final look at the yard, she shook her head in disgust and headed back to her house. She needed coffee. Or maybe a stiff drink would be better. So what if it wasn't even nine o'clock in the morning yet.

AFTER BREAKFAST ON SUNDAY MORNING, Walt and Danielle went outside to straighten up the patio after the previous night's storm while Joanne stayed inside to clean the kitchen. Delighted the storm had left behind a clear blue sky, Danielle cheerfully wiped down the patio furniture with a terry-cloth rag while Walt picked up debris that had blown into the yard. Overhead, the sun shone brightly, yet it was still chilly, and both Walt and Danielle wore jackets.

"It looks like Pearl has a mess on her hands," Walt said as he plucked a soaked newspaper flyer from a bush. It had blown into their yard during the storm. He shoved it into the trash bag.

"Where do you think all that mud came from?" Danielle glanced toward Pearl's house. Before coming downstairs, she had looked into her neighbor's yard from an upstairs window. After seeing the mess, she had expected her yard to have suffered similar damage and was relieved when she found only minor cleanup was required on her side of the fence.

"I don't know." Walt glanced around, looking for any more debris.

"I wonder if she's going to have Craig take some of those trees down. There are at least two dead ones back there. I think she's lucky the storm didn't take one of them down instead of just some branches. It could have landed on her house and caused serious damage."

Walt picked up the last piece of stray debris and shoved it in the plastic bag. He glanced toward Pearl's backyard and said, "I wonder if she's going to change her mind on taking out those rosebushes. When I walked back to check on the garage, I looked over into her yard. It actually looks as if a few of them have moved several feet."

"How does that happen?" Danielle frowned.

"I assume all that water. I'm just glad none of it came over here."

Danielle shrugged. "Well, luckily for us, there's that dip in her yard. Glad the rain stopped or our yard might look like Pearl's."

"We haven't had a storm like that in a long time. But it looks as if we're going to have a sunny Easter."

Danielle paused a moment, the damp rag in her hand. "If Pearl was not such a difficult woman, I would have invited her to join us for Easter dinner. She's all alone. I can't imagine she has plans today." Danielle shrugged and added, "But maybe I'm wrong and she has all kinds of friends."

"I'm afraid even if you did invite her, she wouldn't take the invitation in the spirit in which it was given, and she would assume you were simply trying to rub salt in her wounds over the fact her efforts to shut down Marlow House didn't go entirely as she intended."

With a cheeky grin she said, "Well, I certainly wouldn't invite her to Easter dinner just to rub it in—but it would be a perk."

Walt crooked a disapproving brow at his wife.

She looked back at him and batted her eyes innocently. "I was teasing. Really." Unable to keep a straight face, she giggled.

IT HAS BEEN WRITTEN cats typically sleep sixteen to twenty hours a day. Max, being an older cat, slept in the upper range, leaving just four hours a day to attend to non-sleep-related cat duties. His more wakeful times came in the evening, when he liked to roam, yet the previous night's storm had kept him inside.

Spending the night inside proved boring with all the guest room doors shut and no spirits around to converse with. Even Walt slept all night these days. Bored and with nowhere to go with a storm raging, Max had gone back to sleep. He woke again for breakfast and then went back to the parlor for another long nap.

Sunday's afternoon sun was high in the sky when Max finally woke up again and decided to venture outside. The people staying at Marlow House had gathered in the living room around the fireplace, making all sorts of noise with their human way of conversing.

With a yawn, Max sauntered panther-like down the hallway and into the kitchen, heading toward the pet door. Several minutes later he slipped outside, sending the metal door swinging back and forth as he continued on his way. As he walked by the side patio, he heard birds chirping and looked up, wondering where the sound came from. He enjoyed watching birds. There was a time he would have gladly hunted one for Danielle and brought it to her as a gift to show his admiration, yet Walt had told him not to bring her dead birds or rodents. Humans were peculiar creatures, Max thought.

Max spied his favorite tree along the fence next to the unfriendly neighbor. It provided an excellent view of the surrounding area. With little effort he made his way to the tree and climbed high into its branches, finding his favorite perch. Once there, he nestled down and surveyed the grounds. Motion caught his eye from the rear of the neighbor's yard. Crouching on the branch, he watched.

Had Max come out earlier, he would have seen a river of mud and the gaping hole from the missing rosebush filled with water. But the water had all receded, and the once soggy dirt was now damp with no signs of water or mud puddles. The cat watched in fascination as a large black bird swooped down from another tree, landing by the hole left behind by the stolen rosebush. Something in the hole intrigued the bird. It persistently pecked at its prize, attempting to pick it up before dropping it back into the hole.

Mesmerized by the bird, Max watched, trying to determine what it was trying to pick up. Once again the bird managed to grab hold of the object, only to lose it again. But this time Max caught a glimpse of the prize—it looked something like a spider. A large spider, maybe as large as a human hand.

The sound of the kitchen door opening and closing, followed by human voices caught Max's attention. He looked away from the bird toward Marlow House. The two girls staying there had just stepped outside. They each carried what appeared to be a plate of food.

TAMMY LED the way to the patio table, her sister close behind her. They each carried a slice of Danielle's double fudge chocolate cake on a small plate.

"I think I could get used to this," Tammy said as she sat down at one of the patio tables. She chose not to sit at the table under the overhang, wanting instead to enjoy the afternoon sun. Her sister joined her at the table.

"That breakfast this morning was amazing," Brenda said. "I think Danielle should open a restaurant."

Tammy took a bite of the cake and closed her eyes as she let out a little moan. "Or a bakery," she said as she opened her eyes and prepared to take another bite.

Max looked back to the bird just in time to see it take off in flight, and in its mouth was the spiderlike object it had finally managed to latch onto. The bird flew over the fence with the prize in its beak, making its way over Marlow House's side yard and directly over the two girls sitting at the table.

Neither sister was aware of the black cat with white-tipped ears sitting in the branches of the nearby tree at the edge of the yard, watching them and the bird about to fly over their heads. Nor were they aware of the bird—or the strange spiderlike object that was about to slip out of the bird's beak.

Brenda had just taken a bite of her cake when something dropped from the sky and landed in the center of her plate. She let out a startled cry just before hearing a bird shriek. Tammy looked up and watched as a large black bird flew off. She looked down and immediately realized what had happened. The bird had been flying over with what appeared to be some twigs—probably to make a nest—and had dropped it.

"I can't believe that just happened." Tammy laughed.

"This is so gross. Did that stupid bird have to drop it in my chocolate cake?" Brenda wrinkled her nose and started to pick up what appeared to be a tangle of twigs. Just as she gently lifted the object from the gooey chocolate fudge frosting, the sisters realized what she was holding. They both let out a scream, and Brenda dropped it back into her cake.

The bird had not been carrying twigs for a nest. It had been carrying the skeletal remains of a human hand—one now covered in chocolate frosting.

NINETEEN

"This is definitely a first," Officer Brian Henderson said as he stood by the patio table and carefully examined what appeared to be the skeletal remains of a human hand. Wearing gloves, he gingerly lifted it up from the slice of chocolate cake. Standing next to him were Joe Morelli and Danielle, and across the table from him were the Owen sisters, anxiously watching and listening to what he had to say. Sitting at the patio table under the overhang, listening in at a discreet distance so as not to get in the way, were Walt and the rest of the raffle guests.

"I told them not to move anything," Danielle explained. "When they came in the house and told me what had happened, and I came out here to see, we left everything exactly as it was."

Joe looked across the table at the teenage girls. "And you say a bird dropped it?"

Tammy nodded. "Yes. It all happened so fast. I saw something fall from the sky, I looked up, and this big black bird was flying away."

"Is it real?" Brenda asked. "Is it what we think it is?"

"It looks real. But it is rather hard to say with all this chocolate frosting on it," Brian said, carefully slipping what appeared to be the skeletal remains of a human hand into an evidence bag. "But we will need to take this back to the lab and see what they say."

"If it's real, where is the rest of the body?" Brenda asked, looking around nervously.

"And where did it come from?" Tammy asked.

"Good questions," Brian said. "But if you say a bird dropped it, I have no idea how far a bird might fly carrying something like this. Did it pick it up in this neighborhood, a mile away? Or maybe it's something that washed up on the beach and isn't even from this area. But I'm sure the lab will be able to answer some of those questions."

As Brian and Joe prepared to leave a few minutes later, Tammy and Brenda walked to the rest of the guests, who were eagerly waiting to talk to them. Walt left the group and joined Danielle and the two officers.

"What happens now?" Danielle asked.

"Like I said, the lab needs to examine this," Brian told her. "It looks real, but it could be a piece of a broken Halloween skeleton the bird picked up in some trash."

"Doesn't look like plastic to me," Danielle said.

Brian glanced at the evidence bag and cringed. "No…it doesn't. But I can always hope."

"I'm really sorry you two had to come over. I'm surprised you're working on Easter Sunday," Danielle said.

"I just worked this morning and was getting ready to go home and pick up Kelly. We're having Easter dinner with my sister and Craig," Joe explained. "But when a call came in that a hand fell from the sky at Marlow House, I had to come along. I swear, Danielle, the strangest things happen here."

"I hope Kelly or your sister doesn't get mad at me for making you late," Danielle said.

Joe glanced at his watch. "No. I have plenty of time."

Danielle looked at Brian and asked, "What are you doing for Easter dinner? You have to work all day?"

Brian shrugged. "I get off in about an hour. But it's just another day. Probably have some leftover pizza."

"You could join us for Easter dinner," Danielle offered.

Brian shook his head. "No, you have enough on your hands." He glanced over to the group huddled by the other patio table.

"You should come," Walt told him. "We have plenty of food. And since we're having dinner in the dining room, you don't have to worry about any hands falling in your food."

NEXT DOOR, Pearl stood in the corner windows of her bedroom, using binoculars to peer into her neighbors' yard. Standing behind the curtains and peeking around them so as not to be seen, she watched as two police officers appeared to be questioning Walt and Danielle. She recognized one of the men, Brian Henderson. He had been the investigating officer on her stolen rosebush. He was also the one who had given her his business card when she had caught Lily Bartley breaking into Marlow House. Of course, they had all insisted Lily hadn't broken in. But Pearl knew what she had seen and found the entire incident peculiar. There were a lot of peculiar things about this neighborhood now that all these outsiders had moved in.

She turned her attention to the group of people now huddled at the table on the patio, away from the police officers and the Marlows. Something had obviously gone on next door that had required them to call the police. A few minutes earlier she had watched Officer Henderson interrogating two teenagers, and then he put something in a plastic bag that he was now taking with him.

What is going on over there? Who called the police? What did he put in that plastic bag? I bet it is drugs. Yes, that has to be it. They are doing drugs next door! I knew something like this would happen.

"SO YOU'RE TAKING Danielle up on her offer to come over for Easter dinner?" Joe asked as the pair walked from Marlow House to the police car parked out front.

"Danielle usually puts on a good spread, kind of hard to say no. But if she's serving chocolate cake for dessert, I might pass on that," Brian said.

Joe chuckled. "I don't know. Danielle bakes a pretty good chocolate cake."

Now at the police car, Brian opened the back door and set the evidence bag on the back seat. Just as he closed the door, he heard a woman call out.

"Woo-hoo, Officer Henderson!"

Standing by the police car, Joe and Brian looked down the street to see Pearl Huckabee rushing in their direction.

"Afternoon, Mrs. Huckabee," Brian greeted her when she reached them.

"Aren't you arresting anyone?" she asked, slightly out of breath from running.

"Umm, for what?" Brian asked.

"It was drugs, wasn't it? I saw you confiscating contraband next door. I told you there was going to be a problem allowing those Marlows to operate an illegal motel. And it is illegal, if you ask me. Operating without a business license. Some people think they can skirt the law by finding a loophole. Hopefully this will make the city see I was right, that they need to shut down Marlow House once and for all before this happens again. Something like this can blow up out of control, and then you'll really have a problem on your hands. I was right all along. Why aren't you arresting anyone?"

"I have no clue what you are talking about. What drugs?" Brian asked.

Pearl glanced to the back car door where she had seen Brian deposit the plastic bag. "Isn't that what was in the bag?"

Brian shook his head. "No. I don't know where you got that idea."

"Then why are you here? Something happened. I have a right to know what is going on. If the Marlows are allowing strangers to stay next door to me and bringing illegal activities into this neighborhood, then I want to know! I have my rights."

"We aren't here because any of the guests did something wrong," Brian told her.

"Then it was something the Marlows did?" Pearl asked.

"No. Walt and Danielle did nothing wrong. But we need to go now," Brian said as he reached for the handle of the passenger door.

"Why were you called here? As a citizen, I have the right to know when the police are called to my neighborhood. I have a right to protect myself," Pearl insisted.

"Ma'am, a bird dropped a suspicious object in Danielle's backyard, and she wanted us to see it," Joe explained.

"What kind of suspicious object?" Pearl asked.

"It hasn't been officially identified yet," Brian explained as he opened the passenger door. "So we really can't say. But I'm sure when it is identified, you can read about it in the police report in the newspaper. Now, we really do need to get back to the station. Happy Easter, Mrs. Huckabee."

Pearl frowned as both men climbed into the police car. She watched silently as the vehicle pulled away a few minutes later, disappearing down the street.

EASTER DINNER WAS to be served in thirty minutes. The guests gathered in Marlow House's living room, enjoying appetizers and beverages—cocktails and wine for the adults, and soda for Brenda and Tammy. Chris and Heather had arrived twenty minutes earlier, joining the raffle guests for the evening. They had just been updated on the strange events of the afternoon. In the fireplace, flames flickered and danced, and several guests stood nearby enjoying its warmth. Faye sat on one of the chairs with a glass of wine, a knit afghan draped over her knees to keep her warm.

"I don't believe it's real," Faye told them.

"It sure looked real," Brenda grumbled.

Faye shook her head. "I suspect it is exactly as that one officer suggested. Nothing more than a broken piece from some Halloween skeleton that the bird picked up from the trash."

"You're probably right," Chris agreed.

"But the other is better story fodder," Jonah said with a laugh. "Very Alfred Hitchcock. But having a piece of garbage drop from the sky, not very exciting. But I have to agree, it's not real."

"You didn't get a good look at it," Brenda argued.

Danielle was about to voice her opinion when the doorbell rang. She left her guests to answer the door while they continued to debate the subject.

"I'm glad you decided to join us," Danielle said after she opened the front door to Brian Henderson.

"Thanks for asking me," Brian said as he stepped into the house. "I'd like to talk to you alone for a minute before we see the others."

"Sure." Danielle shut the front door and motioned to the parlor. "We can talk in there."

Once alone in the parlor, the door shut, Brian said, "It was real. And it wasn't a bear."

"A bear?" Danielle frowned.

"Sometimes skeletal remains of a bear claw can be confused for a human hand. But I didn't think it was a bear skeleton when I looked at it. But I was hoping it wasn't real."

"So it wasn't part of a Halloween skeleton?" she asked.

He shook his head. "Not unless someone was using a real human skeleton as a Halloween decoration."

"So what now? Look for the rest of the skeleton? Run DNA tests to identify him? Or her?"

"We won't know anything for sure until they finish their tests. But they think it's old."

"How old?"

"Old enough that there isn't a sense of urgency. Typically, when older skeletal remains are found, it doesn't have the same urgency as remains buried within the last fifty or so years. Chances are, no one is currently looking for the person, and if there was foul play, the guilty party is probably already dead."

"So you think it's that old?"

Brian shrugged. "It won't be conclusive until they run some tests. But it's going to take a few weeks before we know more."

"Either way, it's pretty creepy," Danielle said with a shiver.

Brian glanced over toward the sofa. "Creepier than a dead body in here?"

"Gee, do you always have to bring that up?" Danielle asked.

"Or the dead body at the base of the attic stairs?" Brian asked, glancing up to the ceiling.

"Oh, shut up."

"Or the dead body in one of the upstairs guest rooms…"

Danielle rolled her eyes. "Enough already. You want a drink?"

Brian laughed. "Yeah. I could use a drink."

TWENTY

The late afternoon sunshine streamed in the parlor window at Marlow House. Walt sat alone in the room, smoking a thin cigar and contemplating his life and recent choices. Effortlessly he blew out smoke rings, watching them as they drifted up to the ceiling and disappeared. Angela had once been fascinated with the trick, but she soon grew bored with it—as she did with everything else. Taking another drag off the cigar, he drew in the smoke without inhaling. After forming an O shape with his mouth, he used his tongue to expel some of the smoke in a series of rings. Like the others, they floated upwards and vanished.

He could hear the housekeeper singing as she cleaned the floors in the entry hall. She was always singing some quaint Irish song. Katherine was Irish too, but he couldn't recall her ever singing while she worked. Tossing his cigar in the nearby ashtray, he wondered how long this new girl was going to be here. Angela had obviously brought her in to replace Katherine while she was away. He would be happy when Katherine returned. He didn't care for strangers coming and going in his home, and Katherine did her work without making a lot of noise.

The woman was singing a new song now. It was about whiskey and loose women. Walt chuckled and wondered what Angela would think if she heard the lyrics. He found it amusing the new housekeeper was so free with her music; it wasn't as if she assumed she was alone in the house. Just minutes earlier she had cleaned the parlor while he sat on his chair watching her. She was a bold thing, shamelessly belting out provocative ditties while flashing him impish grins. If the woman wasn't old enough to be his mother, he might assume she was actually flirting with him.

The singing stopped. Walt sat there a moment and listened. He then heard the front door slamming shut. He suspected the housekeeper had left for the day. When cleaning Marlow House, she typically saved the entry hall for last, exiting out the front door so as not to leave footprints on the newly polished wood floors.

Walt leaned back in his wingback chair and picked up the cigar from the ashtray. He would enjoy some quiet time before Angela returned home.

"Hello, Walt." A female voice broke the silence.

Startled by the unexpected sound, Walt looked up and found Maisy Faye standing in the open doorway from the entry hall, smiling in his direction. She wore a stylish pillbox hat atop her blond curls; it sat at a sassy angle. The hat matched the full-length gray coat she wore over her red and white polka-dot dress. Maisy's blue eyes fairly sparkled in that mischievous way she had, and the corners of her mouth tugged upwards in an impish grin. Her white gloved hands held a small handbag.

"Your housekeeper let me in," she explained, stepping into the room. "And I could smell your cigar, so I assumed I would find you in here. I hope it's okay if I came in."

"You're always welcome, Maisy Faye." Walt motioned to the sofa across from his chair. "Please, come sit down and keep me company while I wait for Angela."

"She's not back yet?" Maisy asked as she took a seat on the sofa, making no attempt to remove her coat. She sat primly, her back straight.

"No. Sometimes I wonder if she ever will."

Maisy laughed at the suggestion. "Don't be silly, Walt. I ran into her just a little while ago. I don't think you need to worry. She isn't going anywhere."

"You didn't happen to ask my wife what's taking her so long?"

Maisy shrugged. "She was busy arguing with someone. You know how she loves to argue. I didn't want to interrupt."

"I suppose she will be home soon enough, and then she can argue with me."

Maisy flashed Walt a smile. "I don't know why anyone would want to argue with you. If you were my husband, I would just want to make you happy."

"You're sweet, Maisy. But I suspect Angela would not agree with you."

"Oh piffle. Angela doesn't know what a good thing she has! And I told her so!" She looked to the front window briefly and back to Walt. "Have you seen George lately? I still haven't met him."

"No. He hasn't been by in a while. But I suppose he's busy these days, married and now a father."

"I think you will make a wonderful father someday," Maisy told him.

Walt fiddled absently with the cigar in his hand. He looked down at it, making no attempt to smoke it. "I'm not sure that is ever going to happen."

"Can't Angela have children?" Maisy blurted. She immediately blushed after the words left her mouth. "I'm sorry. I shouldn't have asked that. Sometimes things just slip out of my mouth before I think."

"So what are you doing today?" Walt asked, changing the subject.

"I stopped in to say goodbye," she told him.

"Goodbye? Where are you going?"

"I heard from my mother. She's having my father come and get me. I'm going home," she explained.

"When will you be back?" Walt asked.

Maisy shrugged. "I don't think I will be back."

"Not coming back? But I'm going to miss you," he said.

She flashed him a soft smile and lowered her eyes briefly. "You are so sweet."

"I'm not sweet. Hardly sweet," he grumbled.

"I think you are. And I've enjoyed our talks. I'll miss them."

"Then don't leave," he told her. "Stay."

"I suspect your wife will be relieved when I leave."

"Angela doesn't care," Walt insisted. "She understands our friendship is purely platonic."

"I need to go, Walt. My parents want me to come home. They say it's time."

Walt let out a sigh. "I suppose I'm being selfish. But I am going to miss you."

"And I'll miss you. You have no idea how much I've enjoyed our time together. I don't think you realize how helpful you've been."

"I'm just glad I was able to help."

Maisy stood up. "Be happy, Walt. You deserve happiness."

Walt looked up to Maisy, studying her a moment. "You look content. You want to go home, don't you?"

Maisy nodded. "I…I didn't think I wanted to. But I think it's time."

"And that beau of yours, will you see him?" Walt asked.

Maisy shrugged. "Mother says he has been asking about me. Wanting to know when I'm coming home—if I am."

"So he's waiting for you still?" Walt asked.

Maisy grinned. "Yes. He is."

"He loves you, Maisy. Real love never dies—even when two people are parted. And you still love him, don't you?"

Maisy nodded shyly. "I do."

WALT'S EYES FLEW OPEN. He stared up at the ceiling. If not for the nightlight plugged into the nearby socket, the room would be completely dark. He felt movement in the bed. It took him a few moments to get his bearings.

"Danielle?" It was more a question—an urgent question.

"Walt?" The lamp on the other side of the bed turned on. Danielle, now sitting up in bed, looked over at Walt. "Did you have a nightmare?"

Rubbing sleep from his eyes, Walt sat up in bed and shook his head. "Not a nightmare exactly. But it was a strange dream."

"The way you called out to me, it sounded like you were having a nightmare."

Now sitting up in bed next to Danielle, Walt looked over to her and said, "I dreamt about Maisy Faye."

Danielle arched her brow. "Are you talking about the elderly woman sleeping in our downstairs bedroom, or that attractive blonde I should be worried about?"

Walt chuckled. "I don't think you have anything to worry about. But no, it wasn't about Faye. And to be honest, it felt more like a memory than a dream."

"Was it a dream hop?" Danielle asked.

Walt shook his head. "No, I don't think so. Although I imagine the Maisy Faye of my dream is probably dead by now, considering I knew her when I was still married to Angela."

"Did you figure out who she was?" Danielle asked.

"No. Not really. But so much was familiar in the dream. Like I had experienced it before."

"Déjà vu?" Danielle asked.

Walt nodded. "I suppose. It was like I was watching a movie that I had already seen."

"So who was this Maisy Faye? What did you learn about her?"

"She looked just like I remember. But there was nothing between us. So it's not like she was a girl I dated in college and just couldn't quite remember."

"How do you know that?"

"I made a comment in the dream about how we were just platonic friends. Oh, and Angela, I was married to Angela in the dream, and Maisy knew her."

"You did say you thought Maisy might have been one of Angela's friends."

"I got the impression she was more my friend than Angela's."

"Why is that?" Danielle asked.

"Just by what was said. At least I have a general time of when I knew her—assuming the dream was more a memory. And like I said, it felt like a memory."

"Where were you in the dream?"

"I was in the parlor, here, in Marlow House. And another thing, in the dream there was another housekeeper. Katherine still worked here, but she was away for some reason, and the new housekeeper was someone Angela hired to fill in. Funny thing, now that I'm awake, I can't recall Katherine ever leaving while I was married to Angela, or being replaced, even temporarily, by another housekeeper. But the woman was so familiar. I know I've seen her before. I remember her songs. It was a memory."

"Her songs?" Danielle frowned.

"Yes, the housekeeper, the one filling in for Katherine, she would sing these little Irish ditties. You know, funny little songs. She had a thick Irish accent. Plump woman, probably in her fifties, with red frizzy hair and ruddy freckled cheeks. I can remember her cleaning Marlow House. At least…I think I do. But I know she was cleaning the house in my dream."

"Walt, it was also a *dream.* Just because a dream might show something that actually happened in real life, it doesn't mean the dream will portray the event exactly as it occurred. For example, this plump housekeeper who liked to sing, she might have cleaned the house of some friend of yours, or maybe she was a waitress somewhere. It could be anything, even something you watched on TV."

"I suppose. But the dream felt so real, as if I was reliving a memory."

"So tell me about your Maisy. What did you learn about her?"

"For one thing, she was not my Maisy. I was married to Angela, and she had a beau back home."

"She wasn't from Frederickport?"

Walt shook his head. "No. I don't think so. I'm pretty sure she was just visiting for some reason. She was preparing to go home and stopped by the house to say goodbye. I remember feeling sad that she was leaving—like I was going to miss her—but also happy, because I knew she was anxious to see her family and boyfriend again."

"Well, at least I no longer have to worry about your Maisy Faye," Danielle cheerfully announced before leaning over and dropping a quick kiss on Walt's lips.

"Why is that?" Walt asked with a chuckle.

"Because you just said she had a boyfriend. And it certainly didn't sound like you were jealous she was going back to him."

TWENTY-ONE

Danielle took her place at the end of the table while Joanne brought out the rest of the food for breakfast. Removing the napkin from beside her plate and placing it over her lap, Danielle looked up the table at Walt, who smiled back at her. Faye sat to Walt's right, and Jonah sat next to his left. The couple from Portland sat on Jonah's side of the table, while the sisters sat across from them. The guests began filling their plates, passing the serving platters to their right after they had taken what they wanted.

As Danielle accepted a platter of bacon, she asked, "What does everyone have planned for today?"

Juanita, who was in the process of buttering a biscuit, paused a moment and looked over at Danielle and said, "Now that the rain has stopped and the weatherman promises a day of sunshine, we plan to do some exploring along the beach."

"I'm also going to take advantage of the sunshine." Faye spoke up. "But I plan to enjoy it from Marlow House's patio."

"Just watch out for those birds," Brenda grumbled.

"I suspect those bones were fake," Faye suggested. "Or from an animal."

"I'm afraid they were human bones," Danielle said uneasily. Everyone at the table paused a moment and looked her way, waiting for a further explanation.

"Brian told me last night. But I didn't want to say anything during dinner and spoil the evening. Everyone seemed to have finally put that out of their minds—at least for a while."

"Not me," Brenda said. "It's all I could think about."

"And they are real? Are you sure?" Jonah asked.

"Yes. But they're old," Danielle said. "While the police obviously want to figure out where they came from—and who they belong to, I don't think it's as urgent as it might have been if whoever they belonged to might still be alive today had they lived out their life."

"I bet the bird picked them up on the beach," Tammy suggested. "I know bodies have washed up on the beaches not far from here."

"I disagree," Jonah said. "I don't think they washed up on shore."

"Why?" Brenda asked.

"If they are as old as Danielle said and they were intact, I don't think old bones, especially fragile hand bones, would hold up in the ocean that well."

"Jonah has a point," Walt agreed.

"Maybe we should talk about something else over breakfast?" Danielle suggested.

Walt chuckled. "I think you're probably right. So what does everyone else have planned for today?"

"After breakfast I'll be locking myself in my room and working on my book. I must say staying in Marlow House has certainly amped up my creative juices," Jonah said.

"We were kind of hoping Danielle would give us the grand tour. We haven't been through the entire house yet," Tammy said. "I would love to hear more about its history. And, well, I always heard it was haunted."

"Certainly." Danielle flashed the girls a smile. "But you might be disappointed. The haunting of Marlow House is somewhat overrated." She turned her smile to Walt and added, "If we ever had a resident ghost, I suspect he has moved on by now."

"You know, girls." Faye spoke up. "I grew up in the house next door to Marlow House. I will have to respectfully disagree with Mrs. Marlow. I witnessed a number of unexplained—possibly paranormal—activities over here when I was growing up. On numerous occasions." Faye looked over to Danielle and gave her a wink.

AS WALT LISTENED to the exchange, he felt something rub against his calves. He looked down and spied Max weaving in and out between his feet.

Didn't you already have breakfast? Walt silently conveyed to the cat.

Max, who was now by the side of Walt's chair, sat down and looked up. He blinked his golden eyes at Walt and meowed.

They will be here a few days…What?…You want to know what it was?… Why?…Next door?

Walt abruptly tossed his napkin next to his plate and looked down the table at his wife. "Excuse me, Danielle, do you think I can have a word with you—in the—" Walt was about to say in the kitchen but remembered Joanne was there, so he said, "—the hallway?"

"Now?" Danielle frowned.

"Yes. I'm afraid I just remembered something. It is about one of the repairmen who was supposed to be here today."

Danielle's frown deepened, but instead of asking any questions, she politely excused herself and walked out to the hallway with Walt.

"We don't have any repairmen scheduled for today," Danielle whispered when they were out of earshot of their guests.

"Max told me where the bird picked up the hand."

Danielle cringed. "Do you have to say hand? Sounds so creepy."

"That's what it is. Or was."

"How does he know where the bird got it?"

"Max saw the bird pick it up—and he saw the bird drop it. A few minutes ago he asked me what it was. He couldn't tell from where he was sitting at the time, but he was curious, considering all the commotion over it."

"So where did the bird get it?"

"From Pearl's backyard. You know that rosebush someone stole from Pearl?"

"Umm…yeah…"

"And the hole they left behind?"

Danielle nodded.

"It was not the only thing left behind. The bird picked the hand up from the hole."

"Ewww…next door? You don't think someone stole the rosebush and left it there, do you?"

"No. But I think they disrupted the ground, and then with all the rain, it worked its way up."

"From where?"

"I assume from under the ground."

"I was going to go down to the station and talk to the chief anyway. I'll tell him what Max saw."

"MORNING ,CHIEF," Danielle greeted as she knocked on the doorframe of the open doorway into Police Chief MacDonald's office. He looked up from his desk where he was working and gave her a welcoming smile and waved her in.

"Good morning, Danielle. I heard you had an interesting Easter."

"To say the least." Danielle took a seat facing him.

"Brian tells me you invited him to dinner last night. That was nice. He said he had a great time."

Danielle shrugged. "I should have invited him earlier. I didn't even think about it."

"Why should you think about it?" the chief asked.

"He doesn't really have any family."

He chuckled. "You and Brian have come a long way."

Danielle leaned back in the chair. "He's no longer trying to send me to jail. At least, not at the moment."

"He said you put on an amazing dinner last night. This morning he was singing your praises. Keep feeding him, and I imagine he won't be so anxious to lock you up."

Danielle rolled her eyes. "Way to a man's heart—and the path to freedom—food. Who knew?" She chuckled and then asked, "So how was your Easter?"

"It was good. The boys and I spent it with my sister and Bruce. Sissy had an Easter egg hunt for the boys. I think Eddie felt too cool to look for eggs, but once Evan started filling his basket with them, he changed his mind. Probably helped that Sissy didn't use real hardboiled eggs. She hid those plastic eggs and put money and chocolate inside."

Danielle laughed. "Heck, I would be all over that. Money and chocolate."

"So, what do I owe the honor of this visit? I assume it's to see what's going on with those skeletal remains that fell out of the sky."

"Yes, it does."

"We still don't have any idea where they came from, but—"

"I know."

"And we may never know for sure—"

"No. I didn't mean *I know you have no idea where they came from.* What I meant, *I know where they came from.*"

The chief sat up straighter in his chair. "You do?"

Danielle nodded. "Max was sitting in the big tree in our side yard."

MacDonald slumped back in his chair. "Max? Your cat? The one who wants to bite me?"

Danielle nodded again. "Yes. He was watching this big bird digging around in a hole in Pearl's yard. I assume you know about the rosebush that was taken from her backyard. Brian went over to talk to her about it. Anyway, Max saw the bird pull something out of the hole where the rosebush had been. He flew off, over our yard, and then dropped it. Max saw the entire thing."

The chief groaned.

"What's wrong?" Danielle frowned. "I thought this would help. Brian told me it was going to take weeks before the tests are finished on the bones, and because they were so fragile and old, he wasn't sure how much you could learn by the tests. But this way, if there is a body that went with those hand bones, you might be able to find it in Pearl's yard."

"The problem being, I don't think Pearl Huckabee is going to let us just go digging around in her yard."

"Can't you just get a warrant? After all, the skeletal remains of a hand were found there," Danielle argued.

"And just how are we supposed to get a search warrant?"

Danielle considered the question a moment and slumped back in her chair. "I see what you mean. I don't imagine a judge is going to approve a warrant based on a cat's deposition."

MacDonald chuckled. "I don't think so."

"Gee, if I had known earlier, I would have claimed to have seen the bird coming over from Pearl's house. But that's not going to work now," Danielle said glumly.

"I suppose I could stop over at Pearl's this afternoon and tell my own white lie."

"About what?" Danielle asked.

"Brian went over to Pearl's cousin's house to question him about the missing rosebush, but he wasn't home. One of the neighbors said he'd left and claimed he was heading out of town. And the car he was driving, it wasn't a truck, like Pearl saw leaving down the alley. In fact, according to vehicle registration, he doesn't own a truck. From what I understand, he's still not back."

"So what kind of white lie?" Danielle asked.

POLICE CHIEF MACDONALD stood alone on Pearl Huckabee's front porch, waiting for her to open the door. He glanced around, noticing the muddy area off to the side of the house between Pearl's property and Marlow House.

"Police Chief MacDonald?" Pearl coolly greeted him when she answered the door a moment later.

"Morning, Mrs. Huckabee."

Pearl glanced at her watch. "It's more like afternoon. Why are you here? Is this about whatever trouble went on next door? Didn't I tell you all, Frederickport is asking for trouble letting those Marlows run an illegal motel out of their home."

"Umm…no…actually, I'm here about your missing rosebush," he explained.

Pearl opened her front door a little wider and stepped out on the porch with the chief. "Are you here to tell me you caught the culprit? Do you have my rosebush? Was it that scoundrel cousin of mine?"

"Umm…no, ma'am. Officer Henderson has been trying to contact your cousin, but he has been out of town."

"Yes. He already told me that. So why are you here, then?"

"I was wondering if I could go in your backyard and have another look at where they took the rosebush."

"Why would you want to do that?" She frowned.

"I would just like to take a personal look at the crime scene."

"Are you saying Officer Henderson did not do a thorough investigation when he was here?"

"No. Of course not. In fact, he is one of our best officers. I just thought a second pair of eyes on the scene might give a new perspective on who might have taken your rosebush."

"I'm already fairly certain who took it. And I don't see how you digging around in my garden is going to accomplish anything helpful. Plus, we had quite a rain last night, and I had a pipe break. It is a mess in the backyard. If there was any evidence, it has been washed away."

"But I would still—"

"I really am busy," Pearl interrupted. "I don't want you going back there. You will just end up tracking mud all over. Now good day."

Pearl stepped back into her house and slammed the front door shut, leaving the police chief once again alone on the front porch.

TWENTY-TWO

Brenda and Tammy stood in the Marlow House library, looking at the reproductions of Walt's and Angela's portraits. Marie Nichols was also there, but only Danielle knew of the ghost's presence. Marie had been following the three for the last half hour as Danielle took the girls through a complete tour of the house.

"I still say you should have shown them the hidden staircase," Marie said as she watched the girls. "I suspect that's the type of thing they were hoping to see here."

Danielle glanced over to Marie, who floated nearby on an invisible chair, but withheld comment.

"It really is sort of creepy how much your husband looks like him," Tammy said as she stared intently at Walt's portrait.

"Tammy, that's not very nice," Brenda scolded. "But it is kind of freaky. And how can you sleep in the attic knowing he was murdered there?"

Danielle shrugged. "I try not to think about it."

"That would really freak me out," Brenda said with a shudder.

Tammy looked at Danielle and said, "I kind of thought we might experience—I don't know—some sort of ghostly activity while we were here. Like those paranormal shows we watch, when they stay overnight at a house that's supposed to be haunted, and unexplained stuff happens."

"Well, the skeletal remains of a hand did fall out of the sky," Danielle reminded her.

"That was outside," Brenda said. "While it was pretty freaky, it was a bird not a ghost."

"Maybe I should do something?" Marie suggested.

Danielle looked quickly to Marie and then glanced to the girls. They were both still staring at the portraits. She shook her head at Marie.

"Come on now, Danielle, it will be fun!" Marie said cheerfully. "I could make a book float across the room? Or perhaps have the door open and close by itself?"

Danielle flashed the spirit a stern look.

Marie put out her lower lip in a pout. "You are rather a party pooper, Danielle."

The doorbell rang.

"I'm going to go get that," Danielle said quickly.

"Thanks for the tour, Danielle," Tammy said. "It was fun, even if Marlow House really isn't haunted."

"You're welcome," Danielle said, flashing both girls a smile before heading out of the library.

"After yesterday, I'm sort of glad nothing spooky has happened in the house," Brenda said after Danielle left. She turned from the portraits and headed for the door.

"I don't know," Tammy said with a shrug, following her sister, "I think it would be cool to see a ghost."

Unable to resist the temptation, Marie focused her attention on the vase sitting on the table next to the door leading into the hallway. Just as Brenda was about to step out of the room, her back to the table, the vase lifted up into the air, hovered there a brief moment, and then settled back on the table.

Tammy let out a shriek and froze.

"What's wrong?" Brenda asked, turning to her sister.

Tammy pointed to the vase, her hand shaking. "It…it…it was flying!"

"Flying?" Brenda frowned.

Tammy nodded quickly.

"Don't be lame," Brenda said with an eye roll as she headed out the door.

"HEY, CHIEF," Danielle greeted after she answered her front door a few minutes later. Police Chief MacDonald stood alone on the front porch.

"I spoke to your neighbor. She wouldn't let me look at her backyard."

Danielle glanced over her shoulder to make sure she was alone, and then looked back to the chief. "You want to come in?"

He shook his head. "No. I just wanted you to know I wasn't able to look in her yard. I need to get back to the station."

"You know, Chief, I keep wondering, whose bones did that bird have? I have to assume the rest of the body—or skeleton—is over there. Or was. Who is buried next door?"

"That's what I want to know too."

"Maybe Craig will find something," Danielle suggested.

"Craig?" The chief frowned.

"From what I understand, Pearl hired Craig to clean up her yard. Of course, I also heard she told him not to touch her rosebushes."

AFTER SAYING goodbye to the chief, Danielle went to find Faye. When giving Brenda and Tammy the house tour, she had noticed the elderly woman sitting on the side patio. Danielle walked into the kitchen and looked out the back window. She spied Faye sitting in a lawn chair next to Walt. Faye wore a bulky sweater and slacks, with a knitted afghan thrown over her knees to help keep her warm. Before going outside, Danielle prepared a pot of hot tea and a platter of cookies.

"Enjoying the sun?" Danielle asked ten minutes later as she carried the tray with the cookies and tea out to the patio.

Faye looked up and smiled. "What do we have here?"

"It looked as if you could use some refreshments." Danielle set the tray on the nearby table.

"How lovely," Faye said.

Walt reached out and gave Danielle's hand a quick touch in silent greeting. She flashed him a smile and then asked Faye, "Would you like any sugar or cream?"

"Just plain for me, thank you," Faye told her.

"Faye has been telling me what it used to be like here at Marlow

House when she was growing up next door," Walt explained as he watched Danielle pour them each a cup of tea.

"Really?" Danielle handed Faye a full cup. "And how was that?"

"No one lived here back then," Faye explained. "I remember sometimes my sister and I would watch the upstairs windows, and we would swear we saw the curtains move. Of course, it was probably just a draft. But at the time, the thought of ghosts next door sounded far more exciting."

"Did you know the people very well who bought your house?" Danielle asked.

"Not really. I remember she was a stubborn woman. I didn't particularly care for her." Faye sipped her tea.

"Why was that?" Danielle asked.

With a sigh, Faye set her tea on its saucer, holding it with both hands. She looked over to Danielle. "I was hasty in selling the property. My father had died unexpectedly. He fell at work." Faye shook her head. "Foolish man. He had no business going up and down those stairs each day, considering his bad leg. At the time… well, I was young. I didn't want to keep living in my father's house. I wanted my own home. And when I realized I had not thought it through, I tried to cancel the sale. But they wouldn't have it. I know it was her. I don't think he even wanted the house."

"The couple who bought it?" Danielle asked.

Faye nodded. "I can't recall their last name. It was so long ago. They had two little girls. She was a bit of a shrew, as I recall. He was a traveling salesman, gone a lot. I remember once when they came over to look at the house shortly before the sale was to close, and I got the feeling he just wanted out of there. He was planning to leave on another business trip, but she made it perfectly clear she expected to be moved into the house before he took off again." Faye paused and took a sip of tea.

"I suppose they might have felt they couldn't afford to cancel the sale," Danielle suggested.

"I offered to pay them for the inconvenience. It was a good amount, as I recall. And it wasn't as if there weren't other houses for sale in the area. And it was my home. She wouldn't even consider it. After I offered to pay them something, he was very interested. For a while there, I thought he was going to get her to agree to cancel the purchase."

"I believe those were the grandparents of our new neighbor," Walt said. "The woman who bought your old house."

"Yes, that's what I understand. Norman made another offer on the house a while back, but they seemed obsessed about keeping it in the family. Something about those rosebushes."

"What about the rosebushes?" Danielle asked. "I mean, do you know anything about them? The bushes in the backyard look dead, but Pearl refuses to take them out, says they belonged to her grandmother."

"The woman was very active in the local garden club back then. I remember once hearing how she cultivated some new rose. Of course, we never ran in the same circles, so it's just what I heard around town."

"How soon after they moved in did her husband leave her?" Danielle asked.

"Oh, you heard about that?" Faye asked with a smile.

"Yes. Someone mentioned it."

"Within that first year. Molly Shannon did some cleaning for the funeral home. She also cleaned Marlow House."

"Molly Shannon?" Walt asked.

"Yes. From what I always understood, the owners of Marlow House back then paid Molly to clean once a week. I ran into Molly at the funeral home a couple of months after I moved out and asked her about the new owners. I wondered if she ever saw them when she came over here to clean. She told me that a few weeks after they moved in, she heard a lot of fighting over there, in the backyard. She looked outside and saw both of them shouting at each other while their little girls stood on the porch and cried. She thought it was awful them fighting in front of the children like that."

"Was that when he left her?" Danielle asked.

"All I know, a few weeks later when Molly came over to clean Marlow House, she saw the two little girls playing in the front yard alone. She asked them how they were doing, and one of the little girls told her their father had died."

"Died?" Danielle asked.

"I asked Leo about it. After all, we were the only funeral home in town. He told me he heard a different story, that the man had left his wife. Some even said he had another family in Washington."

"Faye, by any chance do you remember what Molly looked like?" Walt asked.

"Yes, of course. She was a short little thing, rather plump. I remember she had the frizziest red hair and a freckled face. Not particularly attractive, but she always seemed so happy. Always singing. I found her songs quite amusing. Why do you ask?"

TWENTY-THREE

The remainder of the week proved uneventful. When Sunday rolled around again, Marlow House seemed so quiet. All the raffle guests had checked out the previous day. Joanne had finished cleaning the house that morning and had left for home twenty minutes earlier. Walt was upstairs working on his new book, and Danielle was downstairs in the kitchen with Max and Sadie, who napped nearby. She sat at the kitchen table, drinking a cup of hot tea while pondering the events of the last week and wondering who —if anyone—was buried in the backyard of Pearl's house.

Sadie broke the silence when she jumped up suddenly and gave a woof, her tail wagging. She ran to the pet door and rushed outside, only to return a moment later when the door opened and in walked Lily.

"Welcome home. Looks like someone is happy to see you," Danielle said as she watched Sadie dance around Lily's feet in greeting.

Lily laughed, petting the dog as she walked into the house, closing the door behind her. On the other side of the kitchen Max lifted his head sleepily from where he had been napping and looked at Lily. After a bored yawn, he put his head down again, closed his eyes, and continued with his early afternoon nap.

"It is always good to be welcomed," Lily said cheerfully.

"There is more tea in the pot," Danielle offered, not standing up. "It's herbal. No caffeine."

"Sounds good. But I do miss my caffeine." Lily walked to the cabinet and helped herself to a clean cup.

"When did you get home?" Danielle asked as she watched Lily walk from the counter to the table with her cup.

"About fifteen minutes ago. Ian took the luggage in the house and went to go take a nap. He's exhausted. We didn't get much sleep last night. I told him I'd come visit with you a while and get Sadie." Lily started to sit down at the table when Danielle stopped her.

"Don't sit down!"

"Why?" Lily looked down at the empty chair. "Is Marie or Eva sitting there?"

Danielle laughed. "No. They aren't here. I just wanted to look at you. Your baby bump, it's really showing!"

Grinning, Lily reached down with her free hand and patted her belly. "I know. I'm about four months now, and in a couple of weeks I'm scheduled for the ultrasound. Hopefully I'll be able to find out if it's a boy or girl." Lily sat down.

Danielle picked up the teapot and began filling Lily's cup. "Walt thinks it's so strange how you'll get to know if the baby is a boy or girl months before it's born."

"Where is Walt?"

Now finished filling the cup, Danielle set the pot back on the table and leaned back in the chair. Before answering the question, she glanced up briefly to the ceiling and then looked back to Lily. "He's upstairs working on his new book. He didn't get much work done this last week with a full house. Which we need to consider before we do this again."

"So how did it work out?" Lily asked.

"It was an interesting week," Danielle said with a chuckle before taking a sip of tea. "But tell me first, how was your trip?"

"It was nice, but we didn't think the baby shower through very well."

Danielle frowned. "What do you mean?"

"They gave me a huge baby shower. I saw people I haven't seen in ages. Family and friends. I got a ton of stuff. I don't think I have anything left to buy."

"Why do you say you didn't think it through?" Danielle asked.

"We couldn't bring everything back with us. Not flying."

"So what did you do?" Danielle asked.

"My parents are coming for a visit before the baby is born and bringing everything with them. I swear, they're going to have to rent a U-Haul."

"You don't sound very happy about it."

Lily shrugged. "I love my folks, but I was just looking forward to some quiet time before the baby arrives. You know, after school ends and I get my classroom cleaned out. Just coming home and taking my time fixing up the nursery. Enjoying my last nights of real sleep. Although, I imagine that will be more difficult to do as I get bigger. Even now it's not comfortable sleeping on my stomach." Lily let out a sigh and then asked, "Now tell me, was the raffle a success? Did you make a lot of money for the art department?"

"That part was a success. Even if I were running this as a B and B and donating my profits, it wouldn't even be half of what they raised. I figure if we keep doing this, what it's actually costing us is less than what I was already donating each year. This way, a lot more money goes to charity."

Lily lifted her cup in a brief salute. "Well, good for you!"

The kitchen door opened unexpectedly and in walked Heather Donovan. She wore a dark green jogging suit, running shoes, and her black hair was fastened atop her head in a messy knot. In her hand she carried a large paper to-go sack.

"Lily, you're back!" Heather greeted her as she walked in the kitchen, closing the door behind her. Sadie jumped up from where she had been under the table and greeted Heather.

"Got back about twenty minutes ago," Lily said. "Danielle was just about to tell me about her raffle guests."

"Did she tell you about the dead body next door?" Heather asked as she tossed the sack on the table and took a seat.

Danielle glanced questioningly at the paper bag.

"Dead body?" Lily squeaked.

Momentarily ignoring Lily's question, Heather looked at Danielle and said, "I brought tacos from Beach Taco. Thought you might be hungry. And I didn't want to eat alone." She looked at Lily and added, "There is plenty for everyone. Even Walt and Ian. Where are they?" Heather glanced around as if one of the men might instantly appear.

"Dead body?" Lily repeated.

"Oh yeah. Next door. Buried under the roses." Now sitting at the table, Heather pulled out a wrapped taco and handed it to Danielle. "So where are Walt and Ian?"

Danielle accepted the taco and said, "Walt's working in the attic, and Ian is taking a nap."

"Dead body?" Lily shrieked at the top of her lungs.

Both Heather and Danielle froze a moment and looked at Lily, who was clearly agitated and impatient for Heather to explain.

"We only assume there is a dead body under the roses," Danielle explained as she unwrapped her taco.

"And why is that?" Lily demanded, ignoring the taco Heather had just set before her on the table.

"The hand came from her yard, so we have to assume the rest of the body is there," Danielle said.

"Hand? What hand?" Lily asked.

"Not a hand exactly. It was the skeletal remains of a hand," Danielle corrected. She looked at Heather and said, "Thanks for the tacos."

Picking up her teacup and then slamming it on the table, splashing tea all over, Lily shouted, "Stop torturing a pregnant woman! It is not good for the baby! What dead body?"

"It all started when a bird flew over our yard and dropped a hand—well, the skeletal remains of a hand—into a piece of cake one of our guests was eating at the time," Danielle began.

"A bird?" Lily stammered, her eyes wide.

Danielle continued with her story, catching Lily up on recent events.

"So you really think the rest of the body is there?" Lily asked when Danielle finished the story.

"Or maybe whoever stole the rosebush put it there," Heather suggested.

Lily cringed. "Well, that is just a creepy thought. So why hasn't the police department gone over Pearl's backyard?"

"The chief needs a warrant since she refuses to let him on her property. I talked to him the other day, and he told me the judge refused to give him one. The judge seems to think the bird could have picked that up anywhere, and he told the chief he wasn't about to start issuing warrants for the entire neighborhood, considering the age of the bones. If whoever the bones belonged to had died more recently, the judge would be more inclined to issue the warrant."

"That's just stupid," Lily grumbled.

Danielle shrugged. "I don't think the chief is too concerned about it. Joe's brother-in-law, Craig, has already been hired to clean up Pearl's yard. The chief had Joe tell Craig about the bones, asking him to be on the lookout when he is working in this area. Of course, Joe doesn't know Max saw the bird take the bones from Pearl's yard. From what I understand, Craig is supposed to start over at Pearl's sometime this week."

"Who do you think the bones belonged to?" Lily asked.

"I think it could be Pearl's grandfather," Danielle suggested.

Heather nodded. "I agree. After what you told me about him."

"Too bad we just can't ask Pearl about her grandfather. Just because he left her grandmother, it doesn't mean he wasn't in her life when she was growing up. If he was, then chances are those aren't his bones," Lily suggested.

"Yeah, well, good luck with that conversation," Heather said with a snort.

Danielle set her cup on the table and smiled up at Heather and Lily. "Or we could talk to her cousin who lives in town."

"You mean Ruby? I thought you already did," Heather said.

"No, not Ruby. From what she told me, I don't think she would know anything. I was thinking of our suspected rosebush thief. Pearl's cousin. He lives next to Presley House. Or where Presley House once stood."

Lily looked to Danielle and asked, "What do you hope to find out by talking to Pearl's cousin?"

"We could go over there under the pretense of looking at the Presley House property." Danielle glanced to Heather and back to Lily. "After all, Heather used to own the property. And when we're there, figure out some way to initiate a conversation with the guy."

"I thought you told me the other day he was out of town?" Heather asked.

"According to the chief, he's back now. Brian went over and talked to him. But of course the guy denied knowing anything about a rosebush. And he doesn't have a black truck, or even any rosebushes in his yard, so it didn't go anywhere. But if we could figure out some way to initiate a conversation about how he used to own the house next door to us, maybe we can get him to talk about his family. We could save a lot of time if we can rule out the grandfather. He might know where Pearl's grandfather ended up after he left his family."

"You mean, like in the backyard next door?" Heather asked.

TWENTY-FOUR

Walt looked up from his computer when Danielle walked into the room carrying a paper sack. He stopped typing and smiled in her direction.

"Lily and Ian are back," she told him as she walked into the attic apartment.

"Glad they made it back safely, but I guess this means they've picked up Sadie?"

"Lily is downstairs, but Ian's at their house taking a nap. Heather's downstairs too. The three of us are going to walk over to Presley House. We're taking Sadie with us." Danielle set the sack on the desk. "Oh, and this is for you."

"What is it?" Walt asked.

"Tacos. Heather brought them."

Walt opened up the sack and looked inside. "That was nice of her." He then paused a moment and looked back to Danielle. "Presley House? You do know it isn't there anymore."

Danielle flashed him a grin. "We're kind of hoping we might run into Pearl's cousin. His house is right next door."

Walt turned in his desk chair to face her. "Why do you want to do that?"

"We told Lily about the bones—and we're trying to figure out who they belong to. Heather and I think it could be Pearl's grandfather. Maybe he really didn't leave his wife all those years ago. Maybe she killed him and planted his body with the rosebushes."

"You don't think her great-grandson is going to know if she killed him or not, do you?" Walt frowned.

"Of course not. But just because Pearl's grandparents divorced, it doesn't mean he dropped out of his kids' lives forever. I figure if Pearl's cousin remembers stories about his grandfather after his grandparents broke up, then it probably isn't his body in the backyard."

"Assuming there is a body—or the rest of the skeleton over there," Walt reminded her.

"Heather suggested the cousin might be the one who put the bones in the hole after taking the rosebush."

"And you want to go talk to him?"

Danielle shrugged. "We don't really think he put them there. But you know Heather…"

Walt started to stand up. "Maybe I should go with you."

"No." Danielle reached out and placed one hand on Walt's shoulder, gently pushing him back in the chair. "You keep writing. We will be fine, and we have Sadie with us." She leaned over and gave him a quick kiss.

"Sadie isn't exactly a guard dog," Walt reminded her.

"Maybe we should stop at Chris's and borrow Hunny?" Danielle joked.

"Hunny looks ferocious, but that would be like taking an unloaded gun with you."

"I don't know about that. I have a feeling she would rise to the occasion if we were threatened. But I really don't think we need her." Danielle gave Walt another quick kiss.

"If those bones weren't as old as Brian says, I might disagree. Enjoy your walk and stay out of trouble."

"ARE you sure you're up to this?" Heather asked while Lily hooked the leash on Sadie's collar. They stood in the kitchen waiting for Danielle to return from the attic.

"Why wouldn't I be up to it?" Lily asked. "And after sitting on my butt all morning, first in the airport, then the plane and then the car, I could use a walk. And when the sun is shining this time of year, it's best to enjoy it before it disappears behind some rain cloud."

Heather looked at Lily's protruding belly and shrugged. "It just might be a little too much, considering your condition."

"I'm pregnant, not disabled," Lily snapped.

"You guys ready to go?" Danielle asked as she walked into the kitchen the next moment.

"Yes, but you'd better be prepared to carry me back," Lily said as she opened the door, Sadie's leash in hand. "You know how fragile I am."

Heather rolled her eyes at Lily's comment and followed her and Sadie out the back door, Danielle trailing behind them.

As they headed to Andy Delarosa's neighborhood, Lily told Danielle and Heather about the baby shower, about the gifts she had received, and her trip to visit her family. Heather told Lily of the changes to the Glandon Foundation headquarters now that the contractor had started work. By the time they reached Delarosa's neighborhood, Danielle was telling them about her week with the raffle winners.

RETURNING FROM CHURCH, Millie Samson started to turn into her driveway when she spied three young women walking down the sidewalk with a golden retriever. She recognized Danielle first. After parking her car, she went to say hello.

"Afternoon, Millie," Danielle greeted her.

"What are you girls up to today? Enjoying this fine weather?" Millie asked. She stood at the sidewalk near the end of her driveway.

"Lily just got home from visiting her family for spring break, so we decided to take a little walk with Sadie," Danielle explained. "We thought we would come see if they've done anything with the Presley House property."

Millie shook her head in disgust. "It's still a vacant lot. I heard it's gone through a couple of owners since it burned down." She looked at Heather and said, "I always thought you might buy the property back."

"Me?" Heather frowned. "Why would you think that?"

Millie shrugged. "I know you used to own it. And I heard about the unfortunate business over the property tax. I just assumed now that you are working for the Glandon Foundation, you might be buying it back."

Heather glanced down the street at where the house in question had once stood, and then looked back to Millie. "Maybe the foundation has money, but I don't. Anyway, I figure the property is probably cursed."

"Oh, don't say that!" Millie scolded. "I really want to see someone rebuild on the lot. It will be good for the neighborhood."

"Maybe. But it won't be me." Heather shrugged.

Millie looked to Danielle and said, "I ran into Elizabeth Sparks at church this morning, and she told me the raffle was a success. Congratulations. Are you planning any future fundraisers?"

"We're working on a few ideas," Danielle told her.

"I also heard Faye Bateman was one of the winners," Millie said.

"It was actually her son who had the winning ticket, but he gave it to his mother. She had never been inside the house before in spite of growing up next to it all those years. She's a very nice lady," Danielle said.

"I don't think I've seen Faye since Leo died," Millie murmured.

"Leo?" Danielle frowned.

"Her husband. He was the funeral director before he passed and his son, Norman, took over. They used to go to our church. But after Leo died, Faye stopped going."

"Leo is the one who took over the funeral home after Faye's father died?" Danielle asked.

Milly nodded. "Yes. From what I understand, he had worked for the Morton Funeral Home before he got another job in Portland. When Mr. Morton died unexpectedly, Faye eventually offered him the job after the man who was working for them didn't work out."

"That's not a family business I would want to take over," Heather grumbled.

"Maybe not, but it seems to be a very lucrative business," Millie pointed out.

"I guess someone has to do it," Lily said.

"So how was Faye?" Millie asked. "How did you handle her smoking? I understand you don't allow smoking in Marlow House."

"Smoking?" Danielle frowned. "She didn't smoke when she was with us. And I never smelled any tobacco on her."

"Well, good for Faye!" Millie said. "She finally stopped smoking. Faye was a notorious chain smoker. That woman always had a cigarette in her hand. The minister at church had to remind her to put it out. But it's how she dealt with stress. She always wanted to quit. I'm glad she finally did."

"Stress?" Lily asked.

"Yes. She told me once at church, she started smoking after her father died, and then her sister took off, and she was alone trying to oversee a business she had no business running. And of course, once she started that nasty habit, she just couldn't kick it."

"MAYBE FAYE BATEMAN should be a poster child for the tobacco company," Heather suggested after they left Millie's and headed toward the property she once owned.

"No kidding. Didn't you say she was ninety-five?" Lily asked. "Gosh, my favorite uncle died in his early sixties from smoking."

"There is always the exception. But it doesn't surprise me that she was once a smoker," Danielle said.

"Why do you say that?" Lily asked.

"It's not a nice thing to say," Danielle began, "but her face. Smoking really ages a person—and she looks every bit a hundred, if not older."

"She is pretty wrinkled—and leathery—but you have to give the old gal credit," Heather said. "She carries herself like she's on the way to the Oscars. Really nice clothes, jewelry, and I don't think I've ever seen her without perfect hair and her nails done."

"She's also pretty sharp," Danielle added. "I have to say, if I lived as long as Faye Bateman and was given the choice of a youthful face or having all my mental faculties, I certainly wouldn't choose a pretty face."

"Not me," Heather grumbled. "If I someday look in the mirror and see an old woman looking back at me who looks like Faye Bateman, I'd rather not know that woman is me. If I had all my wits about me, I'd know it was."

"Then you have nothing to worry about," Lily teased. "You don't have all your wits about you now."

"Oh, shut up. But you have a point." Heather chuckled.

THEY STOOD at the center of the vacant lot, looking around while Sadie, now off the leash, sniffed curiously, exploring new and familiar smells. Since the fire, everything had been removed—even the concrete foundation and traces of the basement where Danielle and Lily had been held captive by a misguided teenage ghost.

"They've filled everything in. You wouldn't even know a house had been here," Lily said.

"What are you doing over there?" a male voice shouted.

The three women looked toward the sound of a voice—it came from a young man standing on the adjacent property.

"That has to be Andy Delarosa," Heather said under her breath for just her friends to hear. "He has the same nasty attitude as his cousin Pearl."

"Hello," Danielle called out cheerfully to the man, giving him a wave.

Lily hastily reattached the leash to Sadie's collar and watched as the man stomped toward them.

"Unless you're buying this lot, I don't think the owners would appreciate you hanging around," the man said as he approached them.

"I used to own this property," Heather told him unapologetically. "It was in my family for years."

"Are you Heather Donovan?" he asked, suddenly sounding far more friendly than before.

"You know who I am?" she asked with a frown.

"Sure. I know you used to own Presley House. I heard what happened. That really sucks about losing it for taxes. You also own that house over on Beach Drive."

"Umm…how do you know that?" Heather asked.

"I used to own the house next door to you." He reached out and offered her a hand in greeting. "My name is Andy Delarosa."

She accepted his hand and then said, "You used to be neighbors with my friends too. This is Danielle Marlow and Lily Bartley."

By Andy's grin, it was obvious he was familiar with their names. "Nice to meet you! Wow. I'm a huge fan of your husband's. I think I've watched all of his specials," Andy told Lily. He then looked at Danielle and said, "Yours too. I'm normally not much of a reader, but someone told me about *Moon Runners* and how it took place in this area, and wow, it was great. I hope they really do make a movie out of it."

"So how come we have never met you before?" Danielle asked after they all exchanged additional pleasantries.

Andy shrugged. "Well, to be honest, I owned the house with my cousins. And let's just say that was a major pain in the butt. So I never really went over there."

"Your cousin Pearl owns it now," Danielle said.

"Yeah, well, sorry about that," he said with a snort.

"You don't like Pearl?" Lily asked innocently.

"What is it they say, you can't pick your relatives?" he said.

"Umm…now Pearl's grandparents originally owned the house, is that correct?" Danielle asked sweetly.

"Yeah. Pearl's grandmother—I guess she would be my great-grandmother—left it to her two daughters. Pearl always carried on about how it was so unfair her parents couldn't afford to keep her share and was forced to sell to my grandmother. Which was total BS."

"What do you mean?" Lily asked.

"According to my parents, they could afford it, but Pearl's mom had some major issues with her mother and, after she died, was happy to sell her share of the house to my grandmother," Andy explained.

"I'm curious," Danielle said. "I've always heard about Pearl's grandmother. What happened to her grandfather?"

"You mean the bigamist?" Andy said with a snort.

"Bigamist?" Heather asked.

Andy nodded. "Yeah, my family is all kinds of messed up. Nuts on all branches of our family tree. I guess my great-grandmother found out the old man had another family. He was a traveling salesman. Apparently he didn't like to be alone when he was on the road." Andy laughed.

"Did he end up with this other family?" Lily asked.

"Nah. From what I understand, he ditched them both. Took off, never paid any child support. He's the infamous scoundrel in our family tree."

"Never had anything to do with any of his kids? Grandkids?" Danielle asked.

"Nope. One of the cousins who's into genealogy found the other family, but no one knows where he ended up. But I imagine with everyone taking DNA tests these days, we'll probably find he landed with another family, which means there are more nutty cousins out there."

"You seem to find it all rather—amusing," Heather observed.

Andy shrugged. "They're really nothing to me. To be honest, as much as I would've liked to have kept the Beach Drive house and moved into it—great location—I was happy to sell just so I wouldn't have to deal with any of the cousins again. Like I said, a bunch of nuts."

THIRTY MINUTES LATER DANIELLE, Heather, Lily and Sadie started on their way back home. When they were out of earshot from Andy, Heather said, "Well, that was too easy."

"No kidding," Lily agreed.

"It is looking more and more like those bones might belong to old gramps," Heather said.

TWENTY-FIVE

On their walk back to Beach Drive, the three friends decided to have an early dinner barbecue at Marlow House. Lily, whose refrigerator and pantry were empty because she and Ian had been gone all week, loved the idea. Heather hated eating alone, so she quickly agreed, and Danielle offered to run to the store to pick up some steaks. Danielle had lots of leftover salads, side dishes and desserts from Easter week that needed to be eaten up, so there wasn't anything else they needed to prepare. On the way home they stopped at Chris's house and extended a personal invitation for him and Hunny. When they reached Marlow House, Lily headed home with Sadie to see if Ian was still napping and let him know the plans, while Heather went on to her house to shower and change.

PEARL OPENED her front door late Sunday afternoon to find Craig Simmons standing on her doorstep. She glanced over his shoulder and spied his truck parked out front with a trailer hitched up behind it, filled with concrete pavers.

"Afternoon, Mrs. Huckabee," Craig greeted her. "I have the pavers I picked up Friday. I'd like to leave them here if that's okay, because I'm planning to use my truck to bring the Bobcat over in the morning. I'd like to get started early."

Pearl looked over his shoulder again and frowned. "I don't think you can leave that in the front."

"I was thinking around in the alley, by your back fence. That's where most of them are going anyway."

Still standing in the open doorway, her hand on the edge of the door, she looked back to Craig. "I don't think you should leave them in the alley. Someone might steal them. I told you someone came in that way and pulled up one of my rosebushes. And in broad daylight. The thief got away with it."

"Maybe just inside the fence?" he suggested.

Pearl considered the question a moment and then nodded. "Fine, I'll meet you back there and unlock the gate."

WALT AND DANIELLE returned from the grocery store and pulled up the alley, heading for their garage. En route, they passed Craig Simmons's truck backing into the open gate leading into Pearl's backyard.

"Looks like Craig is dropping something off," Danielle noted as they drove by. "Wonder if he's going to start working this week."

"And if he does, what will he find?" Walt asked as he brought the Packard to a stop in front of the garage and pressed the remote to open the garage door. A moment later they pulled the vehicle into the garage and closed the door.

After they got out of the car, Walt scooped up the large bag with the beer and steaks, and Danielle said, "I'll meet you in the house. I am going to go say hi to Craig."

"No, you aren't," he said with a chuckle. "You're going to snoop and see when he's starting over there."

"That too." Danielle grinned and gave Walt a quick kiss.

"Hi, Craig," Danielle greeted the landscaper a few minutes later as she walked up to his now parked truck. Craig, who was in the midst of unhooking the trailer from the hitch, looked up and flashed her a smile.

"Hi, Danielle."

"Pavers, huh?" Danielle asked as she stepped up to the back of the truck and looked down at what Craig was doing.

"I'm putting a small patio in the backyard," he explained.

"Doing anything with the rosebushes?" she asked, glancing to them.

Standing upright, the trailer now unhitched, Craig briskly wiped his hands off on his denim pants. "No. She doesn't want me to touch them." He lowered his voice and added, "Just between you and me, they're dead. When I was here the last time, one of them looked as if it might make it, but someone stole it."

"I heard about that. Why would anyone rip up an old rosebush? Wouldn't it be easier to just buy a new one that isn't already half dead?"

Craig shrugged. "People do steal plants, but normally not ones most people would get rid of."

Danielle glanced to the backyard again. "Did Joe tell you about the skeletal remains a bird dropped in our yard?"

"Yes. I imagine that freaked out your guests." He chuckled. "Any idea where they came from?"

"No. I assume Joe told you to keep your eye out when you're digging around in this area?"

"Yeah. But I won't be doing much digging here."

"No?" Danielle frowned.

Craig shook his head. "Nope. Bringing over the Bobcat in the morning and leveling the backyard. The rain and a water leak caused a mess. But I need to do that before I start laying the pavers."

"Oh…so no digging?"

"No. Why? You don't think that bird found the bones in Mrs. Huckabee's yard, do you?"

Danielle shrugged. "Well, the bird did fly from this direction."

"I bet anything that bird picked it up on the beach. Crap is always washing up." Craig glanced at his watch. "I'd better get going. I need to pull the truck out so I can lock the gate. But I don't know why she bothers. Someone backed into it, and anyone can climb through it."

When Danielle headed home a few minutes later, she couldn't stop thinking about how Craig was going to be grading Pearl's backyard and there was a good chance the bones—if they were there—would never be found. So engrossed in her thoughts, Danielle opened the gate leading into her backyard and failed to close it properly.

IAN AND WALT stood by the barbecue, each with a beer bottle in hand, while Chris manned the grill. Heather, Danielle and Lily sat nearby in patio chairs, discussing what may or may not be buried next door. Off on the nearby lawn Hunny and Sadie romped while Max and Bella perched in a nearby tree, watching the dogs.

"I think the chief was counting on Craig finding those bones, but I don't think that is going to happen," Danielle said.

"We still don't know if there are more bones over there," Chris reminded her.

"He needs to try for a search warrant again," Lily said.

As the friends debated the matter, Sadie took off running toward the garage, a tennis ball in her mouth, Hunny close on her tail. None of the humans were particularly concerned the dogs were no longer in view, considering the yard was fenced.

Hunny chased Sadie to the back gate. When they arrived, Sadie noticed the gate was ajar and dropped the ball. Curious, she ran out into the alley, followed by Hunny, who failed to pick up the ball Sadie had dropped.

PEARL WALKED into the spare bedroom across from hers so she could look out the window at the backyard. She wanted to see where Craig had parked the trailer with the pavers. When she got to the window and looked outside, her attention was immediately diverted to two dogs who were wildly digging up the soil behind her rosebushes. The dogs, both in a fit of frenzy, sent dirt flying, their butts wiggling in the air as they furiously tore up her yard. She immediately recognized the invading canines. One was the golden retriever from across the street, and the other was the pit bull from up the street. Just minutes earlier she had looked out her bedroom window and peered into the Marlows' backyard. She had seen the couple from across the street, the man who owned the pit bull, and the woman who lived on the other side of her all over there, and the dogs had been in the Marlows' backyard.

But the mutts were no longer in the Marlows' backyard. They were now behind her rosebushes, tearing up the ground. Furious, she wanted to go downstairs and take care of those dogs herself, but she was not foolish enough to take on a pit bull, not even with her baseball bat. Instead of informing the negligent pet owners of what their dogs were doing, she decided the best course of action was to call the police. She would call animal control, but she knew they were not open on Sundays. Perhaps if the police filed a report, animal control would do its job and seize the two menacing dogs.

CHRIS WAS JUST TAKING the steaks off the grill when Hunny came streaking across the yard, Sadie close behind her. They were no longer playing with a tennis ball, but instead each had their own prize. The dogs, covered in muddy dirt, each carried in their mouths a suspiciously long bone. They were certainly not the type of bones sold at the local pet store.

"What do they have in their mouths?" Heather asked as she stood up and looked to the dogs, who were in the middle of the yard, their tails wagging, looking as if they were prepared to take off running for more play.

"Is that what I think it is?" Danielle said.

"Sadie," Ian called out. "Sit!"

"Hunny!" Chris yelled, setting the platter of steaks on the picnic table. "Stay!"

Walt walked over to the two dogs with Chris and Ian. The three women trailed after them. Hunny and Sadie, now sitting, dropped the bones on the grass. The dogs looked up to the men, panting, their tongues hanging out of their mouths and tails wagging.

"Where did you get those?" Walt demanded, now standing over the dogs.

"Oh, my god," Heather groaned. "That looks like part of a human leg."

All six gathered around the dogs when they heard someone call out, "Hello!" They looked to the sound of the voice. Walking in their direction was Brian Henderson, and close behind him was Pearl Huckabee. They had obviously entered through the front side gate.

"I understand Sadie and Hunny were over in Mrs. Huckabee's yard," Brian said when he walked up to the six friends. They continued to stand around the dogs.

"They tore up my yard!" Pearl said. "You need to take those dogs in. They are dangerous! They are a menace."

Once Brian reached the group, they all took several steps back, giving Brian an opportunity to see what the dogs had brought over.

Brian looked down at the bones; his eyes widened. "Is that what it looks like?"

"I think it may belong to the hand," Danielle told him. "You might want to check out Pearl's yard. See if you can find the rest of him."

"What are you talking about?" Pearl snapped, shoving past Brian. She froze once she saw what they had been looking at. "What's that?"

"Bones, obviously," Heather said. "It looks like it's from a human leg."

"Where did they come from?" Pearl asked.

"From your backyard," Heather told her.

"They did not!" Pearl shouted back.

"Mrs. Huckabee, you did tell me you saw the dogs digging in your backyard," Brian reminded her.

Walt, who had been silently conversing with the dogs, looked to Brian and said, "From what I gather, the dogs slipped out our back gate—we must not have closed it properly." He glanced over to Danielle and then looked back to Brian. "They got into Pearl's backyard through her broken gate. And you know dogs and bones—if they find them, they will dig them up. And I suspect there are more where these came from."

"No!" Pearl shouted. "You are making this up! There are no human bones in my yard!" She turned to Brian and said, "I want you to arrest those dogs, do you hear me? Arrest them right now!"

TWENTY-SIX

The six friends from Beach Drive had finished eating by the time more responders arrived, which was good for them, since it started to rain and they were able to move inside with less hassle—but bad for the responders, who had to search Pearl's yard in a downpour.

Wanting to remain dry, the friends all retreated to one of the upstairs bedrooms at Marlow House so they could watch the action. All but Danielle stood at the window. They passed around a pair of binoculars to get a closer look. Danielle sat on the bed with her laptop open.

Having her turn with the binoculars, Lily peered into Pearl's backyard. The rain had subsided to a drizzle. What appeared to be bones were being pulled from the ground and then placed on sheets of plastic that had been spread over one section of the ground.

Lily glanced over at Danielle and then looked back through the binoculars. "I don't know why you don't want to watch this. It looks like they've found gramps."

"That's who I'm looking for too," Danielle said.

"What are you doing?" Walt asked.

"Andy mentioned one of his cousins had done some genealogical research. I was just wondering if any of it was posted on Ancestry," Danielle told him.

Lily handed Heather the binoculars and then walked over to Danielle and sat on the side of the bed. "Did you find anything?"

Danielle looked up to Lily. "Actually I did."

"Nancy Drew is at it again," Chris said with a chuckle.

Danielle flashed Chris a quick smile and then looked back down at the laptop. "I found Darin and Betty Burnette, Pearl's grandparents. Pearl's on the family tree—at least, I assume it's her. But it says *private*, so they don't have her name or any information, which is what they do for someone who is still alive. But since all her first cousins have passed, they are listed by name, as well as her parents. Darin's other family is on here too. Looks like he had two children from that marriage. Either they are still alive, or whoever created this tree didn't input death information, so it just says *private*."

Chris turned from the window and walked over to the bed. "If you found Darin on the tree—with his first name—that must mean whoever put that information in there knows when he died—which would lead me to believe he isn't the one buried next door."

Danielle shook her head. "No. There's a note attached to his profile. It states the death date is only a guess. When inputting the data, it's not uncommon to estimate the death date when you assume the person is dead and want the information to show up in a search."

"Is there anything else on him?" Lily asked.

"Oh…this is interesting," Danielle muttered, her eyes on the monitor.

"What?" Lily asked.

"Whoever inputted the information writes how they discovered Darin had another family, and he deserted both of them. The person speculates he might have had a third family out there that he ended up with."

"Or maybe one of his families decided to keep him close by," Lily said as she stood and walked to the window. "In the backyard."

IT WAS ALMOST dark and the rain had stopped. They could see the police and all the responders were preparing to leave, but yellow police tape partitioned off a large portion of Pearl's backyard. Curious to learn what they had found, Ian, Chris and Walt left the women in the house while they went outside to see if Brian would tell them anything.

By the time they reached Brian, he was just about to get into his squad car.

"You found who went with the hand?" Chris asked when they reached Brian.

Brian turned from his car, which was parked in front of Pearl's house, and faced the three men while the other vehicles from the police and coroner's department were driving off.

"Oh…yeah. And then some," Brian said with a weary sigh.

"Then some?" Ian asked.

"There was more than one body planted at your neighbor's. The only good news, it looks as if they have been there a long, long time."

"More? How many more?" Ian asked.

"At least two, but there could be a third. And since we had to stop, not only because it's getting dark, but because more rain is expected tonight, it's possible we'll find more. I'm leaving someone here to keep an eye on the place so no one tampers with what appears to be a crime scene—a very old crime scene. We'll be back in the morning."

"Three or more?" Chris asked. "Holy crap."

"Two for certain. The two femurs your dogs brought over are believed to be from the same body, considering their size. We found two other femurs. Yet we're not certain they go together, considering some irregularities with one of them. It's possible it's from a third body that was buried at a different time."

Walt glanced up at Pearl's house. She stood in the upstairs bedroom window looking down at them. He looked from Pearl to Brian and asked, "I assume you told Pearl?"

"Yes. She, by the way, is convinced you put them there," Brian said.

"What?" Ian asked.

Brian glanced at Ian and smiled. "Not you." He looked at Walt and said, "Walt and Danielle. Or more likely Danielle. You know, when she was fixing up Marlow House and unearthed all the skeletons and decided to move them next door. Which is why Pearl's back gate is broken. That's how Danielle got in to bury the bones, she smashed in her neighbor's gate."

"You are kidding? Right?" Walt asked.

Brian shook his head. "No, I'm not. But I don't think she actually believes that. She's rattled, trying to make sense of it all. And she has to find someone to blame. And for whatever reason, you are not her favorite people. And she really doesn't like any of your dogs."

ON MONDAY MORNING Danielle and Walt decided to have breakfast at Pier Café. The rain had stopped, and once again the sunshine instead of rain clouds brightened the sky. As Walt backed the Packard out of the garage, they noticed several police cars driving up to the alley entrance of Pearl's property.

"Looks like they are here to do some more searching," Danielle said. "I wonder if they'll find more bones."

"Considering all the mediums who live on Beach Drive, it's amazing none of the spirits attached to those bones have contacted any of you," Walt said as he drove the Packard down the alleyway, heading to the pier.

"No surprise. According to Brian, they're really old. So I imagine those spirits moved on long before we arrived. And hey, you were here for almost a hundred years, and you weren't aware of them. I wonder if Eva knows anything."

"When I was a ghost, I didn't get out much," Walt joked.

Danielle pulled her phone from her purse. "I'm going to see what the chief has found out."

Walt was just pulling into the parking lot near the pier when Danielle finished her call.

"He didn't really tell me much more than what Brian told you last night," Danielle said as she slipped her phone back in her purse. "Other than it will probably take weeks before they even know how old the bones are, much less learn anything that will help identify who they belonged to."

"Why is that?" Walt asked.

"Budgets and priority. I guess the labs are currently understaffed, and skeletal remains that might be over a hundred years old—"

"They are that old?" Walt asked.

Danielle shrugged. "He said it's hard to tell considering their condition. But if they're over fifty years, they don't take priority."

Ten minutes later Walt and Danielle sat at one of the booths at Pier Café. They had just picked up their menus when Carla walked up to their table with a pot of coffee.

"I can't even imagine all those dead bodies buried right next door to you!" Carla started the conversation as she righted the clean mugs on their table and began filling them with coffee.

"Not bodies exactly," Danielle corrected. "And it looks like they've been there for decades."

Setting the coffee pot on the table and placing her other hand on a hip, Carla said, "You think it's an old Indian burial ground?"

"I doubt it," Danielle said. "How did you hear about it?"

"It was on the radio this morning." Carla glanced at the menus. "Do you know what you want yet?"

"Why don't you give us a few minutes," Walt suggested.

"Okay." Carla picked up the coffee pot and flounced away.

"You're Walt and Danielle Marlow, aren't you?" the elderly man in the next booth asked.

Walt looked over to him and said, "Yes, we are."

"I'm your new neighbor, Bud Caine." The elderly man extended his hand over the back of the booth in greeting.

Walt shook his hand and Danielle asked, "Really? Where did you move into?"

"I'm in the house three doors up the street from you."

"Glad to see all our dead bodies haven't scared you away," Walt said with a chuckle.

"Actually the house has been in our family for years. I just moved into it last week."

"Would you like to join us?" Danielle offered.

Fifteen minutes later Walt and Danielle sat in the booth with their new neighbor, Bud Caine. The three had just given Carla their order, and she had just left to turn it into the kitchen.

"I actually grew up in Frederickport," Bud explained. "That house belonged to my parents. My wife and I lived there for a while after they died, but she was never fond of the beach. Too damp for her. So we moved to Nevada, rented our house here out with Adam Nichols. You know him?"

"Oh yes. Adam is a good friend," Danielle explained. "And so was his grandmother."

"I was sure sad to hear of Marie's passing," Bud said with a sigh. "I used to have quite a crush on her before I met my Janie. Marie was a few years older than me, but a cute little thing and sassy. Never did understand why she married Nichols. He could be sort of a jerk."

"What brought you back to Frederickport?" Walt asked.

"My wife, Janie, passed away last year," Bud began.

"I'm so sorry," Danielle said.

Bud shrugged. "She was pretty sick. I suppose it was a blessing. But I miss her. We never had any kids. And most of our friends seemed to be dropping like flies, so I figured I would come back here. I always missed Frederickport, and frankly, I was never a fan of the desert. But it was a good place for Janie."

"I suppose you know the people who lived next door to us, where they found the bones," Danielle said.

Bud nodded. "Oh yeah. The ones I knew the best were the Mortons. Daisy was a close friend of my older sister. My parents never approved of her. She was a wild thing, always smoking and running with a different boy each week."

"Her sister, Maisy, still lives in town," Danielle told him. "She and her son still own the funeral home."

Bud nodded. "That's what I heard. I never knew the twins personally. They were quite a bit older than me. But my sister kept in touch with Daisy over the years."

"After she left Frederickport?" Danielle asked.

"Yes. Daisy eloped not long after her father died. She never came back, which I guess I can understand, considering the circumstances surrounding her marriage."

"That she married her sister's fiancé?" Danielle asked.

Bud nodded. "So you know about that?"

"Yes. Adam told me about it. Marie had told him," Danielle explained.

"After destroying whatever relationship she'd had with Maisy, I always wondered if Daisy felt it was worth it. She became a widow fairly young. Never remarried. But she traveled all over the world, would send my sister postcards and letters, up until my sister passed away."

"Do you know anything about the people who moved into the house after Maisy sold it?" Danielle asked.

"I remember the woman—can't recall her name—she had two little girls, and I heard her husband either died or left her. She was active in the local garden club back then. My sister was too, which is why I remember. According to my sister, the woman had developed some sort of new rose—it was quite the deal back then. That's about all I really knew about her—other than she wasn't very friendly. Aside from her involvement in the garden club, she kept to herself and never had much to do with any of the neighbors other than screaming at any of the kids who stepped on her property. She was kind of sour, from what I remember."

Walt and Danielle exchanged glances, each thinking the same thing: *just like her granddaughter Pearl.*

TWENTY-SEVEN

The next two weeks flew by, and nothing new had been reported about the skeletal remains. No one had seen Pearl outside her house since the discovery, but the neighbors did occasionally get a glimpse of her peering out one of her windows, which some found both creepy and reassuring—reassuring because then they knew she wasn't somewhere in the house dead or dying.

On the second Monday morning of May, Joanne Johnson was busily vacuuming the first floor at Marlow House while Danielle reorganized the kitchen pantry, with Walt sitting at the table drinking coffee and unofficially supervising. They had been at the project for about fifteen minutes when Joanne entered the kitchen carrying what appeared to be a ruby earring.

"I found this under the bed in the downstairs bedroom," Joanne told Danielle as she handed her the earring.

Taking the delicate piece of jewelry in hand, Danielle looked at it. "This is Faye Bateman's. I saw her wearing them."

"Did she ever mention losing it?" Joanne asked.

"No. She must not realize she lost it." Danielle placed the earring in a teacup on the counter so as not to lose it. "I'll take it over to her house when I go out later."

Walt looked at the housekeeper, raised his coffee cup, and said, "Joanne, why don't you sit down and take a break. Have a cup of coffee. You've been on your feet all morning."

"Walt just made a fresh pot," Danielle added.

"Thanks. I think I will." As Joanne reached for a coffee cup, she asked Danielle, "Would you like some?"

"Yes. And we should probably finish up the cinnamon rolls," Danielle said cheerfully.

Minutes later the three sat at the kitchen table, drinking coffee and sharing two cinnamon rolls.

"Has there been any news about the remains found next door?" Joanne asked.

"Nothing new. But I keep thinking it has something to do with the rosebushes," Danielle said. "First someone steals one, and then a bird finds those bones in the hole the rosebush was taken from."

Joanne frowned at Danielle. "How do you know that?"

Walt and Danielle exchanged quick glances, and Danielle wished she could take back her comment. She obviously could not tell Joanne it was what Max had told Walt. Instead she said, "I'm just speculating. I mean, we know the dogs dug up the bones there, and I just assume the rosebush being taken is what exposed the soil in the first place."

"I remember hearing something about those rosebushes," Joanne said as she set her cup on the table. "The woman who planted them supposedly created some new rose."

"I've heard the same thing," Danielle said. "She was involved with the local garden club."

"I don't really know much beyond what I heard about her creating some new rose, but you know who might know more is Toynette from the nursery. That nursery has been in Toynette's family for years, and I know her mother was the president of the local garden club before she passed away."

"Maybe I'll stop at the nursery after I drop the earring off to Faye," Danielle said.

AFTER JOANNE RETURNED to her housekeeping, Danielle called Faye Bateman to let her know she had found her ruby earring and wanted to drop it off. Faye insisted Danielle join her for lunch that afternoon, telling her she wanted to thank her again for the stay over spring break, which she had enjoyed.

Danielle arrived at the Bateman home a few minutes past noon.

She was shown to the sunroom by Faye's housekeeper, where they were to have lunch. Faye looked regal sitting in a velvet upholstered wingback chair, wearing a floor-length midnight blue dress, with diamond earrings dangling from her earlobes and her platinum blond hair recently coifed. She didn't stand when Danielle entered the room but extended her hand in greeting.

Danielle accepted Faye's hand, giving it a gentle squeeze, and then handed her a small plastic bag holding the ruby earring.

"Thank you so much for bringing this over. I didn't even realize it was missing. It belonged to my mother. I would hate to have lost it," Faye said as she accepted the small bag and then set it on the table next to her. She motioned to a chair, asking Danielle to sit down.

A few minutes later, after they had both been served lemonade by Faye's housekeeper, Faye asked, "Has there been any news about those remains found at my old house? I just shudder to think they may have been there all along when I was growing up."

"That's entirely possible, considering they say they could be over a hundred years old. Of course, they say they might be half that age."

"Which would mean the woman I sold the house to could be the person who buried them there," Faye said with a shiver.

Danielle looked up from Faye as she sipped her tea while doing her best not to voice the thought that had just popped into her head.

As if reading Danielle's mind, Faye gave her a smile and said, "Because it's obvious it couldn't have been anyone from my family who buried any bodies on the property."

Danielle arched her brow, yet again resisted comment.

Faye's smile widened and she gave a little chuckle before saying, "Because, dear, my family has been in the funeral home business since before I was born, and if we had any dead bodies to dispose of, it certainly wouldn't be done in our backyard."

Danielle broke into a grin. "You do have a point."

"And I assume the authorities should be able to identify those remains. I asked Norman, and he said they can use skeletal remains to get DNA. So hopefully they will be able to find out who those poor people were and give them a proper burial."

"True. But that will only work if someone they're related to has given DNA. And considering the possible age of those bones, any DNA on file would likely be a distant cousin, which would make it difficult to make a positive ID. Unless, of course, their sibling or child has DNA on file. I suppose that's possible."

WHEN DANIELLE LEFT Faye's house, she headed to the nursery to talk to Toynette. Just as she pulled into the nursery parking lot, she spied Carla from Pier Café loading several houseplants into the back of her car. Danielle pulled up beside Carla's vehicle and parked.

"Hi, Danielle," Carla greeted her as she slammed the trunk of her car shut. "Any news on the dead bodies?"

"Skeletal remains," Danielle corrected. "And no. They had to send the bones to a lab out of town, and it will take a while before they know anything."

"I went out a couple of times with the guy who used to own that house," Carla said as she twirled a lock of her purple and pink hair. "Andy Delarosa. I'm just glad to know those bones are older than he is. I'd hate to think I dated a serial killer."

"I've met Andy. He owned the house with his cousins."

Carla rolled her eyes while still twirling a lock of hair. "When I first went out with him, he made it seem like he owned the house himself. He's kind of a player."

Danielle studied Carla a moment and then impulsively asked, "You don't happen to know anything about the rosebush that was stolen from that house, do you?"

Carla grinned and glanced around quickly and then whispered, "You mean the one Andy took?"

Danielle arched her brow. "He did?"

Carla nodded and giggled, releasing her lock of hair and placing her hand on one hip. "One of Andy's friends, Ted, asked me out after I stopped dating Andy. Ted is a nice guy, but he really isn't my type. But he stops in the café every week and flirts with me. I think he figures I'll finally agree to go out with him. The last time he was in, he told me Andy borrowed his truck and used it to take one of the rosebushes from his old house. He was kinda pissed at Andy because he left the back of his truck all muddy. And he couldn't figure out why he would want to take some plant from a house he had just sold." Carla paused a moment and then added, "But please don't tell anyone I told you that. I wasn't supposed to say anything. Ted doesn't want to get Andy in trouble. They're still friends."

"You dated Andy. Do you have any idea why he would steal the rosebush?"

Carla shrugged. "It might be something to do with the stuff they found in the attic. When I first went out with Andy, he led me to believe he owned the house. But then he said something about selling it and how it was going through escrow. That's when he admitted he owned it with some cousins. They sold it to another relative and were selling it with all the furniture. But at the last minute they decided to get some trunk in the attic that had belonged to Andy's great-grandmother. I don't know what was in the trunk, but when I saw Andy after he went to look through it with his cousins, he was kinda pissy, and later that night had too much to drink and said, '*Those damn rosebushes, if I had only known.*' I asked him, '*Known what?*' He never said. But we stopped dating not long after that."

DANIELLE FOUND Toynette sitting on a bench at the rear of the nursery, taking a break. Danielle had seen the woman around town and at the nursery, yet had never talked to her before. She guessed Toynette was in her late fifties, a tall slender woman, wearing denim jeans, navy blue sneakers and a plaid flannel shirt, with her gray hair cropped short and covered with a baseball cap to help shade her blue eyes.

"Oh yes, I remember my mother talking about Betty Burnette," Toynette said after Danielle introduced herself and explained why she was there. The two sat side by side on the bench. "Mom used to say the woman had a way with roses, but was at a complete loss when it came to dealing with people. Betty was active in the garden club, but always seemed to rub people the wrong way."

"Do you know if she really developed a new rose?"

"Mother said she did. But Betty didn't patent her rose. It was during the war. I don't think she could afford it. Of course, this was before I was born. According to Mom, someone else patented Betty's rose years later. Maybe that's who she buried in her backyard." Toynette chuckled.

"You think Betty Burnette buried those bodies?"

Toynette shrugged. "I was just joking. But according to Mom, Betty seemed to only love her roses—and later her grandchildren. I guess she had some issues with her daughters, but she turned out to be a doting grandmother. I guess some people make better grandparents than parents."

"They say the bones could be a hundred years old. If the lab finds that's true, then I doubt Betty or anyone in her family was responsible for those remains being there."

"True." Toynette nodded and leaned back on the bench. They were silent for a few moments. Finally, Toynette said, "My mother hated driving by that house."

"She disliked Betty so much?" Danielle asked.

"No." Toynette shook her head. "Before Betty lived at the house, it was owned by the Morton family—the ones from the funeral home."

"Yes, I know. In fact, I just saw Faye Morton—or Bateman—before I came over here."

"Faye goes by her middle name now. When my mother knew her, she went by her first name, Maisy. That was when she was engaged to my uncle Kenneth, Mom's older brother."

"Your uncle was the Kenneth who married Maisy's twin sister?" Danielle asked.

"You know that story?" Toynette asked.

Danielle nodded. "Yes, a little. But I've never mentioned anything to Faye that I know."

"That's probably a good idea. I never met my uncle Kenneth, but I know it broke my mother's heart. She loved her older brother—and she really loved Maisy. She couldn't stand Daisy. And she never understood why her brother did what he did. After they eloped, Mom never saw him again. But he did send her a postcard about a year after he left. All he said was *sorry*. Nothing else."

"Wow." Danielle let out a sigh.

"After Uncle Kenneth eloped, Maisy wanted nothing to do with Mom. It really hurt her, but she understood. Maisy felt betrayed by the man she had loved, and Mom was that man's sister."

TWENTY-EIGHT

Pearl stood in her backyard and surveyed the change. All her grandmother's rosebushes were gone. It had been a little over three weeks since the dogs—and then the police—began digging up her backyard. After they were done, there was no way to salvage the roses. She refused to admit that they had been beyond redemption before her neighbors' dogs had dug up the old bones. As for those bones, the police still did not know who they had belonged to.

Work on the new back patio had been delayed, but Craig had managed to finish it yesterday. Pearl almost regretted having Craig build the new patio. She wasn't sure what she was going to do with the area. It was now a big rectangle patch of nothing—a paver patio surrounded by damp dirt.

Turning from the backyard, she headed toward the front of her property, walking along the pathway next to the wrought-iron fence separating her land from the Marlows'. On her way there she picked up a rake she had forgotten to return to the toolshed. When she reached the toolshed, she went inside, leaving the door open.

Rake in hand, Pearl looked down at the wood floor and groaned. Mud from the recent storms had been tracked inside, leaving the shed floor covered in dirt. She set the rake in the corner and picked up the broom.

"That's the house where the bodies were buried," Pearl heard someone say. Glaring angrily, she looked out of the toolshed toward the street and spied two women walking down the sidewalk toward the pier. She didn't recognize them and suspected they were tourists. The afternoon breeze had helped carry the woman's voice up from the sidewalk. Shaking her head in disgust, Pearl turned her back to the street and began sweeping.

ABOUT TWENTY MINUTES EARLIER, next door at Marlow House, Walt and Danielle sat silently in the parlor, each reading a book. The only sound came from the steady ticking of the wall clock. Curled up on one end of the sofa, Danielle turned the page of her book. Walt, who sat across from Danielle in a chair, looked up and set his book on his lap.

"You want to walk down to the pier and get an ice cream cone?" Walt asked.

Danielle looked up from her book and smiled. "Ice cream? That does sound good." She glanced up at the clock; it was a quarter to three.

Walt looked over to the clock, noting the time. "Doesn't Lily have her doctor's appointment today?"

"Yes, after she gets home from school. They're supposed to find out if it's a boy or girl today." Danielle closed her book and tossed it on the table.

"I still can't believe they'll be able to find out if it's a boy or girl so soon," Walt said, standing up and setting his book on the table with Danielle's.

Some fifteen minutes later, they walked out the front door of Marlow House, on their way to get ice cream. They noticed two women heading down the sidewalk, walking in the direction of the pier. Beyond the two women was Heather Donovan, walking in their direction.

When Danielle and Walt pushed through their front gate, the two women were already walking by Pearl's house. A few minutes later, as Walt and Danielle passed by the side gate into their property, a police car pulled up and parked nearby, just as they came face-to-face with Heather. Driving the vehicle was Joe Morelli, with Brian Henderson in the passenger seat.

"Where are you off to?" Danielle asked Heather as she and Walt stopped to talk.

"I'm going to Chris's house to pick up something. Where are you two going?" Heather asked.

Just as Danielle told Heather they were walking down to the pier for ice cream, the two officers started getting out of their car.

"Hi, Joe, Brian," Danielle called out.

"Any news on who was buried next door?" Heather asked.

"Not yet," Joe said, slamming his car door shut.

A moment later Brian joined them on the sidewalk, and they all exchanged brief pleasantries. "Here on official business?" Danielle asked.

"Yes. While we wait to hear back from the lab, we're trying to get some more information from anyone who ever lived at this house," Joe explained.

"I have a good idea who one of those bodies might be. But not sure about the other two—if there are really three," Heather said.

"We only found two skulls, so I suspect it will turn out to be two people," Brian said.

"So who do you think it is?" Joe asked Heather.

"I think it's Pearl's grandfather. Danielle thinks that too. Don't you, Danielle?" Heather said in a loud voice. "And the other body might be one of his other wives. The guy disappeared about seventy years ago—after his wife found out he had another family. I say Pearl's grandmother found out and got rid of him. And Danielle looked up Pearl's family tree online and found out he pretty much dropped out of sight around that time, never to be seen again."

"All lies!" Pearl shouted when she unexpectedly stepped out onto the sidewalk. She looked as if she might start swinging at any minute. She turned to Danielle and said, "I don't know what you are doing snooping into my family's business!"

"There were at least two bodies buried on your property," Walt reminded her. "You can't really blame us for wanting to find out who they were."

"I just bought this house! You can't possibly think I had anything to do with burying them here!" Pearl shrieked.

"Certainly not," Danielle said quickly. "And no one was suggesting you had anything to do with those remains. You weren't even born then."

"I don't appreciate you slandering my grandmother!"

"I think we should go," Walt said. "Brian and Joe came here to talk with Mrs. Huckabee. I think we should let them do their job."

"I DON'T KNOW why you need to talk to me again," Pearl said five minutes later after she showed the two officers into her house. The three sat at her kitchen table.

"Your family has owned this property for over seventy years," Brian reminded her. "And Heather is not wrong in suggesting someone from your family—or someone they knew—might be the ones responsible for what we found buried in your backyard."

"Well, I certainly don't know anything about it."

"What do you know about your grandfather?" Joe asked.

Stubbornly folding her arms across her chest, Pearl glared at Joe. She sat in silence for a few moments and then said, "I know for certain he was not one of those unfortunate people buried in my backyard."

"How do you know that? You weren't even born at the time he went missing," Joe asked.

"For one reason, he did not go missing. And for another, I knew him."

"You knew your grandfather? The one who bought this house with your grandmother?" Brian asked.

Pearl nodded. "Yes. My mother loved her father. She was angry at my grandmother for making him leave and then telling everyone he had died. Mother said Grandma told her and my aunt, *your father is dead to us.*"

"But your mother saw him again?" Brian asked.

"Years later. Frankly, I understand why my grandmother kicked him out. But I also understand how my mother resented Grandma for so many years—blaming her. She was just a child and didn't really understand."

"You say you saw your grandfather?" Brian asked.

"Yes. After my grandmother died, my mother and aunt went through my grandmother's things. Mother found a letter from her father. She used it to track him down. My father took us to see him—my grandfather was living in Nevada. I imagine they regretted making the trip—taking me to see him. It didn't work out very well. He wasn't the man my mother imagined all those years. He was the man my grandmother had kicked out. He died a few years later and was buried in Reno. He was going by another name. That was the name he was buried under."

"Do you remember what that name was?" Joe ask.

Pearl shook her head. "No. I don't remember."

"Do you remember what year he died?"

Pearl shrugged. "No. I can't even recall what year it was we went to see him. It was so long ago."

Brian opened his notepad and flipped the page. He read whatever was on the page and then looked up to Pearl. "From what we have, your grandparents purchased this property from the Mortons, and after your grandfather left, it was put in your grandmother's name."

"Correct." Pearl nodded.

"After your grandmother passed away, the house went to your mother and her sister?" Brian asked.

"Yes, but my parents sold their share to my aunt not long after my grandmother died."

"It then went to your cousins, your aunt's children, after she died, correct?" Brian asked.

"Yes. After each cousin passed away, their share went to their children," Pearl explained. "But they couldn't seem to get along, so they sold it to me."

"In all those years, was the house ever rented out?" Brian asked. "We haven't been able to find any information on any tenants of the property."

"No. It never was, as far as I know. And after my grandmother died, the house became a vacation home for the family members who owned it. No one ever lived here full-time. So anyone could have buried anything on the property during all those years, considering the house was frequently vacant."

"YOU KNOW, unless those bones are not as old as the coroner thinks, those bodies could not have been buried in her backyard after the grandmother died," Joe said after getting back into the police car with Brian and closing the door.

"I know. Unless they were put there right after she died," Brian said.

"Do you think she was telling the truth about her grandfather?" Joe asked.

"I was wondering that myself. Especially since she conveniently forgot when her grandfather died and what name he was using."

WALT AND DANIELLE were eating their ice cream cones and walking back to Marlow House when Joe came driving toward them from Pearl's. Instead of driving by, he pulled the car to the side of the road and stopped. Brian rolled his window down.

"I feel bad Pearl overheard Heather, but I think it could be her grandfather," Danielle told the officers when she and Walt stopped by their car.

"Pearl claims her grandfather was alive and well when she was a teenager—so if she is telling the truth, then it's not him," Brian told her.

"Hopefully you can figure this out when the lab is done with the bones. What now?" Danielle asked.

"We're going over to one of the previous owners of the property, see what he might know about the house's history," Brian explained.

"You mean Andy Delarosa?"

"You know who that is?" Brian asked.

Danielle glanced at Walt and then looked back to Brian. "I should probably tell you something before you go over there."

"What's that?" Brian asked.

"Remember that rosebush someone stole out of Pearl's yard? Well, he's the one who took it."

"Maybe, but we can't prove it. Why do you think he took it?"

"Please don't say anything to Carla," Danielle began.

"Carla?" Brian groaned.

Danielle then repeated the story Carla had told her. "I wasn't going to say anything about it, because I figured it was some family issue, and Carla asked me not to say anything. But the more I think about it, you should probably know as much about that family as possible, if you're to figure out who was buried in the backyard."

TWENTY-NINE

Brian and Joe found Andy Delarosa working in his front yard, spraying vinegar on his weeds. As they came up his front walk, they quickly surveyed the area and once again didn't spy a single rosebush, much less the one that had been taken from Pearl's yard.

"Officers," Andy said when he saw them as he set the sprayer on a nearby bench, "what can I do for you?"

"We have a couple of questions we need to ask you," Joe began.

"Let's go inside," Andy suggested.

"We have a witness who claims to have seen you take the rosebush out of Pearl Huckabee's yard," Joe said after the three were sitting in Andy's living room.

"Umm...who?" Andy asked, moving restlessly in his chair while absently wiping his palms along the sides of his jean-clad thighs.

"I tell you what," Brian began. "At this point we have other questions about that rosebush, and we don't really care to pursue charges against the thief—not if we find out what we are looking for. To be candid, the witness is reluctant to come forward—but I know we can make her talk if it comes to that."

"What do you want to know?" Andy asked hesitantly.

"Do you know why anyone would want to steal that rosebush in the first place?" Brian asked.

Andy considered the question for a moment and let out a sigh. "Well—I suppose it is possible any of my cousins might have wanted to take it—since they all knew. But it would have been for nothing anyway."

"Knew what?" Joe asked.

Andy let out another sigh and sat back in his chair. "The house was owned by me and my cousins. We planned to sell it fully furnished. But then, right before the close of escrow, we remembered the old trunk in the attic. My grandmother had put all her mom's stuff in it after her mother had died. We'd never bothered to look inside. Most of it was junk, but there was her notebook on her roses."

"The rosebushes in the backyard?" Joe asked.

Andy nodded. "We'd always heard how my grandmother's mom was obsessed with her roses. In her notebook, we found out how obsessed she was. I guess she had developed a new kind of rose. One of my cousins said that was something that could be patented and you could make a fortune on. I'd never heard about rose patents."

"So that's why you took the rosebush?" Joe asked.

"I'm not saying I took anything. But if someone took it, that's probably why. Of course, whoever took it didn't know that someone else patented the rose not long after she died. But even if they hadn't, all the rosebushes—even the one someone took—were too far gone."

"What do you know about your grandmother's father?" Brian asked.

"The one who was a bigamist?" Andy asked with a laugh. "Is that who you think was buried over there?"

"Is that what you think?" Joe asked.

Andy shrugged. "I have to admit, the thought crossed my mind when I first heard what they found. But then I heard they found the remains for two or possibly three people buried back by the roses. If it was two, I suppose it could have been old gramps and another one of his wives."

"According to one of your cousins, she knew your great-grandfather, so it couldn't have been him."

"You're talking about Pearl, right? Sounds like something she would say. The woman is delusional."

"So you never heard anything about your great-grandfather after he and your great-grandmother split up?" Joe asked.

"Thing about my family, they don't get along, but they still have this genealogy obsession—like great-granny obsessed with her roses. If you can't stand your relatives, why in the heck do you care about a bunch of dead ones? Am I right?"

"And you're saying the family members who've researched your family tree never found out what happened to your great-grandfather?" Brian asked.

Andy nodded. "That's right. Nothing. He vanished into thin air after deserting two families. But I heard you're having those bones tested for DNA, so if one of those was old gramps, then you'll be able to find out."

"There's DNA on file?" Joe asked.

"Personally, I'd never do a DNA test, but I know more than half of my cousins have."

WALT AND DANIELLE sat anxiously at the table at Pearl Cove with Ian and Lily, impatiently waiting for Lily to tell them what they had learned at the doctor's appointment that afternoon.

"Well? Come on, tell us!" Danielle urged after the server brought their cocktails and left the table. "You really don't expect us to wait until dessert for you to tell us, do you?"

Lily smiled sheepishly and looked from Danielle to Walt and back to Danielle, while Ian chuckled under his breath and took a sip of his cocktail.

"We don't know," Lily blurted.

"You don't know?" Danielle groaned. "You mean that little stinker was turned from the camera? Refused to flash the ultrasound?"

Lily shrugged. "Umm, no. He—or she—was right there fully exposed—or so says our doctor. But we told her we don't want to know. We're waiting until the baby is born to find out if it's a boy or girl."

"You're kidding?" Danielle asked.

Walt grinned. "Not knowing until the baby is born is how it used to be."

Lily looked over to Walt and said, "You know, you're the reason I started rethinking this ultrasound. It's not like I was planning to decorate the baby's room super gender specific and needed to know ahead of time so I could start decorating. I'm going with Snoopy—a rainbow on one wall, and Snoopy dancing on his doghouse on another." Lily paused a moment and looked at Ian. "Or maybe we should see if we can do Snoopy sitting on the doghouse writing on his typewriter, like in the cartoons. Keep in theme with his—or her—writer dad."

"I love Snoopy. I didn't know that's what you decided on," Danielle said.

"Snoopy is a classic. He makes me happy, and I figure it would be great for a boy's or girl's room," Lily explained.

"And you really are not going to find out until the baby is born?" Danielle asked.

Lily looked down at her baby bump and gave it a gentle pat. "I've read that knowing the gender of your baby before it's born will help a mother bond with the baby. When I told Mom that, she laughed at me and asked me if I seriously thought she would love me any more if she had known my gender before I was born. She said her love for me—for all of her children—was already limitless." Lily looked up and smiled.

"I don't mind waiting to know," Ian said. He leaned over and gave Lily a quick kiss on the cheek.

"And to be honest, I'm kind of glad Mom and Dad are coming for a visit before the baby is born. For some reason, Mom does not seem as annoying these days."

"That's because you're starting to relate to her," Marie said when she appeared suddenly the next moment, standing by the table.

"Marie!" Danielle said in surprise.

"Where?" Lily asked, looking around.

"I just stopped by to see if it was a girl or boy. I remember you saying Lily was going to find out today. But I just heard they don't know—and won't until the baby is born, which is how it used to be. But I need to run; Eva is waiting for me!" Marie vanished.

"Where is she?" Lily asked again.

"That was a quick visit," Walt said with a chuckle.

"She's gone already," Danielle explained.

FIFTEEN MINUTES later Danielle and Lily were in the women's

restroom at Pearl Cove, when they ran into Toynette from the nursery.

"Danielle! How are you doing?"

"Hi, Toynette. This is my friend Lily. Toynette owns the nursery," Danielle explained.

"Nice to meet you, but if you will excuse me!" Lily said hurriedly before rushing into one of the stalls.

Danielle giggled. "These days when Lily has to go—she has to go!"

"I remember when I was pregnant—" Toynette stopped talking suddenly and whispered, "Oh my, she is pregnant, isn't she? Did I just step in it?"

Danielle grinned. "Yes, she is pregnant."

Toynette let out a sigh of relief. "Good. Nothing more embarrassing than assuming a woman is pregnant when she isn't. I was just going to say, when I was pregnant, it seemed I was always in the bathroom!"

Danielle chuckled.

"By the way, any word on those remains they found next door to your house? I haven't heard anything about it in weeks."

"No. They're still waiting for the lab reports to come in. But when they do, hopefully they'll be able to use DNA to identify the remains."

"It is amazing what they can do these days with DNA testing. It seems like everyone is getting tested to see where they came from. I had mine done, but there was no real surprise. I always knew Mother's parents were from Norway, and my father's father was Swedish. My results were over ninety percent Scandinavian."

By the time Lily came out of the stall, Toynette had left the restroom, and she was alone with Danielle.

"I've seen her at the nursery," Lily said as she washed her hands.

"Oh, I don't think I told you. Do you know who her uncle was?" Danielle asked.

"No, who?"

"Kenneth Bakken. Faye's ex-fiancé, the one who ran off with her sister."

THIRTY

Heather woke up on Saturday morning relieved she didn't have to go into work. Since Chris had started the remodeling of the offices and interviewing new employees, her time with the Glandon Foundation felt more like work than it ever had before. Surprisingly, she liked it.

Yawning, she rolled out of bed and picked up her cellphone off the nightstand and looked at it. It was in that moment she realized it was the beginning of Memorial Day weekend. She had been so busy she hadn't given the holiday a thought. There would be no guests at Marlow House this weekend, and she wondered how busy Frederickport would be.

Looking at the date again on her cellphone, she remembered Lily was supposed to have had her ultrasound last week and realized she hadn't heard any news if the baby was going to be a boy or girl. She had been so busy at work, not even taking last weekend off, that she hadn't seen Lily or Danielle. And while she knew Chris had talked to Danielle several times during the past week, he had never mentioned what Lily and Ian had found out at the ultrasound.

Standing up, Heather stretched. Before taking her morning jog, she decided she would first stop off at Marlow House. She needed to tell Danielle about the humane society anyway. That way she could also find out about the baby.

THIRTY MINUTES later Heather opened her front door to leave and was startled when Bella slipped around her feet and dashed outside.

"Bella, get back here!" Heather shouted at the calico cat.

Ignoring Heather, Bella ran to the large tree near the property line and climbed up it, perching on one of the branches overhanging Pearl's front yard.

"I told you to keep that cat out of my yard!" Pearl shouted from her front porch. The middle-aged woman had just stepped outside to retrieve her morning paper when she noticed the cat sitting in the nearby tree looking down at her. Scurrying over to the property line, Pearl wagged a finger at Heather, who was trying to coax Bella from the tree. "I will not sit around and let that filthy animal turn my yard into a litter box!"

"A litter box might be an improvement over a cemetery!" Heather snapped back. "I'm surprised the police didn't dig up your front yard. I wouldn't be surprised if there are more bodies buried there!"

"You should be the one to talk," Pearl snapped back. "I know about your family. Wasn't your grandfather something like a serial killer?"

Heather narrowed her eyes at Pearl, and instead of shouting another insult, she said in a low menacing voice, "That's right. And you might want to remember that before you threaten my cat again. After all, I have a rather convenient graveyard next door where I can bury your body."

With a gasp, Pearl turned abruptly and rushed back to her front door. She ran inside and slammed the door shut, locking it behind her.

"YOU THREATENED TO KILL HER?" Danielle asked Heather a short time later as the two sat with Walt at the kitchen table, drinking coffee and eating cinnamon rolls from Old Salts Bakery. Heather had just told them about her morning encounter with Pearl.

"I didn't exactly threaten to kill her, just dispose of her body,"

Heather said with a shrug. "And it wasn't my grandfather who was the killer. It was his father. I'm surprised she even knows about any of that."

"I will have another talk with Bella," Walt promised.

"I'm not sure it will do any good. She is such a little troublemaker." Heather ripped off a piece of cinnamon roll and popped it in her mouth.

Danielle looked at Heather and chuckled.

Heather paused a moment and frowned. "What?"

"I just think it's funny to eat a cinnamon roll before going on your morning jog."

"I would think that's when you should go jogging," Heather countered, breaking off more of her roll.

Danielle flashed her a grin. "True."

"I didn't just come over here to complain about Pearl or steal your cinnamon rolls. I hadn't heard how the ultrasound went. So what is she having? Boy or girl?" Heather asked.

"They decided they don't want to know," Danielle said. "They're waiting—the old-fashioned way."

"Hmm...really? Well, crap. I was planning to get her some adorable baby clothes for her shower—something super cute boy or girl. I can't really do that now."

"I think I'm going to get the baby some outfits after its born. Something to give Lily when she comes home from the hospital," Danielle said.

"Hmm, that would work. I'll do that too. Very tricky of Lily. This way she'll get more gifts." Heather took a sip of her coffee.

"From what Lily told me, she got so much at the shower in California, she doesn't really need much," Danielle said.

"Diapers—she will need lots of diapers. Trust me," Heather said.

"Very true," Walt said with a chuckle.

"Anyway, the other reason I'm here, I wanted to give you this." Heather paused a moment and licked off the sticky cinnamon roll frosting from her fingers before digging a folded piece of paper from her pocket. She handed it to Danielle.

"What's this?" Danielle asked, unfolding the paper.

"It's about the humane society. They outgrew their current site. Plus, the building needs to be condemned. Chris donated land, but they have to raise money for construction costs. You know how he feels about these kind of projects being supported by the community. I was thinking it might be a fundraiser you would like to spearhead. Maybe tie it in with your annual July Fourth celebration."

"We hadn't really thought about what we might do—if anything—for the Fourth this year," Danielle said.

"Oh, you have to do something. Anyway, just imagine how it will piss Pearl off if the entire community shows up at Marlow House for the Fourth."

Danielle chuckled. "Heather, you are awful. We can't do something just to irritate our neighbor."

"Don't be such a little goody-goody, Danielle. I'm not saying do it to piss her off. The humane society is a great cause. I'm just saying pissing her off will be an added benefit." Heather grinned and popped the rest of her cinnamon roll in her mouth.

"You are a brat." Danielle laughed.

Heather shrugged.

"I like the idea of a fundraiser for the humane society," Walt said. "We need to start planning now. It's only a little over a month away."

Danielle groaned. "We really can't make this a habit—planning last minute charity events."

"You'll get in the groove," Heather told her. "An annual fundraiser for the humane society for the Fourth might be kind of a cool tradition. And while it'll be a pain to pull it together this year, it will be easier next year—and the year after that."

"If we do decide to do it, it will be sort of ironic," Danielle said.

"Ironic how?" Heather asked.

"Think about it. What do dogs hate? And what do they have every Fourth?"

"Fireworks?" Heather asked.

IT WAS the last day of May. It was also Walt and Danielle's first wedding anniversary—commemorating their first and official wedding when they had eloped. While most of their close friends knew their Valentine's Day wedding was only a formality, an event that allowed them to all gather and celebrate Walt and Danielle's love, they also knew the pair had started their life together months earlier.

The doorbell rang. Danielle, who stood in the hallway, glanced at the clock before going to answer the door. They needed to leave for their dinner reservation in thirty minutes. She wondered who was here.

A moment later she opened the door and had her answer; it was Police Chief MacDonald.

The chief looked Danielle up and down, noticing her high heels—something he had only seen her wear on several occasions—a dress he had never seen her in—diamond earrings dangling from her earlobes, and the heart locket he had given her on her Valentine's Day wedding.

He let out a low whistle. "Wow, you look great. I take it I'm catching you and Walt on your way out?"

"It's our official wedding anniversary," she said with a grin. "We're having dinner at Pearl Cove, but we aren't leaving for another thirty minutes." She opened the door wider. "Come on in."

"Not if I'm interrupting." He remained standing on the front porch. "We got the results in on the skeletal remains, but I can tell you about them later."

Danielle threw the door wide open and waved him in. "Please, I've been waiting to hear what they found."

Five minutes later the chief sat with Walt and Danielle in the parlor.

"The remains were for two people, a man and a woman."

"Why did they think there might have been a third person?" Walt asked.

"It wasn't so much that they suspected there was a third person, but they didn't feel confident without further tests to say two of the thigh bones were from the same person. Not only was a portion of one femur missing, the level of deterioration appeared different than the rest of the bones. They believe it had something to do with the soil around that area."

"Do they know how they died?" Danielle asked.

"The man, from blunt head trauma. The woman, she was shot. But we knew that already."

Danielle frowned. "You did?"

The chief nodded.

"Keeping secrets from me?" Danielle grumbled half-heartedly.

"So do you have any idea who they were? Do you know their approximate ages?" Walt asked.

"They were young adults," the chief said. "Probably in their twenties."

"Were they able to do any DNA tests?" Danielle asked.

"Yes, but if we were hoping some close match would come up, that hasn't been the case so far," the chief explained. "The matches that did come up were distant cousins, and no relatives from the northwest. The woman is believed to have blue eyes, and over eighty percent of her ethnicity was Great Britain. They believe the man had brown eyes, and sixty percent of his ethnicity came up Italian."

"And no close relatives showed up?" Danielle asked.

"Not surprising. They believe those bones are about seventy years old," the chief said.

"Maybe so, but it would not be out of the question for one of their siblings, their children or grandchildren, or even a cousin to have taken a DNA test in the last few years," Danielle suggested.

"Maybe so, but considering the age at the time of death, it is entirely possible they never had children," the chief reminded her. "So that limits the possibilities. And even if they had siblings, those siblings might have died before DNA testing became common."

"Now what?" Walt asked.

"Now that we know they were killed about seventy years ago, we know they could have been buried there when the Mortons still owned the property—or after Pearl's grandmother bought it," the chief said.

"Any chance it's Pearl's grandfather?" Walt asked.

The chief shook his head. "No. Andy told Brian and Joe his cousins had their DNA tested—and he was right. There was no match with any of them. Plus, when Brian was searching on the grandfather, to find out if he was really buried in Reno, he learned he had blue eyes. Our mystery man had brown eyes."

"I find it hard to believe the Mortons were responsible for those bodies. Like Faye told me, her family was in the funeral business, and if they had to get rid of some bodies, it wouldn't be in the backyard," Danielle said.

"Actually, there have been instances where a funeral home will illegally dispose of a body to cut costs and pocket more of the burial expense," the chief explained. "Faye should know that."

"Yeah, but in their own backyard?" Danielle frowned.

The chief shrugged. "It has happened before."

"Do you think that could be what this is?" Walt asked.

"We're checking it out, but considering both victims appear to have been murdered, I doubt it," the chief said.

"Maybe Maisy caught Daisy and Kenneth together, and in a fit of anger killed them before they had a chance to run away with each other. She might have panicked and buried them in the backyard. Maybe that's why she wanted to buy the house back," Danielle suggested.

"That thought crossed my mind. But I've seen a picture of Kenneth Bakken's parents. They were from Norway and both blue-eyed," the chief said.

"That's right. Two blue-eyed people will have a blue-eyed child," Danielle muttered.

"Plus," the chief reminded her, "Daisy kept in touch with her friends over the years, so the woman's remains can't be hers."

"Kenneth also sent his sister a postcard about a year after he left," Danielle added.

"If it's not Daisy and Kenneth, or Pearl's grandfather and a mystery woman, who was buried next door?" Walt asked.

THIRTY-ONE

Finally, alone in the classroom, Lily did what she had been dying to do since her students had come in from the last recess of the day. She shoved one hand under her blouse and scratched her protruding belly. Standing by her desk, still scratching the itch, Lily let out a sigh of relief followed by a burp. The heartburn was annoying but an improvement over the morning sickness she had experienced earlier in her pregnancy.

No longer scratching, she gently rubbed her belly and then gave it a light pat before removing her hand from under her blouse and then giving the garment a gentle tug at its hem. Her belly was not overly large for being almost six months pregnant, yet considering her petite stature, it seemed larger. Already a busty girl, she was even more so now, which was why she had opted for traditional maternity clothing similar to what her mother had worn, which consisted primarily of loose-fitting smock-like blouses and dresses. Tight or form-fitting maternity clothing gave her figure a more provocative look, which she felt inappropriate for a second-grade teacher.

Surveying the room, she felt a brief pang of sadness. She would miss teaching, but if she later wanted to return, she knew she could. Today was Friday, June 9, the last day of the school year. Ian had left for California earlier in the week to meet with a producer and his agent, and wouldn't be returning until that evening. Since he was out of town, Danielle had promised to meet her after school and help her move some boxes to the library.

"I'm here!" Danielle announced a moment later when she walked into the classroom. She had come prepared to work, wearing her old jeans, a work shirt, and comfortable shoes. Once she stepped into the room, she frowned and glanced around. "Where is everything?"

Lily nodded to the six cardboard boxes stacked neatly by the door. "That's about it. And the aquarium." Sitting on her desk was an aquarium. The water had been removed, yet everything else remained, including the fish, which were now swimming around in plastic bags of water.

Danielle glanced around the room. "Wow. Everything is taken down, even your bulletin boards." She looked back at the boxes. "How in the world did you fit everything into those boxes? I've been in your classroom before. Where are all your books, games? No way did they all fit in there." Danielle briefly pointed to the boxes as she asked the question and then walked to Lily.

"I raffled everything off," Lily said with a grin.

"Raffled?"

Lily nodded. "Yeah. For the last few weeks I've been letting my students earn raffle tickets. Keeps the little darlings in line." Lily chuckled. "I didn't really want to bring all that stuff home. I know I could have given it to another teacher, but this was more fun, and the kids loved it. I made sure they all went home with something. So my books, CDs, games, a few stuffed animals, all got a good home."

"But not the aquarium?" Danielle asked, looking to the desk.

"I'm giving that to Evan. He helped me pack up everything this last week. Came in every recess."

"He's a good kid," Danielle said.

"Yeah, he is." Lily smiled.

"So what's in the boxes?" Danielle asked.

"Some things I'm leaving for the other teachers—mostly seasonal stuff for the bulletin boards. They told me to go ahead and leave the boxes in the library."

"Are we dropping the aquarium off at Evan's house?" Danielle asked.

Lily glanced up at the wall clock. "No. The chief said he would pick it up. He should be here in about five minutes."

"Okay, you want me to start moving the boxes to the library?" Danielle asked. "You don't need to be lifting anything."

"If you want to. But I need to go over there anyway to drop off my class diary, so I can go with you after the chief gets here."

"What's a class diary?" Danielle asked.

"It's something this school does. I think it's pretty cool. At the end of each year, the students have to write a one-page essay on the school year. The pages are inserted in a binder for that year. I'll show you when we go to the library. It's fun to read those old books. A lot of kids whose parents went to school here love to go look up what their parents wrote."

"Would Walt be in there?" Danielle asked.

"No. They didn't start it until the 1930s. But Marie's are in there. Also Adam's. His are kind of funny."

A knock came at the classroom door. The next moment it opened and in walked Chief MacDonald and his two sons.

"Hey, Chief, Eddie, Evan," Danielle greeted them.

While additional greetings were exchanged between the adults, the two boys ran over to the desk and looked in the aquarium. Eddie picked up the castle and examined it while Evan gently poked one of the plastic bags filled with water and a live fish.

"You ready to set up an aquarium?" Lily asked. "I think our little fish are anxious to get back swimming in the big tank."

"I suppose," the chief said, not too enthusiastically. "Not sure if I should thank you or curse you. The last time I had an aquarium was when I was in college."

"Aw, come on, the boys will take care of it." Lily looked at Evan and Eddie. "Won't you, boys?" They both nodded and continued examining the rest of the aquarium accessories.

"Yeah, right," the chief grumbled, walking to the tank.

"Evan helped me take it apart," Lily told him. "So he will be a big help putting it back together. And there is a book in there on how to take care of the fish."

The chief grinned at Lily. "Yeah, I know. Evan has been so excited about getting the aquarium."

"I'm surprised you aren't at work," Danielle told the chief.

"I took the afternoon off, since it's the boys last day at school. After we get this thing set up, I promised them we would go out for an early dinner of pizza."

"Fun." Lily grinned.

THE CHIEF and his sons helped Danielle carry the boxes to the library, and then returned to the classroom to pick up the aquarium. After they left, Lily and Danielle returned to the library to drop off Lily's class diary.

Danielle stood in the library and looked at the binders stored on the bookshelves along the back wall. Danielle had expected them to take up more room, yet the eighty-some binders only occupied a corner section of the bookshelves.

"The students are no longer allowed to look at the books without adult supervision," Lily explained, standing next to Danielle. "The pages are fragile in the older books."

"Can I look at some?" Danielle asked.

"I think you're adult enough…did you wash your hands?" Lily teased.

"Actually I did." Danielle grinned and stepped closer to the bookshelf, looking for the oldest binder. When she found it, she removed it from the shelf and took it with her to a nearby table and sat down.

Flipping through the pages, she read the names. Finally, she came to a page marked Marie Hemmings. There was no essay or text, just a hand-drawn picture of a little girl holding hands with her mommy and daddy.

"Aww, Marie was just in first grade when she drew this," Danielle said. "I wish they had started this earlier, when Walt was going to school here." Danielle turned the page to see what the other students had drawn or written that year, while Lily left to hand her class diary into the school librarian.

Ten minutes later, Lily returned to find Danielle still sitting at the table, looking through the same binder.

"Anything interesting?" Lily asked as she took a seat across from Danielle and then let out a burp.

Danielle glanced up from the open binder. "Lovely."

"Just wait until you're pregnant and your body turns on you," Lily grumbled.

Danielle chuckled and looked back down at the binder. She turned the page. "Hey, here is a familiar name!"

Lily craned her neck to see. "Who?"

"Maisy Faye Morton."

"Is her evil twin in there?" Lily asked.

Danielle flipped the page. "Yep. They both wrote essays." She turned back to Maisy's essay and began to read aloud.

"I liked school this year. I won a certificate for reading the most books in our class. My sister Daisy Faye is in my class with me. We are always in the same class. That is because we are twins, and my father says our school is not big enough for two fourth-grade classes. This year our teacher had a hard time telling us apart. Our father can always tell us apart. He says we look alike but are different. Daisy likes to run and play with the boys. I like to read books. Daisy likes vanilla ice cream. I like chocolate ice cream. Daisy does not like anything chocolate. This summer we are going to visit our grandparents."

"So what did the evil twin write?" Lily asked.

After turning the page, Danielle began to read aloud.

"This year my favorite classes were PE and art. We did not have music this year. At home my father makes my sister and me take piano lessons. He says girls should play the piano. I don't know why. My sister likes playing the piano. I am glad school is almost over. I love summer. In the summer I get to go to the beach and play outside."

Danielle closed the book. "I wonder if any of these people ever come back and read what they wrote?"

"I know the parents who went here sometimes do. A few of them have cringed after their kids read theirs." Lily chuckled.

"I wish they had been doing this back when Walt was at the school. How fun to read his thoughts at that age." Danielle stood up and returned the book to the shelf. "I would love to read what Adam wrote. But we should probably get going."

THIRTY-TWO

The next three weeks went by quickly. Lily spent most of her time cleaning and reorganizing her house in anticipation of the baby's arrival. During this time period, she and Ian also purchased paint for the nursery walls and signed up for a Lamaze class, which was to begin at the end of the month.

Across the street Marlow House prepared for its annual July Fourth anniversary celebration, which was just days away. This year they were using it to raise money for the local humane society's building fund. Walt and Danielle expected Pearl to raise a fuss over the event; however, they just expected it sooner than it actually came. Since finding the remains on her property, Pearl avoided going out, uncomfortable with people coming up to her and asking questions. Therefore, she hadn't heard the news around town. The first article about the event that had appeared in the local newspaper had come out two weeks earlier, but Pearl had spilt tea on that page and totally missed the article. But she didn't miss the second one.

"You can't do this!" Pearl shook the rolled-up newspaper at Walt and Danielle. The two stood in the open doorway with their angry neighbor standing on the front porch glaring at them. Moments earlier the pair had been in the living room and had spied Pearl stomping up to their front door. They decided it prudent to answer the door together.

"You really need to stop doing this," Danielle said calmly. "It is all perfectly legal. We have a permit for the event—and the city is behind us a hundred percent."

"Do you realize how much traffic this street has gotten since—since—" Pearl started to sputter.

"Since remains were found in your backyard?" Walt finished for her.

"All those nosey looky-loos trying to see something," Pearl said, still waving the newspaper.

"And whose fault is that?" Danielle asked.

"It isn't mine!" Pearl snapped. "I had nothing to do with those remains being there. They were already buried in the backyard when I bought the house. And who knows, maybe they were there when my grandparents bought it!" She pointed the newspaper at Walt and Danielle. "But your family owned this house all that time. How do we know your family didn't have something to do with bodies being buried on my property! Someone from Marlow House could have put them there!"

"You are being silly," Danielle said patiently. "And no one is accusing you of being personally responsible for what they found in your backyard. But don't blame us for the additional traffic on Beach Drive."

"But you're doing this." Pearl opened the newspaper and shoved the article at Danielle. "This will bring even more traffic to our street. And when all those people are here, do you know what they will be doing?"

"Having fun?" Walt asked.

Pearl glared at him. "They'll be looking in my backyard. They can't see it from the street, although that doesn't stop them from standing on the sidewalk and gawking. This ridiculous little event of yours will just attract more looky-loos who want a better view into my yard to gawk. This is an invasion of my privacy!"

"You really are being silly," Danielle repeated.

AS IT TURNED OUT, Pearl wasn't being silly at all. Those attending the anniversary charity event days later weren't just animal lovers; many attended simply for an opportunity to get a better view into Pearl's backyard.

American flag bunting; Stars and Stripes flag banners; red, white and blue streamers; carnation floral arrangements; and an assortment of other patriotic ornaments decorated the grounds of Marlow House, as well as inside. Heather took her turn at the side gate manning the ticket booth, while Chris and Ian passed out refreshments. Inside Walt was giving a tour of the house, while outside, Danielle took a break to chat with Lily. The two women stood by the refreshment table, looking toward the portion of the side fence separating Marlow House's property from Pearl's. Attendees to the charity event lined the fence, shamelessly peering into Pearl's yard and pointing. Upstairs at Pearl's house, the angry neighbor looked down at them from a bedroom window.

"I guess she was right," Danielle said as she sipped her lemonade, glancing from Pearl to the people looking into her yard.

"On the positive side, it helped you sell more tickets. Good for the animals," Lily chirped.

"I don't think Pearl cares about that. She's not exactly an animal lover," Danielle reminded her.

With a shrug Lily glanced briefly to Pearl and then looked back to Danielle. "You could always lie and tell Pearl the shelter you're raising money for is a kill shelter. That might cheer her up."

Sputtering from a spontaneous laugh, Danielle spit out a little lemonade, choking for a moment. She coughed and wiped off her mouth with the napkin she had been holding. "That's perverse," Danielle managed to say after she regained composure, unable to keep from smiling.

"The only one who's perverse around here is Pearl," Lily said, her expression now devoid of humor. "If those remains hadn't been there for so long, I wouldn't be surprised to find out Pearl was the one who buried them."

"Looks like a great turnout. Congratulations!" came a male voice.

Danielle turned to find her new neighbor, Bud Caine, approaching her. By his side was a woman who Danielle guessed to be around Bud's age.

"Mr. Caine, so glad you could make it!" Danielle greeted.

"Please call me Bud." He grinned.

"Bud, this is another one of our neighbors, Lily Bartley. Lily, this is Bud Caine; he lives in the house three doors up the street. Lily and her husband, Ian, live across the street."

"Nice to meet you." Lily flashed him a smile.

"I see congratulations are in order for you too," Bud said. "Congratulations!"

Lily smiled again and patted her baby bump. "Thank you."

Bud turned to the elderly woman at his side. She looked familiar to Danielle, but she couldn't place her.

"This is my dear friend Margaret Richards. Margaret and I met in kindergarten."

They exchanged more pleasantries, and Margaret insisted they call her by her first name.

"My older sister and Margaret's were good friends. We used to love to torment them." Bud laughed at the memory.

"I see the old Morton house is certainly getting a lot of attention." Margaret nodded toward the crowd of gawkers at the side fence. "They still haven't identified those remains, have they?"

Danielle shook her head. "Nope. They just know whoever they were, they were probably killed around seventy years ago. They were able to get DNA, but nothing came up to help them."

"Seventy years, that's around the time Maisy sold the house," Margaret noted.

"Around that." Danielle nodded.

"I didn't really know the people who moved in after the Mortons," Margaret said. "But I can't imagine the Mortons had anything to do with it."

"Why do you say that?" Bud asked. "I remember my dad didn't have many kind words for Mr. Morton."

Margaret shrugged. "The man owned a funeral home. I can't imagine someone like that burying bodies on their own property."

'That's what Faye said," Danielle added.

"That's not necessarily true," Lily said. "Ian and I were just talking about this. There was a case in Rhode Island a few years back where a funeral director hid bodies in a storage unit and other locations and then pocketed cremation and burial fees."

"I remember reading about that," Bud chimed in.

"Yeah, the chief mentioned that sort of thing happens sometimes," Danielle said. "The thought had never occurred to me."

"Does that mean the remains might be the results of an improper burial—fraud on the part of the funeral home?" Margaret asked.

Danielle shook her head. "They don't think so. I know they have since gone through death records for that time frame looking for any deaths that match the bodies found—that were handled by the Morton Funeral Home, but nothing came up. Plus, it looks as if the people were murdered."

"I don't know Maisy very well, but I don't see her as a murderer," Margaret said. "Although my sister used to say she wasn't as sweet as everyone said."

"Margaret Richards, you were always such a gossip!" Marie said when she appeared the next moment. Of course, only Danielle could see her.

Arching her brows, Danielle glanced to Marie.

"Well, she is," Marie insisted. "Margaret and Bud were a few years younger than me. Bud had an annoying crush on me, and Margaret was a meddlesome gossip."

"How so?" Lily asked Margaret.

"For one thing, I can't imagine how difficult it was for Daisy, always being compared to Maisy as if her sister was some sort of paragon. Maisy was held up as the daughter who didn't drink, smoke or run around with boys. Stayed at home to take care of their father. But Daisy was just a young woman herself, and she had her own dreams. When Mr. Morton died, everything was left to Maisy. My sister felt so sorry for Daisy being cut out of the will. How could a father do something like that?" Margaret asked. "Of course, poor Daisy had nowhere to go. It wasn't like she had a job or anything, and she wasn't married at the time. According to my sister, Maisy let her stay at the house, even telling everyone she insisted. Said she didn't want to kick her sister out on the street. But the real story, Maisy had all sorts of conditions."

"Conditions?" Lily asked.

"Oh, pshaw. Like I would take anything that sister of yours would say seriously! She was a worse gossip than you!" Marie snorted.

"According to my sister, Maisy tried to run Daisy's life. It was like Maisy believed she was now the parent, since the entire estate had gone to her, and now that she controlled the purse strings, she could control her sister."

"Technically speaking, it was Maisy's money," Danielle reminded her.

"Perhaps. But it wasn't right. In fact, Kenneth Bakken, Maisy's fiancé at the time, could see it too. He was horrified with how Maisy was treating her sister. It's really what ended their relationship and brought him together with Daisy."

"Oh, malarkey!" Marie barked. "I've never heard such a heap of poppycock in my life. Kenneth didn't end up with Daisy because he felt sorry that the poor thing was being mistreated, he ended up with her because Daisy set her sights on him. And as I recall, that girl had a knack of getting whatever she wanted."

Danielle glanced warily from Marie to Margaret, wondering whose version of the story was correct. She felt disloyal to Marie to consider Margaret's version, yet she also recalled there was a time Marie had been convinced Danielle had amorous feelings toward her grandson Adam.

"In fact, I'll tell you something that is not widely known," Margaret said in a hushed whisper. "Just before Daisy eloped with Kenneth, our family was preparing to go to Los Angeles for my cousin's wedding. Daisy came over to our house and asked my sister to mail a letter to Maisy for her when she got to Los Angeles."

"A letter? What kind of letter?" Lily asked.

"She and Kenneth were planning to elope, but Daisy was afraid her sister would interfere. In fact, Maisy had even threatened to have her committed!"

"Committed for what?" Danielle asked.

"Maisy said Daisy was not acting right—that she should see a doctor. Considering all the money Maisy had after her father died, Daisy was terrified her sister would be able to have her committed—locked up forever in a mental institution."

"I wouldn't be surprised if Maisy tried to get Daisy to seek help," Marie told Danielle. "Daisy did act erratically. But caring about your sister and wanting her to get help is certainly not sinister like Margaret is painting."

"What did this letter say?" Lily asked.

"It was a letter telling Maisy that she and Kenneth had eloped and were okay. But the real reason she wanted the letter mailed, Daisy wanted her sister to think she and Kenneth were in California. That way, if she started looking for them, she would be searching in the wrong area. So while Maisy thought her sister was down south, she and Kenneth were heading east."

THIRTY-THREE

August was just days away. Lily and Ian had attended their first Lamaze class, but the next day Ian had been called back to California for another meeting with the producer on his current project. Unhappy with her husband's unexpected business trip, Lily sat glumly in the passenger seat of Danielle's car as the two headed to Adam's office.

"My folks are going to be here next week. What if Adam can't recommend anyone?" Lily asked Danielle. Ian had planned to paint the nursery this week, but his trip to California made that impossible. Lily's original plan was to have the nursery freshly painted and ready for her parents' arrival, when they would be bringing the gifts from Lily's first baby shower, which included the crib and dresser Lily's parents had given them.

"Then I'll paint it for you," Danielle suggested.

"No, you won't. No offense, but you're kind of a crappy painter."

"Well, that's not very nice," Danielle grumbled. "But true."

"I do appreciate the offer," Lily said. "I guess in the big scheme of things, this is not a big deal." She didn't sound convinced.

"Just as long as you don't do something stupid, like try painting it yourself. You know what your doctor said."

"I know. And while I don't always do what my doctor tells me to,

I won't do anything to risk the health of my baby." Lily looked down at her protruding belly and gave it a gentle pat.

Ten minutes later they entered Adam's office. Unbeknownst to Lily—and Adam—he was not alone. Marie hovered overhead in an invisible chair.

"Danielle, Lily, hello!" Marie called out, waving down to the pair.

Danielle glanced up at Marie and flashed her a smile.

Adam stood up from the desk, his eyes on Lily's belly. "Wow. You really are pregnant."

"Well, gee thanks, I think," Lily said dryly as she plopped down ungracefully in a chair.

"I just meant—" Adam stammered.

"I know what you meant. I'm as big as a house."

Marie frowned down at her grandson. "Adam, sometimes you just don't think before you talk." She pinched his right ear.

Adam's right hand flew to his ear. "Ouch!"

"What's wrong?" Lily asked.

Adam rubbed his earlobe. "Did something bite me?"

Danielle looked at Adam's ear and shook her head. "It's a little red, but I don't see any bite marks, and there isn't any bug crawling on you."

"It felt like someone pinched me." Adam frowned and stopped rubbing his ear. "Kind of déjà vu. Reminded me of Grandma. She would do that when she was annoyed with me."

Danielle arched a brow at Marie.

Lily glanced around the office wondering, *Is Marie here?*

Marie shrugged down at Danielle. "I love the boy, but sometimes he says the most oafish things. Lily dear is pregnant; she needs to be pampered."

"We're here to see if you can recommend a painter…someone who might be available, like, now?" Danielle told Adam as she took a seat next to Lily.

Adam sat back down in his desk chair. "A painter for what?"

"Ian was supposed to paint the nursery this week, but he had to go to California again. My folks are going to be here next week, and I really wanted to have the room painted by then."

"Are your parents staying in the room?" Adam asked. "I know your other bedroom is Ian's office now."

"No. They're staying with us, in the downstairs bedroom,"

Danielle explained. "They don't really have a guest room anymore, not with the spare room being turned into a nursery. Plus, the downstairs bedroom at Marlow House is comfortable; it has its own private bathroom."

"Just as long as you don't charge her parents," Adam teased. "Or I'm telling your neighbor you're running a B and B again."

Danielle rolled her eyes. "Har, har. Anyway, who said I'm feeding them breakfast?"

Adam chuckled. "True."

"So do you know anyone?" Lily asked.

"I'm having one of our rentals painted, and the painter I use can't get to it for three weeks. He's really backed up."

Lily groaned. "It is just one room."

Adam looked at Danielle. "Why don't you paint it?"

"She offered," Lily said.

Danielle shrugged. "She won't let me."

"Why not?" Adam asked.

"Because I'm not a terrific housepainter. To be honest, I kinda suck at it."

"You know who was a good housepainter?" Adam asked.

"No. But do you think they can do it?" Lily asked.

"I seriously doubt it. It was my grandma," Adam said.

"Oh, Adam, how sweet you remember," Marie cooed.

"Marie?" Danielle asked.

"Yes. When she was younger, she always did her own painting. At least, the interior. She told me once that before Grandpa, she dated a guy who was a housepainter, and he taught her some tricks."

"He certainly did," Marie snickered. "And it wasn't just about painting."

Danielle's eyes widened; she looked up at Marie.

Marie shrugged again. "I was young once."

"But you know who might be able to do it, Bill. If it's just one room, he should be able to whip it out in a day," Adam suggested.

Lily wrinkled her nose. "Bill? Is he any good?"

"I imagine he's better than Danielle." Adam flashed Danielle a grin then looked back at Lily. "You want me to have him stop by your house?"

"Yeah. I guess. I already have the paint, brushes and rollers. It's all sitting in the room. Ian and Walt moved all the furniture out of the nursery before Ian left." The truth was, Walt did most of the moving—without actually touching anything, while Ian watched in fascination. Of course, she couldn't tell Adam that.

"Bill's in Portland for the next couple of days," Adam began.

Lily groaned. "Then no way he can get it done before my folks get back."

"Sure he can. When he returns, he had some things he was going to do for me, but I can push that back, and he can do your nursery instead. One room should only take him a day."

"You would let him put off the work you need?" Lily perked up.

"Sure. When he returns from Portland, I'll have him stop by and look at the room so he can give you a bid and see if he needs to get anything," Adam told her.

"Hmmm...okay. That could work. Have him call me before he wants to come over. I'm staying at Marlow House until Ian gets back from California."

"When's he coming back?" Adam asked.

"We're babysitting," Danielle said with a grin.

Lily glanced at Danielle. "Funny." She looked back to Adam and said, "Not until next week. The day before my parents get here."

"WAS MARIE IN ADAM'S OFFICE?" Lily asked Danielle as they drove down the street to the museum.

"Yes. How did you know?" Danielle asked.

"I just figured. His ear looked red, like it really was pinched." Lily chuckled.

"Marie was annoyed with his crack, *wow, you are pregnant*."

"That's sort of what I figured. I do love Marie."

"Me too." Danielle pulled the car into the parking lot of the museum.

"You are a sport," Lily said.

Danielle parked the car and turned off the ignition. She looked at Lily and asked, "Why do you say that?"

"Considering all that nonsense the historical society pulled a while back, for you to agree to help with this exhibit."

"They've all apologized. Sort of. And Ben did leave me the Packard, so holding a grudge would seem petty. But mostly, it's for the community, not them." Danielle started to open the car door but paused a moment and looked back at Lily. "By the way, while we're at the museum, would you mind if we stop at the newspaper exhibit?"

"I don't care. What do you want to look up?" Lily asked.

"I know the chief and his people have searched through the records, looking for who those remains might have belonged to. I'd just like to look through the newspapers and see if I can find anything."

"Danielle, that's a lot of newspapers to look through."

"I just want to look around the time Mr. Morton died, up until Pearl's grandmother bought the house."

"What are you hoping to find?"

"I don't know. But I can't help but wonder if whatever happened to those poor people might have something to do with Mr. Morton's death."

"Why would you think that?" Lily asked.

"I don't know. It's something that keeps nagging at me. But if you don't want to hang around at the museum while I look, I can do it another time."

"Nah, I don't have a problem sticking around. I enjoy looking through those old newspapers."

A few minutes later Danielle walked with Lily into the museum and was greeted by Millie Samson.

"Oh, Lily, you look radiant," Millie told her. "How are you feeling?"

"Other than the heartburn, pretty good, I suppose."

"When is the baby due?" Millie asked.

"September 25," Lily told her.

"Really?" Millie looked Lily up and down. "By the looks of you, I would have thought that baby was about to come any time now. Are you sure you aren't having twins?"

"Where is Marie when you need her?" Lily muttered under her breath.

"What did you say?" Millie frowned.

Lily smiled sweetly. "Nothing."

"I'm here to pick up the list of businesses you want me to visit," Danielle interrupted.

Millie turned her attention to Danielle. "Oh yes. I do thank you for doing this for us."

"What exactly is this new exhibit?" Lily asked.

"It's on the local businesses, the ones who have been in the same family for a couple of generations," Millie explained. "I'll go get you that list."

The telephone in the gift shop rang. "I need to answer that first," Millie told them.

"No problem. Lily and I are going to go look at the newspaper exhibit. We'll be in there," Danielle told her.

DANIELLE AND LILY sat together at the newspaper exhibit table, each looking at a large book containing back issues of the local newspaper. They had been silently thumbing through the papers for about fifteen minutes.

"Find anything interesting?" Lily asked, looking up from what she had been reading.

"I found something sad," Danielle said. "Nothing to do with our mystery bodies. It's an article on the suicide of Millie's brother in-law, Lewis."

Lily glanced to the doorway leading to where Millie was, and then back to Danielle. "The one who killed himself over Daisy marrying another man?"

"Yeah." Danielle continued to read to herself. "This is kind of interesting," she muttered, and then looked up at Lily.

"What?"

"I think Leo Bateman was the name of Faye's husband."

Lily frowned. "So?"

"According to this article, the witness who saw Lewis drive off Pilgrim's Point was Leo Bateman, a mortician from Portland. Odd coincidence. He ends up marrying the jilted sister after witnessing the man who was brokenhearted kill himself over the other sister."

"Are you sure it's the same person? From what I remember, the man Faye married was already working for her when Daisy and Kenneth took off, months after Mr. Morton died," Lily reminded her.

Before Danielle could answer, Millie brought her the list of businesses she had been waiting for.

"Here it is," Millie said, handing her a manila folder. "Everything is in here."

Danielle accepted the folder and asked, "Millie, I came across an article on your brother-in-law's death."

"Such a sad thing. But like I said, I never really knew him. It was before I was even dating my husband."

"In the article it said the witness who saw him drive off Pilgrim's Point was Leo Bateman," Danielle began.

Millie nodded. "Yes, that's right. Norman's father, from the funeral home. He's one of the businesses for you to visit for the exhibit."

"According to the article, Norman's father was working in Portland at the time of your brother-in-law's suicide. But someone said he started working for the Morton Funeral Home right after Mr. Morton's death. So I would assume he wasn't working in Portland at the time of the suicide, like the newspaper said."

Millie shook her head. "No. Leo had worked for Morton Funeral home before Mr. Morton's death. But he had left to take another job in Portland. The man who had been hired to take his place took over as funeral director after Mr. Morton's death but he didn't work out. That's why Leo happened to be in Frederickport that day. Maisy was interviewing him to replace the director at the time."

THIRTY-FOUR

The next morning Lily, Walt and Danielle sat at the kitchen table eating breakfast, while Sadie and Max were in the side yard enjoying the sunshine. Danielle reread the list Millie had given her while nibbling on a piece of toast.

"How exactly is this exhibit for the museum a fundraiser?" Lily asked.

Danielle glanced up to Lily from the paper, looking at her from across the table. "It's actually a special exhibit, so it will only be up for one month."

"That way they can do it again next year and make more money," Walt snickered.

Lily glanced from Danielle to Walt, back to Danielle. "And how do they make money from it?"

"Each applicable Frederickport business will have a section in the exhibit. If they make a donation, the Glandon Foundation will double it. So a business doesn't have to donate anything, but with Chris doubling the donation, it gives them an incentive. Marlow House gets an honorary spot, because they see Marlow House as technically being in the same family, since I married Walt. More honorary, because we are no longer a licensed business."

"Plus, Danielle agreed to talk to all the applicable businesses about the exhibit," Walt added.

"Walt and I have to pitch the idea to them," Danielle said with a grin.

"Somehow I got roped into this project," Walt said before sipping his coffee.

"So who are you going to see first?" Lily asked.

"The nursery. I need to pick up some potting soil anyway. We're going in a couple of hours; you want to go with us?" Danielle asked.

"I appreciate the invitation, but I think I'll just hang around here and read. Maybe take a nap. That's all I want to do these days —sleep." Lily yawned.

"Then sleep. In two months, sleep might be a precious commodity for you," Danielle said.

MARIE STOOD ALONE in what had once been her bedroom some ninety years earlier. While she couldn't remember actually living in the house, she was familiar with the property, considering she had owned it all those years until she had sold it to Lily and Ian shortly before her death.

A ghost—an image of a woman in her early eighties (she had actually been older at the time of death, but Marie opted to shave a few years off her appearance, yet not enough that those who could see her and she cared about would not recognize her)—stood in the middle of the room, hands on hips, taking inventory.

As Lily had mentioned in Adam's office, cans of fresh paint sat on the floor. By her estimation it would be more than was needed to paint the room, yet more was better than not enough. Also stacked in the corner were paintbrushes, a roller, roller pan, and an assortment of other items needed to complete the painting project, including drop cloths to protect the floor.

Marie wanted desperately to get something for the baby, but she had learned with her passing, you really can't take it with you. She no longer had money. Of course, considering the energy she had managed to harness, it would be possible for her to lift any baby gift she wanted without getting arrested. However, once she decided to pass over to the other side, she imagined there might be hell to pay —*literally*.

While she didn't have money to buy Lily and Ian a gift for the new baby, she realized she could paint the nursery. Marie smiled at the idea. At the time of her death she had been in no shape for such a project. But now, without her earthly constraints and with her newly harnessed energy, she had no doubt she could complete the project—and do a far better job than Bill.

"I have a room to paint!" Marie said cheerfully, willing the drop cloths to float up from the corner and unfold.

TOYNETTE STOOD behind the sales counter at her nursery, thumbing through the family album she had brought to work to show Danielle. Millie Samson had called her the night before, telling her about the museum project and that Danielle would be stopping by to see her sometime this week. She had just opened the store ten minutes earlier and hadn't had any customers yet.

A moment later the front door to the store opened, ringing the bell. Toynette glanced up to see Danielle walk in with a man. She had never met him before, but she immediately knew who he was: Walt Marlow. She found it breathtaking how much he looked like the man in the portrait on display at the museum—*the other Walt Marlow*.

She had heard around town how he had his own distinct style. Some even suggested he dressed for the part of a 1920s author—his crisply pleated slacks, collared shirt, with its long sleeves pushed up to his elbows, and a fedora hat sitting at a cocky angle atop what looked like a thick head of dark hair. His manner of dress was strikingly different from the men his age who typically came into her nursery. While his clothing was hardly casual by comparison, he appeared quite comfortable and natural with his style, in some ways more so than her customers dressed in denims and T-shirts. While they had never met, she had seen him around town driving the Packard Ben Smith had left Danielle in his will—and some said had once belonged to the original Walt Marlow.

It all comes full circle, Toynette thought to herself before saying, "Morning, Danielle. I assume this is the infamous Walt Marlow?"

"Guilty as charged," Walt said with a smile, glancing around the front of the store.

"Morning, Toynette. Yes, this is my husband, Walt."

"I assume you're here about the museum exhibit?" Toynette asked.

Danielle arched her brows. "You know about that?"

"I spoke to Millie last night. She told me about it and that you might be by."

"I guess that means I don't have to give you my sales pitch. Does it also mean you want to participate?" Danielle asked.

"I would love to. In fact, I pulled out an old photo album. Millie suggested I show it to you, and maybe it will help us decide what I should get together for the exhibit."

Walt eyed the album sitting on the counter. "I love looking at old photo albums."

Toynette perked up. "You do?"

He nodded, hesitantly reaching for the album. "Especially anything on this area."

Toynette smiled broadly and slid the album closer to Walt for him to look at. "My grandparents emigrated from Norway. They started this nursery."

Walt turned the album around so it was right side up for him to view. With Danielle close at his side, looking over his shoulder, he opened the book to the first page.

"That's a photograph of a painting of my grandparents. The ones who started the nursery. The original is hanging at home. I didn't know if the museum would want to display the actual painting or a smaller photograph of it." The photograph showed a blond, blue-eyed couple who appeared to be in their thirties.

"I think it will depend on how much space the museum intends to allot for each exhibit," Danielle said as Walt turned the page.

Toynette pointed at the lone photograph of a young blue-eyed blond woman. "That's my mom."

"She was gorgeous," Danielle murmured.

"She took over the nursery after my grandparents retired. She wanted to be a teacher, but after my uncle left Frederickport, she ended up running the nursery."

Danielle glanced up to Toynette. "Did your uncle Kenneth work in the nursery?"

"Before the war he always worked here with his parents. It was one of the reasons Mom was so surprised when he left like that."

"How so?" Danielle asked.

"She always expected him to take the business over someday. He always talked about it. He enjoyed working outdoors, with plants. And he knew his plants—he could name every one, knew what grew in the area, what wouldn't. But I guess he found something else he liked better." Toynette shrugged.

Walt turned the page. Once again, there was just one large photograph. This time, it was a painting of a man's portrait. He had dark hair, large brown eyes, a dark complexion and a mischievous grin.

"Oh, who is this? He's quite handsome," Danielle said.

"That's Uncle Kenneth. Looking at that picture, I suppose I can understand why Daisy Morton stole him away from her sister."

"But he has brown eyes," Danielle blurted without thought. She instantly regretted her outburst and felt her face growing warm.

Toynette laughed. "That's because he was Italian."

Danielle frowned. "Italian?"

Toynette nodded. "Uncle Kenneth was adopted. My grandparents got him when he was about two, from an orphanage back east. At the time, my grandmother didn't think they could have children. But later, my mother surprised them."

"I had no idea," Danielle said.

Toynette shrugged. "If you take another look at my grandfather's photograph, you'll see Kenneth actually looks a lot like him. It's uncanny. No blood relation, but they look remarkably alike. When my grandparents settled in Frederickport and opened the nursery, Mom said people would comment on how tan Kenneth was from working outside with his father all the time. They didn't realize he was adopted, and my grandparents didn't broadcast it."

"I suppose that was before most people realized two blue-eyed people can only have a blue-eyed child," Danielle said.

"Unless, of course, the husband is not the father," Toynette said with a mischievous grin. "Fortunately, Kenneth looked like my grandfather's mini—aside from the coloring."

Walt turned the page again. Instead of one photograph, the page was filled with snapshots of Kenneth in his uniform, standing with his parents and sister.

"That was right before he left for overseas," Toynette explained.

"He came back a war hero, didn't he?" Danielle asked.

Toynette nodded. "Yes. He lost part of his right leg."

THIRTY MINUTES later Walt and Danielle sat in the Packard in the nursery parking lot, preparing to leave. Noticing Danielle had grown uncharacteristically quiet while talking with Toynette, Walt turned to look at his wife.

"What is it, Danielle?"

Sitting in the passenger seat, she looked to Walt. "I know who was buried in Pearl's backyard."

"Who?" Walt frowned.

"Daisy Morton and Kenneth Bakken."

"DAISY MORTON AND KENNETH BAKKEN?" the chief repeated forty minutes later. He sat in his office with Walt and Danielle and had just finished listening to who Danielle believed had been buried next door to Marlow House.

The chief leaned back casually in his chair, eyeing Danielle curiously. "How do you figure that?"

"You initially discounted the possibility it was Kenneth because we all assumed he was Norwegian, with blue eyes. But Kenneth had brown eyes and was Italian, just like the man whose remains you had tested. And tell me, which leg had a part of it missing—the right or left?"

The chief furrowed his brow and sat up in his chair, placing his elbows on his desktop. His gaze met Danielle's. "The right."

Danielle smiled. "If you will check Kenneth's medical records, I imagine those legs will match. He lost part of his right leg in the war."

"But the letters—" the chief began. "It's well known both Daisy and Kenneth corresponded with family and friends after they supposedly left Frederickport."

"At the Fourth of July party, I met an elderly woman named Margaret Richards. She told me her sister had been a close friend of Daisy Morton. Daisy had come to her, telling her about eloping with Kenneth, and how she was afraid of her sister."

"Afraid of Faye? I thought you told me Faye was the sweet sister; it was Daisy who was the wild one. And that Faye had changed after her sister ran away with Bakken," the chief argued.

"According to Margaret, Maisy was not as sweet as everyone thought." Danielle then told the chief about the letter Margaret's sister had mailed for Daisy from Los Angeles. When she was finished, she asked, "Perhaps Maisy found out about the elopement before they had a chance to leave—and in a fit of rage, killed them both."

"But by that time the letter was on its way to LA to be mailed," Walt interjected.

"And when the letter arrived from Los Angeles, maybe it gave Maisy an idea. She'd arrange to have other letters mailed to friends of Daisy's, so they would believe she was alive. She had the money, could easily hire someone to do it. And from what I understand, Kenneth only sent one letter to his family—and that was not really a letter, more one word, *sorry*," Danielle explained.

"Being twins, she probably felt more comfortable forging her sister's handwriting, but not Kenneth's," Walt suggested.

"And she conveniently killed Kenneth off a year or so later, in another country, so his family wouldn't wonder why he never returned to Frederickport. After all, if he hadn't died, it wouldn't make sense for him to stay away from his parents and sister indefinitely. Toynette said they had been close."

"I'll see if I can find any medical records of Kenneth Bakken that I might be able to use to identify those remains. I'll also see about getting a warrant for Faye's DNA. In the meantime, this can't get out," the chief said.

THIRTY-FIVE

"You actually think this Maisy Faye could have killed her boyfriend and sister?" Lily asked Danielle later that afternoon. They sat on the back porch having lunch with Walt. "Did she seem capable of that?"

"I liked her. She seemed nice," Danielle said. "But she's ninety-five. I have no idea what she might have been like when she was younger."

"I liked her too," Walt said. "But someone killed those people and buried them next door, and the male victim certainly matches Kenneth Bakken's description."

"What I don't understand, after Kenneth supposedly died in Europe, didn't any of his family ever go to visit his grave?" Lily asked.

"You have to remember this was decades before the internet. According to Toynette, they never knew where he had been buried, and they weren't sure how to look. Daisy never stayed in one place, and while she sent letters to friends, she never gave a return address. It was always a one-way conversation."

"Are you still going out to the funeral home to talk to her son about the museum project?" Lily asked.

"Yes. Plus, it will give me the perfect opportunity to ask Norman questions without sounding suspicious. I talked to the chief about it, and he agreed."

"You don't think Norman has any idea his mom might have offed her own sister, do you?" Lily asked.

"I doubt it," Walt said. "Faye seemed to sincerely care about her son. He was born long after any of this happened. So I can't imagine her burdening him with any of that knowledge—if it is true."

LATER THAT AFTERNOON Walt and Danielle sat with Norman Bateman in his office at the funeral home. Danielle had just explained the museum exhibit to him and asked him if he would be interested in participating.

"Most definitely. I'm proud that Morton Funeral Home has been in our family for three generations," Norman said. "And I will definitely make a donation."

"That's wonderful. Do you mind if I ask you some questions about the business so I can get an idea of how we might put together your section at the exhibit?" Danielle asked.

"Certainly. Ask away." Norman grinned.

Once again Danielle was struck with how much Norman Bateman physically resembled the fictitious Norman Bates. Pushing that thought aside, she reached down to her purse and pulled out a notepad and pen. In doing so, her cellphone slipped from her purse onto the floor, unnoticed.

"I understand your grandfather died here after falling down the stairs?" Danielle asked.

"Yes." Norman nodded. "He was alone and his office was upstairs. According to my mother, he had a bad knee. It was a terrible accident."

"He had two daughters, but your mother inherited, is that correct?" Danielle asked.

Leaning back in his desk chair, Norman folded his arms across his chest and nodded. "Like you know, my mother was a twin. According to Mother, her sister, Daisy, was spirited and misunderstood." He smiled softly. "I think it always bothered Mother that her father left the business to her and wrote her sister out of the will. It put a wedge between the sisters, damaged their relationship. As much as Mother loved her father, I don't think she ever forgave him for writing Daisy out of the will."

"Couldn't she have shared the inheritance?" Walt asked.

Norman shrugged. "I suppose she would have—had Daisy stuck around. But the damage was already done, and Daisy was understandably bitter. I don't know how much you know about the story, but she ran off with Mother's fiancé at the time."

"With Kenneth Bakken," Danielle said. "We talked to his niece this morning. The nursery is also participating in the museum exhibit."

Norman nodded. "Yes, Kenneth Bakken. According to Mom, she wasn't heartbroken over Kenneth breaking up with her—despite what everyone thought at the time. She always claimed they really weren't right for each other. Mother said when she met Dad, she knew he was the only one for her."

"Your father used to work for your grandfather and then left for a while to work in Portland?" Danielle asked.

"Yes. My father found a higher paying job in Portland. After he left, Grandfather hired someone to replace him. Of course, when he hired the man, he wasn't thinking of someone to take over the business. At least, not in the immediate future. And when my grandfather died unexpectedly, Mother soon discovered the man he'd hired was not equipped to run the business. She was faced with selling or finding someone to replace him. Then she remembered my father."

"You said your mother knew he was right for her when they first met—was that when he worked for her father, before his death?" Danielle asked.

Norman smiled. "No. While my mother met Dad the first time he worked here, she didn't really know him then, aside from the fact her father thought highly of him and wanted to kick himself when he let him get away. After Grandfather died, and Mother realized the man he had hired to replace my father was not going to work out, she called Dad and asked him to meet her. Dad always said she made him an offer he couldn't refuse. They fell in love not long after he came to work for her, married, and the rest is history."

"When they married, they moved into the house you live in now?" Danielle asked.

"Yes. But if things had been different, we might be neighbors." Norman smiled.

"Because your parents would have stayed at the Beach Drive house?" Walt asked.

"Mother always said she sold the house impulsively—a gut reaction to losing her father. Which is why she wanted to buy it back. But now, well, frankly, I'm glad they never accepted any of our offers."

"Why is that?" Walt asked.

Norman arched his brows at Walt. "Those remains they found. I certainly wouldn't want to be dealing with all that. It's not terrific PR for a funeral director to have remains show up on private property they own."

"But they could have been put there when your mom still owned the property," Danielle daringly suggested.

"I certainly can't imagine my mother or aunt having anything to do with that. Digging two graves? No. And my grandfather? Considering his physical shape at the time, no way. But I've heard stories about the people who bought the property. They seem a little shady to me."

"Like you know, the granddaughter of the people who bought it from your mother lives there now," Danielle reminded him.

"Yes. I understand they were able to get DNA from the remains, so hopefully they'll be able to identify them," Norman suggested.

"They haven't been able to yet," Danielle said.

Norman shrugged. "I suppose testing for DNA doesn't always provide answers. Not everyone is anxious to have their DNA tested."

"Have you ever had it done?" Danielle asked.

"No. I don't have any kids, so I don't really see the point. Plus, my mother is opposed to it."

"Why?" Danielle asked.

"My mother is superstitious. She's opposed to having our DNA tested, insists it will be put to some nefarious use."

Walt and Danielle exchanged quick glances.

"I suppose we're getting off track," Norman said. "What else do you want to ask?"

"Umm…perhaps we can look at those portraits you have hanging in the entry again? It might give me some ideas for the museum when putting together your display," Danielle suggested.

"Certainly." Norman stood.

As Danielle stepped out of Norman's office a few minutes later, Walt at her side and Norman leading the way, Danielle caught a glimpse of a bright ball of light moving down the hallway, disappearing into an open doorway. She and Walt exchanged quick glances.

"Did you see that?" Danielle whispered under her breath.

Walt nodded. By the way Norman continued to chatter on, leading the way down the hall, it was obvious he hadn't seen the bright light. A few minutes later Walt stood in front of the portrait of Maisy and Daisy Morton. Mesmerized, he stared at their faces.

"They really were beautiful," Danielle said, looking up at the portrait.

"That's Maisy Faye," Walt stammered.

Standing beside Walt and Danielle, Norman looked up at the portrait. "My mother hates that name. After my grandfather died, she started using her middle name. She used to say Maisy sounded like a hillbilly."

"I guess some parents like to choose matching names for twins—Maisy, Daisy," Danielle suggested, still looking at the portrait.

"My aunt Daisy always fascinated me. I was an only child, and here my mother had a sister—a twin sister—one she was estranged from, one I had never met. From what I've heard, they were as different as night and day. But they were also the same in many ways—like twins are."

"How were they the same?" Danielle asked.

"For example, Mom and Dad went to Italy one year. And a few months later, her sister was there. We knew, because Aunt Daisy sent us a postcard from Italy. We thought it was bizarre at the time. After all, they hadn't seen each other for years, but they were both in Italy at practically the same time. That's the types of things I hear twins do—doing the same things even though they are miles apart and not communicating. It happened a few other times too. So, while they were different in some ways—like Aunt Daisy being a reader and playing the piano, and Mom preferring to do something more active, they were also doing the same thing—like traveling to the same place at around the same time."

Danielle glanced at Walt to get his reaction to what he was thinking about Norman's comments, but her husband continued to stare blankly at the portrait, as if he weren't listening.

"TRAVELING to the same place at the same time?" Danielle repeated when she and Walt got into her car fifteen minutes later. He sat quietly in the passenger seat, staring ahead. She had been so preoccupied listening to what Norman had to say, she had failed to notice Walt's distant behavior.

As Danielle hooked up her seatbelt, she said, "Gee, what a coincidence. Daisy happens to send letters to all her friends just months after Maisy visits the same area?"

"That was Maisy Faye."

Danielle frowned at Walt. "Who was Maisy Faye?"

Walt turned to Danielle, his expression blank. "One of the women in that portrait. One of them was Maisy Faye."

"Yeah? So?"

"The Maisy Faye in my dream. It was her."

"What are you saying, Walt?"

"The woman I dreamt about. The woman I remembered. The one named Maisy Faye. The one I can't place how or when I knew. It's her. One of the women in that portrait. My Maisy Faye looks exactly like the Morton twins."

"That's impossible. They were practically babies when you died."

THIRTY-SIX

Lily stood at the kitchen counter grating cheddar cheese while Sadie napped in the parlor and Max snoozed in one of the upstairs bedrooms. She looked up when Walt and Danielle walked in the back door.

"I'm making tacos for dinner," Lily announced as a greeting.

"Sounds good," Walt said, snatching a bit of the cheese as he headed for the door leading to the hallway. "Wait until I get back before you start telling Lily."

"Telling me what?" Lily asked as Walt walked out of the room.

"Something freaky happened at the funeral home."

"Did you see a ghost?" Lily asked.

Before Danielle could answer, the landline rang. Both women looked at the ringing phone.

"Another person you have to disappoint?" Lily asked. Since the landline had been used for primarily bed and breakfast business, calls these days tended to be people trying to make reservations, who ended up disappointed when they learned Marlow House B and B was no longer open for business.

Danielle answered the phone. "Hello?…Oh, hi…I did?…Let me check…" Danielle set the handset on the counter and then picked up her purse, opening it. She looked inside while Lily silently watched. A moment later Danielle put her purse down and picked up the handset again.

"Yeah, I did. How long are you going to be there? Okay. I'll leave right now. You'll wait? Thanks!" Danielle hung up the phone and picked up her purse.

"Who was that?" Lily asked.

"Norman Bateman, from the funeral home. My cellphone must have fallen out of my purse in his office. He just found it. But I need to leave right now to get it. He was on his way out, but he promised to wait for me, because all his employees have already left. Tell Walt where I went. Save me some tacos!"

NORMAN BATEMAN EXPECTED Danielle to walk through the front door, not his mother.

"What are you doing here?" Norman asked in surprise. "I told you I would be there as soon as Danielle picks up her phone."

Faye sat down in one of the chairs in the front waiting area of the funeral home and let out a weary sigh. "I needed to get out of that place. The new owner plays the most gawd-awful music. I hate to say this, but I'm going to find a new hairdresser."

"Who brought you?" Norman asked.

"I ran into Susan Mitchell from the bank. She had just finished getting her hair done and offered to take me home. I asked her if she would bring me here instead."

"You should've had her take you home." Norman glanced at his watch.

"Why? You're here. And I was hoping we could stop at the grocery store on our way home. Now tell me about your little visit with the Marlows. What was that all about?"

Norman recounted his visit with Danielle and Walt while Faye sat quietly, digesting all that he was telling her.

"Is something wrong, Mother?" Norman asked.

"It just seems Danielle was overly curious about my sister."

"To be honest, I was probably the one who brought up the subject, not her."

Faye glared at her son. "You know I don't like discussing my relationship with Daisy."

"Yes, I know, Mother."

A smile suddenly replaced Faye's glare. "Why don't you run to the store now, and I'll wait for Danielle and give her the phone.

Then when you come back, we can go straight home." Faye smiled brightly.

THE PARKING LOT was empty when Danielle arrived at the funeral home. She wondered if Norman had changed his mind and had left to pick up his mother without waiting for her to get there. After parking her car, she reached for her purse, intending to retrieve her cellphone so she could call Norman and see if he was inside or had left, before getting out of the car. The moment she grabbed her purse, she realized the absurdity of her actions.

"Real smart, Danielle," she grumbled aloud. Tossing the purse back on the passenger seat, she unhooked her seatbelt. If Norman wasn't here, she would have to go home and call him to make other arrangements to pick up her phone.

A short time later Danielle tried the front door of the funeral home and was relieved to find it unlocked. But when she walked inside, it was Faye Bateman sitting in the front waiting area, not Norman.

"Faye?" Danielle said in surprise.

"Hello, Danielle," Faye said with a smile, making no attempt to stand up. "So nice to see you again. Norman will be back in a moment; he had to step out. Why don't you come tell me about that museum project my son mentioned?"

"I would love to, but I really need to get going. I came to pick up my cellphone. It must have fallen out of my purse when I was here. Your son found it. Do you know where he put it?"

"I'm sorry, dear. Norman didn't say anything about a cellphone. But he will be right back." Faye's hand clutched Danielle's cellphone hidden under the jacket draped over her lap.

"Oh…okay…" Danielle started to take a seat and then paused. "Umm…can you tell me where the restroom is?"

Faye smiled at Danielle and pointed down to the hallway. "First door to the right. But hurry back, dear. I'd love to hear all about our exhibit."

Just as Danielle reached the hallway leading to the bathroom, the ball of light she had seen earlier appeared again. She stopped abruptly and watched wide-eyed as it whirled up and down the hallway. With a gulp she moved hastily to the door leading to the bathroom. Entering the room quickly, she closed the door behind her and locked it.

"I just need to get out of here," Danielle mumbled aloud.

The next moment the ball of light came through the wall. Danielle stood frozen, making no attempt to use the facilities, but instead watched as the light swirled around the room a few moments before it landed before her, and then in a matter of seconds the light transformed into what appeared to be a man. But she knew it wasn't a man. It was a ghost.

"Who are you?" Danielle asked. By his manner of dress, she guessed he had died decades earlier—perhaps in the 1930s or '40s.

The man smiled. "You can see me! I thought earlier you did. Marvelous!"

"Who are you?" she repeated.

"No one of significance, just someone who has no desire to move on. And why should I? This is such a busy place, always someone new to chat with. Of course, none of them are ever someone like you."

"Like me?" she asked.

"Alive," he explained. "I've heard about people like you, who can talk to folks like us. But I have never met one before. Are you a friend of naughty Daisy?"

"Naughty Daisy?" Danielle frowned.

"Oh, the stories I could tell!" He laughed. "You know I was here when old man Morton kicked the bucket. It was about a month after I got here. But I'm not too good at time anymore. So maybe it was a year after they brought me here. I'd been fishing on the pier, fell in. I tell you what, never a good idea to drink alone while fishing on the pier late at night. I guess I was lucky; my body washed up on shore not far from here. My wife was pretty angry with me. But that's another story."

"Why did you stay?" Danielle asked.

"So much going on. My life was pretty boring. Get up every day. Go to work. Come home. Get nagged by the wife, kids whining. Day after day the same thing. But here, so much action! Right after I arrived, I met naughty Daisy, woohoo, a hot little thing. You should see what she was doing with that Leo character. Her dad had a fit! Fired him on the spot when he caught them doing what only a bride and groom should be doing on their wedding night. But I guess it was more than a fling. Leo came back after the old man kicked off and married her."

"Wait a minute—Leo married Maisy," Danielle argued. "Not Daisy."

The ghost stubbornly shook his head. "Nope. It was Daisy, but everyone seems to think she's her sister. That's Daisy sitting out there, waiting for you. She was also here when her pop fell down the stairs. Woohoo, was he angry when he heard what she said to him after he died. Cold girl. Looking down at her father's dead body, only regretting he hadn't died sooner. Of course, she didn't know he could hear what she was saying—or maybe she did." He shrugged.

"Are you saying Daisy had something to do with her father's death?"

He shook his head. "No. He fell down those stairs on his own. She just wasn't particularly sorry to see him go. Now that other guy, both she and Leo helped him drive off Pilgrim's Point."

"Are you saying Lewis Samson was murdered?"

"Oh yeah. At least that's what Lewis told me when they brought him in here. You know, they don't always come in here with their bodies, so I don't get to meet everyone who goes through this place. But Lewis followed his body here. He was pretty angry."

"Why did they kill him?"

"Lewis knew it was really Daisy, not her sister. I don't know what happened to Maisy, I just know Daisy is pretending to be her, and Lewis knew it. I guess when you really love someone, you can tell them from their twin sister. But what a schmuck. Falling in love with some broad who'll snuff you out without blinking an eye. That's naughty Daisy for you."

Danielle glanced nervously to the closed bathroom door and back to the ghost. "I need to get out of here."

"I don't blame you. Someday I'll move on too, but I keep waiting for naughty Daisy to kick off so I can ask her a couple of questions I have been dying to ask." He laughed and then repeated, "Dying to ask!" He laughed again. "Get it? Dying to ask. I should have been a comedian!"

He disappeared.

"Is everything alright?" Faye asked when Danielle walked back into the waiting area several minutes later.

"Umm…yeah…" Danielle muttered.

"Norman called; he said he got tied up and will be another

fifteen minutes. That will give us time for you to tell me all about the museum exhibit and our display."

"I can't stay. I'll have to get my phone later," Danielle said.

"Oh, please don't go," Faye begged, smiling sweetly.

Danielle silently studied Faye for a moment. The elderly woman seemed so feeble and old. No longer a physical threat—but if the spirit was to be believed, she had once been deadly.

If Danielle had thought for a moment Faye's son would be walking in the door at any moment, she would not have uttered the next words. Instead, she would have quickly left and headed straight to the police station.

"Do you like chocolate?" Danielle asked impulsively.

Faye stared at Danielle, confused by the question. Finally, she said, "No, actually, I don't. Why do you ask?"

"You are Daisy Faye. You killed your sister and Kenneth, didn't you? You also killed Lewis Samson. He knew your secret."

"Oh my. You really have figured it all out, haven't you?" Faye seemed unfazed by Danielle's declaration.

"Those remains they found buried at your old house, it's your sister and Kenneth, isn't it? Kenneth wasn't involved with you. He was involved with Maisy. The real Maisy."

Faye shrugged. "I had no idea my sister had sold our house. Especially after she told me I could stay with her until I could afford my own place. Leo and I had it all worked out. We were going to move the bodies and dispose of them so no one would ever know, but then I found out the house had been sold and the new owner was moving in, in just a few days. It didn't give us any time. We had to leave them there. And for all these years no one found them. Until now."

"I guess you almost got away with murder." Danielle turned to leave.

"Where do you think you're going?"

Danielle turned back to Faye and was surprised to find the elderly woman pointing a small revolver at her. Her eyes widened.

"You need to stay here until my son returns," Faye said sweetly.

THIRTY-SEVEN

The first person Norman saw when he walked in the funeral home was Danielle. From the corner of his eye he caught a glimpse of his mother sitting on a chair, but with his attention on Danielle, he failed to notice the gun in his mother's hand.

"Hi, Danielle," Norman said cheerfully. "I would have thought you'd have been gone by now."

Danielle stood quietly, glancing from Norman to his mother.

"Norman dear, why don't you lock the front door in case someone tries to come in," Faye said calmly.

Norman looked to his mother, prepared to ask her why he should lock the door, when he noticed what she was holding. His eyes widened.

"Mother? What are you doing? Is that my gun?"

"I said lock the door, now. So we can discuss this little problem without interruption," Faye instructed.

Swallowing nervously, Norman walked back to the door, stumbling a bit as he did, while his mother continued to point the handgun at Danielle.

Once he locked the door, he said, "Okay, it's locked. Now will you explain to me what is going on, and why are you pointing a gun at Danielle?"

"Because I found out your mother has been impersonating her

sister all these years," Danielle told him. "Daisy Faye is your mother. Not Maisy Faye."

"Shut up, you stupid girl," Faye snapped. While her right hand continued to hold the gun, she pulled her left hand out from under the jacket on her lap. It held Danielle's cellphone.

"What is she talking about, Mother?" Norman demanded.

"I'm your mother. I'm the same woman I have always been," she told him.

"Maybe," Danielle said. "But you've been using your sister's identity all these years—after you murdered her and her fiancé and buried them in your backyard."

Frowning, Norman looked frantically from Danielle to Faye.

"I had to do it, for us," Faye told him. "Your grandfather cut me out of the will because I was in love with your father. If we had listened to your grandfather, you would never have been born. This was all for you!"

"I don't understand," Norman said numbly.

"He left it all to my sister. I didn't mean to kill her, you need to know that. It was all a terrible accident."

"Then we can tell them it was all an accident," Norman suggested.

Faye shook her head. "No, dear. Don't you understand? You will lose all this. Your business, your home. It all came from Maisy's inheritance. Do you actually think they'll let you keep it?"

Agitated, Norman rubbed the heel of his right hand against his forehead. "But how can they prove any of this?"

"That's who they found in the backyard of my old house," Faye told him. "If Danielle tells them what she knows, then they'll make us give them DNA, and then they will know—they will know one of those people they found was my sister."

"What do you want to do?" Norman asked.

"If it was just me, I would let Danielle leave. I'm an old woman; I've already lived my life. But you. You will lose everything. So come, take Danielle's cellphone, and I'll tell you what we need to do."

Danielle warily watched as Norman walked to his mother and took the phone from her. He glanced from Faye to Danielle, back to his mother.

"Listen carefully," Faye told him. "You need to take Danielle's phone and put it in her car. They always track these things, and once they realize she is missing, they will use her cellphone to find her. Then you need to move her car. I'll keep her here, and when you return, we can take care of her. We'll give her a proper respectable cremation."

Norman took the phone from Faye. Holding it for a moment, he looked at it and then looked to Danielle, who stared at him through wide eyes, her complexion chalk white. He nodded at his mother and slipped the phone in his pocket.

"I think we should take care of Danielle first," Norman said. "I don't want her getting away from you while I'm out moving her car." Norman put out his hand for the gun. "If she decides to run for it, you're not as steady with that thing as you used to be."

"What are you going to do?" Faye asked.

"I certainly don't want to shoot her in here—we don't need to get her blood all over the place. I'll take her in the back and handle it. Give me the gun, and you wait here."

Faye smiled up at Norman. "You were always a good boy." She handed him the gun.

Now holding the pistol, Norman walked to Danielle.

"Please, you don't want to do this," Danielle begged. "Like your mother said, she has lived her life, what can they really do to her? And there's a chance you could still keep all this. You don't want to kill someone."

"I seriously doubt I will be able to keep any of this, considering it never belonged to my parents," Norman began. "Plus, I know my mother. Even if she thought I wouldn't lose a thing, she would still insist we do this. There is no way she would allow herself to spend a single day in jail." Norman shoved his free hand in his pocket and pulled out the cellphone. He then handed it to Danielle.

"Call the police," Norman said in a quiet voice. He turned to his mother and slipped the gun in his pocket.

"Norman!" Faye screeched. "What are you doing?"

"I'm certainly not killing an innocent woman," Norman retorted.

"But you're going to lose everything! And I will not spend my remaining years in some prison!"

"If I lose everything, so be it," Norman said calmly. "I don't even know you, Mother."

NORMAN SAT SLUMPED over on the sofa, his forehead buried in the palms of his hands as his elbows rested against his knees. Standing in the room with him were several police officers, who were explaining to him what was going to happen next.

Outside the funeral home, Danielle stood with Walt and Lily, watching as Brian Henderson escorted Daisy Faye Morton Bateman to a squad car, the elderly woman's hands cuffed.

"I'm going to sue you all!" Faye shouted. "I am Maisy Faye not Daisy Faye! If Daisy was buried with Kenneth, I didn't do it! But I know who did!"

As Brian opened the back door of the squad car for her, she said, "It was probably Lewis Samson! He was in love with Daisy! He didn't want her running off with Kenneth! That's who killed them! And he felt so guilty about it he killed himself! That's who did it! Not me!"

"That is actually a pretty good theory for the defense," Danielle commented from the sidelines, out of earshot of Brian or Faye. "If she hadn't held me at gunpoint and plotted to kill me with her son, while basically confirming to me she was Daisy, maybe a jury would buy it."

"I'd like to know why you didn't just leave when you realized she was Daisy and had been responsible for three deaths?" Walt asked. "Was it necessary to stick around and have a chat?"

"How did I know she was going to whip out a gun?" Danielle asked. "She seemed like a harmless little old lady. What could she do, the two of us all alone? I thought I could take her if she tried something. And she said Norman wouldn't be back for at least fifteen minutes."

"And you believed her? A serial killer?" Lily snapped. "A gun in the hand of this not so harmless little old lady."

Walt nodded at Lily in agreement.

"Okay. I admit it was foolish of me to stick around. I should have gone straight to the police station and told the chief what I had learned. But…"

"But what?" Walt asked.

"I wanted to make sure it really was Daisy. Spirits don't always tell the truth."

"How did you plan to do that?" Lily asked.

"I asked her if she liked chocolate. Remember that essay Maisy wrote when she was in elementary school? How she liked chocolate and her sister didn't?"

"While you were off trying to get yourself shot, Walt and I had already figured out Faye was not Maisy," Lily announced.

"And exactly how did you do that?" Danielle asked, looking from Lily to Walt.

"My dream. It wasn't Maisy Faye—a live person—I met. It was her spirit."

"Her spirit?" Danielle frowned.

"Sure," Lily said. "Poor Maisy probably didn't see it coming, so when she left her body, she ended up next door—at Marlow House."

"I don't think either of us understood we were dead at the time. And when Maisy talked about Angela, I think she might have been talking about Angela's spirit. Maisy very well could have gone to the cemetery—perhaps looking for Kenneth's spirit—and met Angela there."

"If you think about it, Dani," Lily began, "that has to be what it was. Walt said the Maisy Faye he remembered looked exactly like the twins in that portrait."

"Sometimes the reality of a spirit who hasn't yet acknowledged his or her death can seem disjointed—a little like a dream. Not a dream hop. But a regular dream. And like our dreams, we just accepted the confusion—the disjointed nature of what was happening—without questioning it," Walt explained.

THIRTY-EIGHT

The Beach Drive mediums and friends gathered around the dining room table at Marlow House that evening, discussing what had unfolded at the funeral home. Walt sat at the head of the table with Danielle to his left. Across from Danielle and to Walt's right, Chris sat. He had provided the dinner, bringing several boxes of pizza, chicken wings, and pasta salad from the local pizzeria. Lily sat to Chris's right, and on the other side of her was Heather. Ian was still in California. Across the table on Danielle's side was Eva and Marie, who were visible to everyone but Lily. While Lily couldn't see or hear the two spirits, she knew they were there.

As food was passed around the table—enjoyed by everyone but the two ghosts—Marie said, "Danielle, please tell Lily I left a gift for the baby over in the nursery. She can see it in the morning."

Danielle conveyed the message.

"A gift? Oh, Marie, how sweet. Where did you get a gift?" Lily asked.

"Tell Lily she'll just have to wait and see."

"She says you'll have to wait and see. That's sweet, Marie. Now I'm curious too," Danielle said.

"A baby gift?" Eva muttered under her breath. "What shall I get the baby?"

"I'm not only sweet, I know what I'm talking about. Didn't I tell you all that stuff Margaret was saying about Maisy was nonsense?"

"Yes, you did, Marie," Danielle conceded as she grabbed a slice of pepperoni pizza and set it on her paper plate.

"Marie did what?" Lily asked.

"She told us Margaret didn't know what she was talking about."

Lily frowned. "I don't know what you mean."

"Remember at the July Fourth party, Margaret said Maisy wasn't as nice as everyone claimed. Basically said Daisy was the nice one—the misunderstood one—and Kenneth fell for her after he saw how poorly Maisy treated her," Danielle reminded. "Back then Marie told us Margaret didn't know what she was talking about. And she was right."

"Yes, I was," Marie said with a nod.

"It's obvious what Daisy was doing back then," Danielle said. "She used Margaret's sister to make people believe she had run away with Kenneth by that letter she had her mail. That worked so well, she got other people to send more Daisy letters back to Frederickport so everyone would assume she was Maisy, and Daisy was off traveling the world."

"It's a good thing I was wrong about Norman," Heather said as she pulled a chicken wing apart.

"Wrong how?" Lily asked.

"He looks so much like Norman Bates in *Psycho*, and the way he seemed to be such a mama's boy. The Norman I imagined he was would have had Danielle crispy in the crematory about now."

"Not a pleasant thought." Danielle cringed. "But I did have one ace up my sleeve. Not sure it would have worked, but I was going to use it."

"And what was that?" Walt asked.

"There was at least one ghost hanging out at that place. I was going to plead with him to contact one of you and send in the cavalry."

"I'm just glad you didn't have to rely on that. As we all know, there's a chance the spirit you met is confined to the funeral home," Walt reminded her. "And he wouldn't have been able to contact any of us."

"Ahh, I have a pretty good idea who you're talking about." Eva spoke up. "Did he by chance tell you he fell off the pier after having too much to drink?"

"Yes." Danielle nodded.

"He's been hanging around that place for as long as I can remember," Eva said.

"I have a question, Eva," Heather asked.

"Yes?"

"You seem to know many of the spirits who hang around Frederickport before moving on. Why is it you never encountered Maisy's spirit? If Walt's dream is accurate, it sounds like she might have ventured down to the local cemetery."

Eva looked over at Walt and smiled. She then looked back to Heather. "As you know, for a number of years I avoided Marlow House. At the time, I thought it best for Walt if he didn't see me. And I also avoided the local cemetery, as that's where Angela was confined. In my hauntings, I never had an opportunity to come in contact with Maisy, and I hadn't heard anything in the spirit realm about her—or the murders. Ghosts aren't all-seeing."

Danielle continued playing interpreter for Lily, keeping her apprised of what Marie and Eva were saying.

Heather considered Eva's answer a moment and then gave it a nod before taking another bite of food.

"Learning Faye was actually Daisy and not Maisy all these years does make a great deal of sense," Marie said. "I'm surprised I didn't figure it out earlier."

"How so?" Danielle asked after telling Lily what Marie had said.

"I always heard how Maisy changed after her sister ran off with Kenneth—how she stopped seeing her friends."

"That's because they were never her friends," Heather said.

"Exactly." Marie nodded. "Or why she started going by Faye. I remember once one of her friends from high school thought it so odd she suddenly hated her first name. She told me that when they were younger and talked about names for the children they wanted to have some day, Maisy had told her she liked her first name, but didn't care for her middle name at all."

"I imagine Daisy felt more comfortable being called Faye. It was a way she held onto part of her identity, even if it was a middle name she had shared with her twin," Chris suggested. "It's bad enough murdering your sister—I can't imagine living with that guilt. But then to have everyone call you by her name." Chris shook his head at the idea.

"For some reason, I don't think guilt played a part in her choice of names," Walt said.

"Also the smoking," Danielle added. "More than one person mentioned how in their youth Maisy didn't smoke, but Daisy did. I knew Faye had been a smoker, but I just assumed it was something she had taken up when she was older."

"That same friend who thought it odd Maisy started going by her middle name once ran into her not long after her sister supposedly eloped with Kenneth. She was surprised to find Maisy smoking and commented on it. Maisy—or more accurately Daisy—told her with all that had happened, being so distraught, she had taken it up. The friend actually found that more understandable than her suddenly going by Faye," Marie said.

"When I asked Faye if she liked chocolate, because of that essay Maisy had written as a child, I probably didn't need to ask the question" Danielle confessed.

"What do you mean?" Lily asked.

"When Walt and I were talking to Norman about his mother and aunt, he said something about how his aunt was a bookworm and played the piano."

"According to that essay, Maisy was the bookworm, played the piano—and liked chocolate," Lily said.

Danielle nodded. "Norman was right about his aunt being the one who liked those things. He just didn't know his aunt was Maisy."

"As much as I hate the fact Danielle could have been killed by asking that question instead of just leaving, the truth is, if she hadn't, Daisy could have gotten away with murder if Danielle had left and simply gone to the chief," Walt said.

"Why do you say that?" Heather asked. "Once they got a warrant for Faye's DNA, everyone would know it was her sister."

"While they were arresting her, she came up with a plausible defense—she accused Lewis Samson of being the jilted lover who killed them in a fit of jealousy and then killed himself from guilt. I suspect had Faye thought of that earlier, it could have been her ticket to freedom. I'm not sure how they could prove she was really Daisy," Walt explained. "Not unless they had her fingerprints on file somewhere, which I doubt."

"See, I did a good thing," Danielle chirped.

Walt glared at Danielle. "Just don't do something foolish like that again."

"So what do you think is going to happen now, with Norman?"

Heather asked. "Morton's estate went to Maisy, not to Daisy. So everything he has basically came to him illegally."

"I suspect it will depend on Maisy's will—if she had one," Chris said. "And there is a good chance Norman will actually be Maisy's rightful heir anyway. It's not like he had anything to do with the murders—and he didn't help his mother cover up the crime."

"Not to mention, when they ran the DNA on those remains, the only hits that came for Maisy were distant cousins, where the results were rated fair, which could mean they may not even be related," Danielle said. "So perhaps there are no close relatives out there aside from Norman and Faye to inherit the estate."

"I hope Norman gets to keep it all," Lily said. "It's not his fault his mother is evil. And when he was put to the test, he did the right thing."

"I have to admit, I didn't see this coming," Heather said.

"I don't think any of us did," Walt added.

"I never thought the Batemans had anything to do with those remains," Heather said as she wiped her hands off on a napkin.

"But he reminded you of the guy from *Psycho*," Danielle teased.

"True. But I seriously thought Pearl's family was responsible. I figured it had to have something to do with those roses, especially since someone stole that plant from her yard and then the remains showed up."

Chris glanced over to her and said, "Sometimes, Heather, a rose is just a rose."

THIRTY-NINE

A phone call woke Lily the next morning. Danielle and Walt were already dressed, awake and sitting in the kitchen having coffee. Sadie, who had also been sleeping on the bed, woke up as Lily rolled off the mattress, grumbling.

"How did you sleep last night?" Danielle asked as Lily stumbled into the kitchen a few minutes later, wearing a robe and her red hair frazzled as she rubbed sleep from her eyes, Sadie trailing behind her.

"Good. And I would have liked to have kept sleeping. But Bill Jones called and woke me up. He's coming over in about thirty minutes and checking out the room to paint." Lily grabbed a cup from an overhead counter and filled it with orange juice. "He's already familiar with the house, so he gave me a price to paint it if I supply everything. It was fair."

"I want to go with you when you go over there. I'm dying to find out what Marie got you for the baby," Danielle said. "What kind of a baby gift does a ghost give?"

IT TOOK Lily a while to get going that morning, and by the time she was dressed and ready to head to her house, Bill was already pulling his truck into her driveway. Together Lily and Danielle walked across the street.

"Morning, Bill," Danielle greeted him as she walked up Lily's driveway.

"Hi, Bill, sorry if I sounded grumpy when you called this morning," Lily began.

He gave Danielle a nod in greeting and then said to Lily, "I guess I woke you up?"

Lily shrugged.

"Adam said you wanted to get the room painted this week. Before I get started, I wanted to make sure I don't need to pick anything up."

"I appreciate you doing this on such short notice. As for waking me up, I needed to get up anyway." She flashed him a smile.

Bill, wearing his trademark worn denims, blue work shirt, and work boots, trailed behind Danielle and Lily as they made their way up the walkway to the front door. A moment later he and Danielle stood quietly as Lily unlocked the door. They then followed her inside.

The three walked through the house and then down the hallway. Lily stopped a moment and frowned at the door to the guest bedroom. It was closed. She was fairly certain she had left the door open before going to Danielle's house. She remembered because as she was leaving with her suitcase and Sadie to go across the street, she had glanced at the nursery and spied the paint cans sitting inside the room and worried the nursery wasn't going to get painted in time. She hadn't stopped to close the door. Or had she?

Dismissing the thought, Lily opened the door to her spare bedroom and walked in without paying close attention. But once she stepped into the room, her eyes widened in surprise. Stunned, she glanced around at the four freshly painted walls.

Frowning, Bill looked around the room and said, "Are you sure you want to paint this room? It looks like it's—" He paused a moment and looked down. There, sitting on the floor, was a neatly folded—and clearly used—drop cloth. Sitting atop it were several cans of empty paint, a used brush, a roller and a roller pan. "—already been painted."

"It has…" Lily said in awe, looking around the cheerfully painted room. "Marie. She painted the nursery."

"Marie? Who's Marie?" Bill asked.

Catching herself, Lily looked to Bill and said, "I'm so sorry to have dragged you over here. I had no idea the room had been painted. A friend must have done it to surprise me."

"You say this friend's name is Marie?" Bill asked as he stepped closer to the walls, inspecting the workmanship.

"Ummm…yes." Lily and Danielle exchanged quick glances.

Ignoring the exchange between the two women, Bill continued on his inspection, walking around the room. "Does this Marie do this professionally?"

"Umm, no. She's…retired," Lily told him, resisting the urge to giggle.

"Well, your friend does beautiful work. A lot of people think they can just slap on paint. Rarely see this quality anymore. Tell your friend if she wants to pick up any side jobs, give me a call."

AFTER BILL LEFT ten minutes later, Lily succumbed to the laughter she had been holding in since Bill offered Marie a job.

"That is just too funny," Lily said.

"Yep. The image of Marie working for Bill is—out there." Danielle chuckled.

"This was the baby gift she was telling me about. I can't believe what a good job she did."

Danielle shrugged. "Well, Adam did say Marie was a pretty good painter in her younger years. I guess that old boyfriend of hers really did teach her a few tricks."

IAN ARRIVED home a few days earlier than expected, and several days later Lily's parents showed up as promised, bringing the gifts from her first baby shower. Lily found herself unexpectedly happy to see her mom and dad. The next few days her mother helped her decorate the nursery.

Danielle threw a second baby shower while Lily's parents were still in town. When it was time for them to return to California, Lily and her mother cried. Danielle, who watched the emotional goodbye, couldn't help but envy the time Lily was given with her mother. Danielle was also happy to see Lily seemed to be appreciating her mother more. It wasn't that Lily hadn't loved her mother before, but sometimes the depths of that appreciation isn't fully realized until the child becomes a parent herself—or the child loses the parent.

The following weeks flew by for everyone—except Lily. As her belly grew larger, the weeks seemed to get longer. The fear she had once experienced about going through childbirth was replaced by a desire to—*just get this kid out of here!*

Lily's due date had come and gone. She and Ian were at Marlow House on the last Tuesday evening of September, originally intending to play a game of Yahtzee. The game was soon abandoned so Lily could get more comfortable on the living room sofa. Outside, the wind shook the tree limbs, hitting them against the house.

"Maybe this will be an October baby after all," Ian suggested.

Lily glared at her husband. "That is not even funny."

He smiled sheepishly and gave her a gentle pat. "I love you."

"You'd better," she grumbled, awkwardly getting to her feet. She wobbled to the open doorway, heading to the bathroom.

When she was out of earshot, Danielle said, "She really does look uncomfortable."

"I know," Ian agreed. "She has been a trooper. And I need to be more sensitive about what I say."

"Especially when you're her Lamaze coach!" Danielle told him.

The next moment Lily returned. She stood in the open doorway, one hand on her stomach. "I have good news and bad news."

"Let me guess, the good news, you're in labor?" Danielle asked excitedly.

Lily nodded, a grin on her face.

"And the bad news?" Ian asked.

"I didn't quite make it to the bathroom before my water broke."

PEARL HUCKABEE STOOD at the corner windows of her upstairs bedroom, looking down at the street. Overhead, a quarter moon helped light the sky. She watched as someone ran across the street from Marlow House to the Bartleys'. A few minutes later, whoever had run over pulled the Bartleys' car out of the driveway and parked in front of Marlow House. She couldn't see what was going on, but a moment later she spied the same car driving down the street, in her direction, with Danielle Marlow's car following close behind. She couldn't tell who was in either vehicle.

Wind continued to shake the tree limbs. She worried about the trees she wouldn't let Craig Simmons trim because she didn't want to spend the additional money. In the next moment, just as the Bartley car was about to drive by her house, a top portion of the front tree snapped off, sending a massive branch, with countless limbs attached, to the street below, barely missing the oncoming vehicles. Pearl let out a gasp. Had the tree limb landed on either car, it would have surely killed the occupants.

Stunned, she stared down at the vehicles, which were now both stopped, the fallen branch and limbs blocking their way. The driver of Danielle's car—it looked like a man—got out of the driver's side of the vehicle and rushed up to the car in front of him. Now standing at the driver's window, he leaned into the Bartleys' car. They were obviously discussing the near catastrophe.

Pearl wondered who she should call. She imagined she would be forced to pay to have the branch hauled away—it had come from her tree. Considering her options, Pearl continued to peer out the window, down at the two cars.

A moment later the man who had gotten out of the back vehicle—who she assumed was probably Walt Marlow—stepped back from Bartley's car and faced the tree limb blocking the road. To Pearl's utter astonishment, she watched as the limb lifted up from the road, moving upward some twenty feet. She stared dumbly at the sight. The next moment the front car raced down the road and under the hovering branch as if it were nothing but a toll gate.

The branch then turned clockwise so that it ran parallel to the street and slowly fell back to earth, settling along the sidewalk in front of Pearl's house.

WALT GLANCED up to Pearl's house and saw her standing in her upstairs bedroom. She had been watching. He turned and rushed back to the Ford Flex, its motor still running, and climbed into the driver's seat.

"Nice trick," Danielle told him.

"Pearl saw," Walt said as he hastily latched his seatbelt.

Danielle peered out the windshield, looking over to Pearl's house. She saw the woman standing in an upstairs window.

"Well, that's going to give her something interesting to talk about," Danielle said dryly.

"It certainly will," Walt said before putting the car back into drive and racing down the street, heading to the hospital.

LILY LOOKED LIKE AN ANGEL, Walt thought. She sat up in the hospital bed, the newborn infant sleeping in her arms, wrapped in a baby blanket, only a sweet pink face peeking out. Ian sat on the side of the bed, one arm wrapped around the new mother—his little family of three. Four if you counted Sadie, and Sadie had to be counted. Family of four. Walt thought Ian might burst from pride the way he looked down at the sleeping babe.

"I thought for sure I was going to have a chaotic Lucy delivery," Lily said with a sigh of relief.

"What's a Lucy delivery?" Walt asked.

Lily smiled up at Walt. "*I Love Lucy*, the sitcom—or any sitcom for that matter—where an episode features the delivery of a baby. Crazy things happen—like a tree falling from the sky, blocking the road." She grinned up at Walt.

"Thanks again, Walt," Ian said.

Walt flashed him a smile.

"Aside from the tree—it has to be one of the easiest deliveries on record," Lily said. "Ian gets me to the hospital, they get me right into a room, and before they can call the doctor, out comes the baby. I didn't even get a chance to yell at Ian when he said something lame while trying to coach me. It all happened so fast." Lily laughed and grinned up to her husband. He returned the smile and kissed her forehead. Walt and Danielle, who stood in the room with them, exchanged a smile before looking back down at the new arrival.

"Can we come in?" came an anxious voice from the open doorway. It was Chris, and standing next to him was Heather.

"We were so worried when we heard about the tree," Heather said, rushing into the room, not waiting for a response. "Oh, the baby is beautiful!" she said excitedly.

Ian stood up to greet the new arrivals.

"Congratulations, old man," Chris said, shaking Ian's hand

vigorously. He then leaned down and kissed Lily's cheek while saying, "You look beautiful, Mama."

"You heard about the tree?" Lily asked. "How?"

"I called them as we were driving to the hospital," Danielle explained.

"And I'm glad she did," Heather told them. "Not long after she called, a police car showed up—it was Joe and Brian. I went out to see what was all the commotion, and you should have heard Pearl rambling on about how the wind picked the tree up into the sky and you guys just kept on driving, and then the tree came down on the sidewalk as the second car drove away. Joe kept looking at Pearl like she had lost her mind, and Brian asked me where you guys were going."

"Forget about our crazy neighbor, I want to hear about this little angel. Have you decided on a name?" Chris asked.

With Ian sitting back on the bed again next to Lily and the baby, the four friends hovered around the hospital bed, looking down at the sleeping infant.

"Yes," Lily said with a grin. "I'd like you all to meet Connor Daniel Bartley."

LATER THAT NIGHT, long after their friends had gone home, Ian finally fell asleep. Lily had been dozing off and on since their friends had said goodbye. The baby had been sleeping for the last hour in the crib next to Lily's hospital bed. Unbeknownst to the sleeping parents, two visitors came to meet Connor Daniel Bartley. Yet, even if Ian and Lily had been awake, they would not have been aware of the visitors.

"He's absolutely beautiful," Marie said wistfully. "There is just something about babies..." She let out a sigh and continued to look down at the sleeping infant.

Standing beside Marie, Eva gazed down at the child and reached out, running a finger over the tiny nose. He wouldn't feel the touch—and sadly, neither could she.

"You really never wanted children?" Marie asked softly, her eyes still on the baby.

"I suppose I might have—if I thought I would be around to watch the child grow up. But I always knew I would die young," Eva whispered. "But I did get great pleasure watching you grow up when you were a baby. Although it was bittersweet when you could no longer see me."

Marie looked over to Eva—a picture of youth and beauty, thinking how peculiar it was now, almost as if their roles had reversed—Marie the older woman, Eva forever young.

"Do you think he'll be able to see us? Hear us?" Marie asked.

Still studying the child, Eva shrugged. "There is a good chance, but we won't really know until he can see more clearly, about a month or so. If he wakes up and smiles at us now, it's probably just gas."

FORTY

The winds of late September had calmed by the first week in October. The days of October moved swifter than those in September had for Lily. Already her baby was four weeks old, and Halloween was just a week away. Although sleep deprived, Lily felt blessed that she had not experienced any postpartum depression. She was also grateful Sadie had adapted so well to the new family member, even insisting on napping by his crib during the day, standing guard. Lily wondered what Walt might have told the golden retriever.

She was also immensely proud of Ian, who didn't make excuses when it was time for a diaper change and even offered to help during feeding time. Of course, she was breastfeeding, so she assumed that offer was just Ian being naughty. She grinned at the thought and felt blessed all over again.

Even Heather, who she had once thought prickly and had gotten on her nerves countless times, had turned into a good friend who seemed quite enamored of little Connor Daniel Bartley, as did Chris, who insisted he wanted to be called Uncle Chris.

Walt and Danielle, they were family, always there when she needed them, even performing impossible tasks, like practically picking up a tree so she could get safely to the hospital. Since the baby's birth, Walt and Danielle had also been busy with a new fundraising project—turning Marlow House into a haunted house for Halloween. After all, they knew a few ghosts who could provide some ambiance.

IT WAS a sunny afternoon and a beautiful setting—even if it was a cemetery. None of the residents of Beach Drive attending the funeral knew the deceased, but it only seemed right they attend the funeral for Maisy Fay Morton and Kenneth Bakken. After all, they were practically neighbors. A noticeable missing resident from Beach Drive was Pearl Huckabee, who never considered attending a funeral for someone who had died years before her birth, even though their remains had been found in her backyard.

The caskets were the finest Morton Funeral Home could provide—not that a fancy box for remains that were barely there could make up for what Daisy had done those many years ago.

Danielle, Lily and Heather stood under a large shade tree with the baby sleeping in the stroller. They watched the mourners—if they could actually be called that, since most of them had never met the deceased—slowly disperse, with some lingering to chat with neighbors and friends. Toynette from the nursery was there, to pay her final respects to an uncle she had never met. She stopped by the three friends under the tree to thank them for coming and to take a quick look at the newest resident of Frederickport.

"This is what it is all about," Toynette murmured, looking down at the sleeping baby.

Not long after Toynette stopped to say hello and then moved on, Millie Samson came by.

"I had to come today, for my late husband, for Lewis," Millie said. "I heard that awful woman tried to blame Lewis for those dreadful murders. I'm just glad the truth finally came out. Bruce was right all along. Lewis didn't kill himself." She stayed a few more minutes to look at the baby and then went on her way.

Walt, Ian and Chris, who had been chatting with some other residents from Beach Drive, returned to the shade tree when Joe and Kelly came walking up.

"Is he sleeping?" Kelly asked, peeking in the stroller. "How is my adorable nephew?"

"Still adorable," Lily said with a grin.

"Your neighbor still insists that tree flew up in the air and stayed there while you drove under it," Joe told her.

Lily shrugged. "I was a little preoccupied at the time. I wasn't really paying much attention to what was going on outside."

Joe looked at Danielle, obviously expecting a comment from her.

"Pearl is just confused." Danielle smiled sweetly. "It all happened so quickly. I imagine she was pretty shook up watching that tree break and then land on the sidewalk. She probably thought it was going to land on one of our cars."

"It was a dramatic entrance for your little guy." Joe grinned and looked down at the baby.

Chief MacDonald joined them a minute later.

"Is it true Morton Funeral Home paid for everything today?" Ian asked the chief.

MacDonald nodded. "That's what I understand."

"And Faye confessed to everything?" Heather asked.

As Heather asked the question, Officer Brian Henderson joined the group.

"Yes, but she claimed it was an accident," MacDonald said.

"What exactly was an accident, Kenneth's bash over the head or Maisy being shot?" Danielle asked.

"She blamed her husband, claims he accidentally shot Maisy, that he never intended to hurt her when the gun went off, and then Kenneth tried to rush to Maisy's side, and he fell because he was using crutches and hit his head," the chief explained.

"Yeah, right," Danielle scoffed.

"She claimed it had been her husband's idea to bury the bodies. He intended to move them, but the house was sold, so they couldn't. And now, her lawyer is claiming mental incapacity, and considering her advanced age, I'm not sure justice is going to be served in this case."

"What about Norman? It's nice that he paid for the funerals, but can he even do that if they decide none of it is his?" Heather asked.

"That's already been determined to some degree. But it has to finish going through probate." Brian spoke up. "Maisy had made a will when she turned eighteen, several years before her father passed away—before she was engaged to Kenneth. In the will she left all her worldly possessions to her children. If she had no children, they were to go to her sister, Daisy, and if Daisy had preceded her, then it was to go to Daisy's children, which would be Norman."

"Funny she would even mention children, considering neither one was even married at the time," Heather said.

"What might be in Norman's favor, the verbiage in the will refers to *future* children in either case. I'm assuming she had them include it that way so she wouldn't be in a rush to have a new will drawn up when she eventually had children. Yet I suspect that once she was married to Kenneth, she would have rewritten her will to include him," the chief suggested. "But who knows what is in a young girl's mind when she writes up her first will."

"Does this mean everything goes to Norman?" Danielle asked.

"Like Brian said, it has to finish going through probate. Unless someone contests the will, I suspect it will be decided Norman was always the rightful heir of Maisy's estate. Even though Daisy was mentioned in the will, she wouldn't be allowed to inherit because of her part in her sister's murder."

A SLIVER of moonlight fell through the nursery window, casting a faint glow over the infant sleeping in the crib. Sadie the golden retriever slept nearby, placing her curled-up body between the doorway and baby. The sound of the baby making a cooing noise followed by a woman's voice saying, "Hello, handsome," caused the dog's ears to perk up. Jumping to attention while emitting a low growl, Sadie faced the crib.

"Calm down, Sadie," Marie whispered. "It's only me."

Sadie looked at the spirit—the image of an elderly woman wearing a floral-patterned dress, with gray hair, and tonight no hat—as she stood over the crib looking down at the baby. Satisfied her charge was safe, Sadie let out a grunt and settled back down.

Connor opened his eyes and stared up into Marie's smiling face. He gurgled and then grinned, wiggling his little hands in excitement.

"You can see me, can't you?" Marie beamed.

The baby cooed as he continued to look up at Marie; their eyes met. He made a noise that to Marie sounded like a giggle.

"Oh, you sweet child, you can see me. You know what this means, don't you? It means Grandma Marie needs to stick around and keep you safe. Oh, yes, she does."

Return to Marlow Houses in

The Ghost and the Halloween Haunt

Haunting Danielle, Book 22

Coming August 2019

For updates and notification of when

The Ghost and the Halloween Haunt

is available for preorder sign up for our newsletter!

Haunting Danielle Newsletter

NON-FICTION BY

BOBBI ANN JOHNSON HOLMES

Havasu Palms, A Hostile Takeover

Where the Road Ends, Recipes & Remembrances

Motherhood, a book of poetry

The Story of the Christmas Village

BOOKS BY ANNA J. MCINTYRE

Coulson's Wife

Coulson's Crucible

Coulson's Lessons

Coulson's Secret

Coulson's Reckoning

UNLOCKED HEARTS

Sundered Hearts

After Sundown

While Snowbound

Sugar Rush

CPSIA information can be obtained
at www.ICGtesting.com
Printed in the USA
LVHW090817011019
632824LV00001B/22/P

9 781949 977417